THE HIGHFIRE CROWN

BLOOD MAGIC

BOOK ONE

JT LAWRENCE

FIRE FINCH

FIRE FINCH

 Created with Vellum

About the Author
JT LAWRENCE

JT Lawrence is a USA Today bestselling author
of 30+ books, and a Kindle Unlimited All-Star. Mother to a
menagerie of chaos, voracious reader, gin fan, and urban
farmer.

Stay up all night
with USA Today bestselling author
JT Lawrence.
www.jt-lawrence.com

amazon.com/author/jtlawrence

tiktok.com/@stay_up_allnite

instagram.com/authorjtlawrence

facebook.com/JanitaTLawrence

x.com/stay_up_allnite

bookbub.com/authors/jt-lawrence

pinterest.com/stay_up_all_night

linkedin.com/in/janita-thiele-lawrence-56533610

SPECIAL THANKS

Immense gratitude to my readers
whose loyalty, support, and generous reviews
give me the courage to face the blank page
over and over again.

I wouldn't be able to do this without you.

I hope you enjoy this new magical adventure!

- Janita (JT Lawrence)

THE HIGHFIRE CROWN

BLOOD MAGIC BOOK 1

CHAPTER I

CRIMSON COPPER MIST

I was running when I caught the scent of it—the crimson copper mist—and I knew I was too late.

My borrowed whalebone corset was grinding into my ribs as I raced up the staircase. Scarlet-lipped Madame Woolf, the proprietor of The Jupiter Drawing Room, had designed the interior of the building with such style and attention to detail that anyone visiting was instantly transported to a Victorian-era brothel, with lush swathes of fabric and glittering stones... and working girls in impossible outfits, a wardrobe decision that I now thoroughly regretted.

Being undercover in the most luxurious neo-gothic bordello in Johannesburg in 2018 was one thing, but a full silk skirt and a marine-ivory exoskeleton that seriously hindered me in doing my job was quite another. I stopped halfway up the cast-iron spiral stairs and ripped off the ridiculous costume. My utility belt, still snug on my hips, was now easier to reach, and I immediately felt more mobile. I sped to the top, out of breath and out of time. I refused to give up; maybe there was still a life I could spare. More importantly: maybe there was still a particular life I could snuff out.

I arrived at the top, glancing left and right, trying to catch a glimpse of my target. The cream brocade wallpapered corridor was bare, but I knew she was there. I could smell her; could sense her burgeoning evil behind the wall. In my mind's eye I saw black mist spilling out from underneath the numbered doors.

I reached for the crossbow on my back and eased off the safety catch. I prowled down the passage, hoping to be able to sense which room she was in, but the dealings of the people inside threw up a screen of emotion that I couldn't get past. I changed my mind about the crossbow and hitched it onto the clasp on my hip, and from the same belt I unclipped my silver wand and pointed it at the first door.

Door number one: let's have some fun.

Usually when I'm breaking in—especially when the mechanisms locking me out are quaint bronze doorknobs—I'll use a gentle fire spell to just melt the metal enough to force entrance. It's an easy, quiet way to gain access; an elegant way to smash and grab. But right then I didn't have time for elegance.

I narrowed my eyes and focused my attention on the bronze handle, and I thought of the victims I had witnessed in my line of work so far. The reckless slaughtering of good, innocent people; loving fathers and brothers and wives and friends, and small children orphaned by careless violence. I had experienced the soul-aching loss myself, had felt—and still feel—the endless grief circling me like a hungry vulture. Thinking of lost fathers, I clutched the pentacle ring that hung on a chain around my neck, and I felt fortified. I gathered the roiling storm in my chest and launched my emotion at the door: eyes unblinking, arm straight, cool wand clutched in my hot palm.

My name is Jacquelyn Denna Knight, and I turn my pain into magic.

"*Fiat Fulgur!*" I yelled, and a bolt of white lightning surged within me, bypassing my heart and shooting out of my hand, hurtling through the wand, and exploding a hole in the door, sending a billowing cloud of golden sparking smoke into the air.

Goodbye, quaint bronze doorknob.

Some wizards like to use wooden staffs, but I prefer the antique wand I stole from my mother. It acts like a conductor: it narrows my focus to a white-hot point, and concentrates the power I pull from the Void. The door flew open under the heel of my boot, and shouts of shock burst from within.

Through the haze of smoking wood and screaming I saw that the couple in the first room was not who I was looking for. I blasted open the next door, and the next, counting the precious seconds I was losing while someone was dying. He may as well have been right there, lips to my ear, taking his last gasping breath. I shuddered, then steeled myself; tightening my grip on the wand. Loud shrieking and angry protestations bowled down the passage, but I paid them no mind. I didn't give a damn about their interrupted passion. I could smell the copper crimson again, and this time I welcomed it, breathed it in deeply. It was like a red ribbon of scent, leading me to room number six.

Room number six, show me your tricks.

I ran to the doorway, stood before it, and raised my wand. The smell was pungent, then, and I knew for certain I was too late.

"*Fiat Fulgur!*" Arm outstretched, the bright current of electricity jolted through my body and shot out of my wand once more. Knowing I was close, my fear intensified the spell, exploding not just the handle but the whole door, and the shards and burning splinters gusted back into the room; a hurricane of sparks. Inside my chest, I felt my heart was in a similar state.

There, on the luxuriously oversized bed, lay a middle-aged man, naked apart from a pair of pink silk boxers. The pillow beneath his lolling head was turning slowly from white to red. I quickly swapped my wand for my crossbow, and entered the velvet- and vanilla-striped room. Two distinct sounds hit me at the same time: a wet gurgle from the man, hinting that he was still alive, and a neat click and slide on the other side of the vintage paneled dressing screen that divided the space. Cool city air crept toward me, and I could hear the traffic beyond; the sound had been the window being opened. Making the decision between saving the bleeding man on the bed and killing the perpetrator before she escaped was impossible, so I relied on my gut instinct instead, which pushed my limbs toward the window behind the screen. My body felt like it was on fire from the spells it had cast in getting there—my wrist was singing with pain—and the foreboding I felt for what I'd find on the other side of the divider. I lifted my crossbow and approached.

I may as well have been walking in quicksand, the time it took me to cross the room. My instinct was pushing me forward, and my sense of self-preservation was holding me back. I didn't want to die, and I *especially* didn't want to die in this room, in this building, at the hands of this hateful creature. I took another step forward, hands perspiring and weakening my grip on the weapon. There was a soft noise, a ruffle of fabric, and a slight movement of shadow beyond the partition. My heart was on high alert, bashing into my ribcage. I swallowed hard, and took another step.

It often feels like this. All brave and ballsy during the chase, bolstered by the sure knowledge that I'm the best in the city at what I do. A flash memory of the sensation of running my hands over the hundreds of notches I've made on my bedpost at home: not of lovers, but of successful kills. But then when you're right there in the room and there's a man dying with his throat opened and leaking, and you're so close to the attacker that you can smell her stale perfume and sour breath... that's when bravery falters and your breath catches. And you don't get used to it, no matter how many times you do it.

The fear sucks the air out of the room.

Then, just as the panic mounts and you think it's too much, your body's primal instincts are screaming *fight or flight*, and, by god, you want to hightail it out of there, a different feeling comes crashing over you and your fear. A hot wave that holds you up, lets you breathe, and with that breath your uncertainty evaporates and you realize that no-one can do this like you can—that you were born for this—and it lights up your body and sets your jaw.

Gripping the crossbow with the new burst of courage, I marched over to the screen and kicked it over.

The satin-skirted vampire was waiting for me.

CHAPTER 2
TWIN MIDNIGHT WHIRLPOOLS

She had deep black eyes, midnight whirlpools that threatened to inhale me. I didn't give her the chance. I pulled the trigger of the crossbow and I waited for the satisfying rushing sound of the arrow leaving the flight groove, and for the vixen's chest to implode, but it didn't. She stood there, framed by the ornate window frame, city lights sparkling like stars in the background. There was amusement in her expression, and a quirk of her bloodied lips, as if she had somehow known that my crossbow would misfire; as if she were able to mesmerize inanimate objects as well as middle-aged men in pink silk boxer shorts. I jammed my finger down again, harder, but nothing happened, except that the vampire used the opportunity to advance on me. In a blur of black satin she was at my exposed throat, only slowing when she saw the tattoo there. I took advantage of the split-second of her confusion to step back and reach for my wand. The crossbow clattered to the floor, spiking my adrenaline and making everything outside of that moment in the corner of that velvet room disappear.

When the vampire saw the silver spellstick, she raised her pale wrist to her forehead and hissed, her pink-stained fangs and blood-breath amplifying the disgust I felt for her and her kin. As hatred and anger swirled up inside me like blue smoke, I gritted my teeth and pointed the wand at her, ready to blast her with every molecule of terror, pain and loathing that I felt vibrating in my body. I was going to pulverize her. I was going to turn her into the lump of hot sparking ash she deserved to be.

And then I hesitated. Something inside me slipped.

Maybe I was knocked off my game by my crossbow jamming a few moments earlier, or the new blood-gurgle I heard coming from the other side of the room. Or maybe it was the fact that I was standing in a vintage brothel in nothing but my underwear in front of a bloodthirsty monster who seemed intent on having me for dessert. Whatever it was, it was a strange, terrible feeling, as if my spiritual center of gravity dropped, and my power dropped alongside it. As if I was cut off from the Void—the source of my magic—with no warning. As if my soul just collapsed right there on the varnished wooden floor, like a discarded bath towel, damp and warm. There was no magic left in my arm, and my wand only threw off a few sparks, as if we were at a toddler's birthday party instead of what was supposed to be a merciless vampire slaying. When I looked up from the fizzling wand I assumed the worst. I was expecting to be turned into a bloody drinking fountain by the vicious creature, my mouth hanging open with the sheer horror of it, my ultimate nightmare in high definition. But she was gone.

The vampire had launched herself out of the window and all I heard or saw of her was the soft flapping of her cape in the night. I stood there, arms limp at my sides, looking out into the bustling neon city below, while the ivory voile curtain billowed around me.

Madame Woolf would not be happy.

What the hell just happened? I felt as if I had been pulled through a dream sequence at high speed. I took a step backwards, stumbled, then sat with a bump on the floor, next to my discarded crossbow, and looked up again at the widemouthed window. I wouldn't let the vampire get away with this. Her actions were pure wickedness: with so many different brands and flavors of synthetic blood on the market there was no need to hurt humans for it, never mind kill them. She was a cold-blooded murderess, one of many in the city—too many—and they were getting increasingly reckless. I swore right there and then to find her and finish her, and any one of her clan that stood in the way.

My head was spinning like a planet in orbit. I drew up my legs and rested my forehead on my knees. I needed to process what had just happened. I needed to go home, to shower and sleep, but there was a shrill beeping coming from my belt that I couldn't ignore. I tried to blink away the post-terror stupor I was feeling, but I needn't have bothered. When I saw the message on my phone my thoughts cleared instantly: my mind was a demolition video played in reverse. It was an emergency alert from Morgan's phone: a ten-out-of-ten, which could only mean that her life or someone she loved was in danger. *One* being a bad hair day, and *ten* being a calamity... and Morgan is not the type to overreact. Anything from eight upwards counts as a panic button click and gets auto-directed to the official emergency services. We're talking armed police, ambulances, and a forensic team with body-bags. Morgan had never sent out a ten-out-of-ten alert for the decade I'd known her, and she'd been through her fair share of crises. The accompanying location pin showed that she was at home, seven and a half kilometres away. If I really bolted, I could be there in ten minutes.

I leapt up with my crossbow, clipped it onto my back, and without a backward glance, I jumped up onto the sill and stepped out of the window.

CHAPTER 3
UNPOPULAR GARDEN ORNAMENT

Morgan's panic button alert kept vibrating on my phone and inside my chest. Fresh adrenaline made me feel like I could fly. I stepped out of the window, leaving poor pink boxer shorts to take his last rattling breath alone. I left the warm flame-yellow light of the brothel and fell into the cool dark night, the fresh air turning my naked skin to braille.

I landed on the top of a balcony, then jumped across and grabbed onto the edge of the flat roof of the apartment block opposite The Jupiter Drawing Room. They must get some interesting views. From there it was just a parkour across and down to Sauer Street, where I had left my motorbike. Passers-by stared as I unlocked the top-box and retrieved my trusty trench coat and smart helmet. I pulled the coat on around my exposed body and belted it tightly. The sense of comfort I felt was about more than preserving my modesty: the coat is made from graphene, a compound more flexible than kevlar and stronger than steel. To add to the tech, it has a protection enchantment, which I keep fresh by casting a new spell every time I go out on a mission. There are some other tricks it can do, too, because the person who made it is a total bonafide genius of the dwarf variety.

I slammed the box shut and jumped on the bike, and was immediately reassured by the feeling of the powerful machine beneath me.

"*Contendis,*" I said into the helmet, and the engine roared to life—a glinting black aluminum lion in the urban jungle. I squeezed the handlebar, rolling it forward, and we took off out of the city CBD, the rushing tarmac beneath me painted orange by the glaring streetlights.

IT TOOK me nine minutes to race to Morgan's house, but they felt like nine hours. My head was crowded with questions, none of which I liked the potential answers to. I almost clipped a swerving taxi because I was distracted, and that made me pull myself together. If I didn't simmer down, I would be no use to anybody. It wouldn't be easy to do magic with mangled limbs.

I PUT my head down and roared out of the city and into the quiet suburb, which was darker than usual because of the overcast night sky. I changed my visor setting to night-vision and the houses popped in green. By "houses" I mean ten-foot exterior walls festooned with glittering razor wire and electric bunting. No picket fences here in Jozi, where crime is as everyday as cereal in a box.

When I pulled up to the entrance of the security complex that Morgan lived in I didn't like what I saw: a trio of badly parked cop cars. Even without a calamity, the security at these places is tight. You need to show your full creds to enter, and they take your digital fingerprint. I've been denied access before because I forgot to bring my driver's license. Soon they'll be asking for iris scans and your pee in a cup. I blasted through the gate and the uniforms jumped and shouted at me to stop, but I didn't have time. My blood was pulsing in my head, my stomach was a stone.

Then it got worse.

Outside Morgan's home flashed the emergency lights of more squad cars, and an ambulance with its back doors flung open. Officials with small straight lines for mouths hurried around, badges glinting, talking to themselves and looking up at the flat black sky, as if it held an answer for them. Yellow emergency police tape cordoned off Morgan's property like a badly wrapped gift.

No, I was thinking. *No, no, no.*

Not Morgan, I begged the same sky the others were blinking at. *Please, not Morgan.*

I don't have many friends. Being a cynical, paranoid hexer with a penchant for straight talk and quick and dirty magic is —surprisingly—not a great recipe for winning friends and influencing people. Besides, I know I spook non-magical humans. I guess it's not easy to have coffee with someone who is haunted, like I am, by what I've seen and what I've done. Sitting across from a damaged person with their finger on a proverbial loaded gun doesn't make for easy conversation.

I slowed down and parked my bike on the neat concrete sidewalk. As soon as I took my helmet off I heard kids crying, and I looked across and saw Morgan's children sobbing into the chest of who I guessed was a social worker. There were another couple of kids there, too, all crying inconsolably while the worried-looking official tried to comfort them.

No!

Dread pulled at me with cold fingers. I started jogging toward the kids, the whole scene flickering bright blue and red with the emergency vehicle lights and my frayed nerves, and I was about to go down on my knees to embrace them when I heard Morgan shouting my name.

"Jax!" she shouted. "Jax!"

I was so relieved it felt like my knees melted. I had to take a second to steady myself, to make sure I didn't fall down. I wheeled around and searched for where her voice was coming from, and then I saw her waving to me from the open-mouthed ambulance. Her face was as pale as the moon and the foil blanket around her shoulders rippled in the breeze. I was so relieved to see her alive that tears stung my eyes. I ran over as fast as I could with my melted knees and launched into a hug.

"MY GOD," Morgan said. "You have no idea how happy I am to see you."

She was wearing pajamas marked with grass stains and soil, sitting on the edge of the ambulance floor, and her dachshund, Pincher, was shivering on her lap.

"What the hell happened?" I asked. "I thought—"

"My neighbor," Morgan said.

"Your neighbor?"

"Liz. Liz Durison. You've met her before. She's your height. Has your hair-color."

"What?"

Nothing was making sense to me; anxiety had short-circuited my brain. Morgan may as well have been speaking in tongues.

She took a deep breath, and put her hand on Pincher's head. "I was locking up the house, ready to go to bed, and I let Pinch out, like normal, but he didn't come back. Next thing he's going bat-shit crazy, barking." Morgan's eyes were electric. "And I got this really bad feeling. So I grabbed my gun and came out here," she gestured to the front lawn, "and then Pincher whines, a sharp high whine, like... like someone kicked him? But he didn't give up, he kept barking and growling at him."

"At who?"

She shook her head, blond hair dyed blue by the flashing police lights. "I don't know."

Pincher looked at me, ears trembling, brown eyes alert. Damn, I wish animals could talk.

"I went out into the front garden, and Pincher wasn't there. I stuck my head over the hedge, to look into Liz's property, and then I saw her, lying on the lawn."

"Dead?"

"Her body's on the way to the city morgue."

"*Filius canis,*" I whispered through gritted teeth, and then when she looked at me for a translation, I said "Son of a bitch."

Morgan hates it when I swear in Latin, but this time she let it slide.

"She was my neighbor," says Morgan, as if speaking aloud would help her understand what had happened. "We used to borrow sugar from each other, for god's sake."

I nodded.

"Our kids used to play together."

I understood that she was shocked by what she had experienced, and I was sure it had shaken her deeply, having someone she saw every day killed and left on the lawn like an unpopular garden ornament. Murdered in a complex she called home and thought was safe, or at least, safe enough. But what was bugging me was that she had seen far worse than this, and had never pressed her ten-out-of-ten panic button. What was different about what happened here?

"Were you very close?" I hoped I wasn't asking her too many questions. Sometimes it was a difficult line to navigate, the one between friend and wizard private eye.

"No," Morgan coughed into her white-knuckled fist. "Hell, no. She was a total bitch."

I frowned at her, trying to work it out. *Why the panic button?*

Morgan understood my unasked question. "The reason I got such a fright... when I saw that dead body on the lawn," she said. "Is because I thought it was *you*."

PINCHER HAD FINALLY STOPPED SHIVERING, and he closed his eyes and put his snout down on her thigh.

Liz Durison, lying dead on the lawn. Same height, same hair color.

"I thought it was you," she said again. "Murdered. Stripped naked." Then a look came over her. "And there was something else."

"What?"

Morgan stood up and passed the sleeping dog to a fresh-faced cop standing nearby, who nodded and headed toward the house. She yanked off the silver blanket and threw it into the back of the ambulance, then picked up her captain's uniform jacket and Beretta. Morgan heads up the Scorpions, a special ops task force recruited by the Council to investigate paranormal crime.

"It's not something I can describe," she said, tucking her gun back into her holster and zipping the jacket up over her pin-stripe pajamas. "I'll have to show you."

CHAPTER 4
BLACK MIST

I was going to ride my bike to the morgue, but then something made me go with Morgan, instead. She still seemed shaken up. I don't know what it is, but I feel protective of her. She may be captain of the Scorpions, and by far the most intelligent and intuitive cop I know—plus, she's an excellent shot—but when I'm around her I just feel like I'm the older sister. Maybe because I'm taller than her, and physically stronger (and usually wearing a triple-layer graphene coat) while she's feminine and petite, and pretty much always wearing lipstick. She's the Muggle to my Mage. She's the light, I am the shadow. (But you shouldn't let her looks fool you. The last orc who underestimated her got a red stiletto heel spiked through his eyeball. I'm pretty sure he'll never look at her the same way again.)

But it wasn't all bravado and selflessness on my side. I had to admit that the bomb-proof exterior, bullet-proof windows and run-flat tires of Morgan's police-issue SUV held a certain attraction for me after the night I had experienced. The leather seats were pretty comfortable, too.

It wasn't a leisurely drive. Morgan put on her blue flashing light and barreled her way through the last of the city traffic, narrowly missing a beggar who wanted to squirt dirty water on her pristine windshield.

"Out of my way!" she shouted, and put her foot down. She suffers from road rage at the best of times, so being in a car with her, while her body worked through the residual adrenaline of her trauma, was not boring. We screeched into the underground parking entrance. She flashed her badge at the attendant, and the boom was barely raised by the time we flew through it, round a dark corner, and into an empty parking bay. I made a note to myself that next time, big sister or not, I'd take my bike.

The morgue's interior was as depressing at its reason for existing. White walls stained by sneaking damp and human traffic. Dusty lightbulbs flickering. Cold stagnant air. I shivered and pulled my trench coat tighter, remembering then that I had nothing but underwear on beneath, which in turn reminded me of my failed mission—the sour breath and stained fangs, and the man bleeding out on the bed—and I shivered again. I rubbed at the tattoo on my neck: a realistic depiction of a vampire bite.

"You okay?" Morgan asked, furrowing her perfect brows at me.

I nodded. "Cold," I said. I wasn't sure if she needed to hear about the murder at The Jupiter Drawing Room earlier that night. Didn't need to know that I had hesitated just before performing my *coup de grace*, and now there was a decidedly vicious vampire out on the town who knew my scent intimately, and could find me in a crowded room.

I also had less lethal problems, but they were problems nonetheless. Madame Woolf would probably have to close her doors, because it turns out, rather unsurprisingly, that bordello customers make easy pickings for reckless vampires, and when the word gets out about tonight, her queue of clients will certainly dry up.

Most vampires manage to keep their bloodlust under control. Most of them are intelligent enough to realize that if they don't toe the line, if they don't follow the rules set out by the Council, that there'll be hell to pay. The Council doesn't mess around; they have agents and assassins hidden in pockets all over the city, and they're not afraid to use them. The rules keep the Realm in check.

A lot of magical species live on the edge of those boundaries, committing petty crimes and dealing in contraband—like the infamous orc mafia do—but they know not to cross the line. Disobey the Council and you may as well take yourself for a nice long walk off a short cliff.

But of course, like in any society, you always get the rebels, the rogues. The beasts who let their desires rule them, even if the consequence happens to be a swift death meted out by the person you thought was your housekeeper. These vamp delinquents don't accept the restrictions placed on their kind, don't buy into the idea of drinking synthetic blood to stave off their hunger. They certainly don't know how to behave in luxurious neo-gothic bordellos. Unfortunately, as far as I knew, no-one had published a brochure on *Brothel Etiquette for Vampires.*

I sighed. No more honey, no more money, which was bad news for me. Woolf would not be happy, and neither would my landlord, who was a particularly smelly orc named Uragh who didn't approve of wily female wizards at the best of times, but especially not when they were two months behind on paying their rent.

MORGAN LED me through the grim morgue corridor and bashed open a pair of swinging doors the color of old army tanks. The room inside was cavernous and crowded with corpses. The dead bodies were tucked away in their refrigerated drawers, but I could sense every single one of them. I felt their fright, their confusion, their unwillingness to let go of the lives they were so attached to. There was a distraught mother who had died without saying goodbye to her three small children, and a teenager who never meant to pull the trigger of his father's revolver. An old man who—

No.

I stopped myself. I cut myself off from the slow, creeping energy of the dead, I had to. I needed to hang on to some sanity, some clarity of mind for what I was about to see.

My eyes rested on the table in the middle of the room. A worn white sheet covering a body that could have been mine.

"Ready?" Morgan asked. Without waiting for my reply, she whipped the sheet away.

LIZ DURISON. I recognized her. Quick flashes of memories of the woman next door. She had been the one who shrieked at her children for getting their clothes dirty while playing outside on a beautiful summer day, the one who never let go of her yapping poodle, the one who had given me a dirty look at Morgan's last neighborhood barbecue for pouring a triple gin into my shot of tonic. She was pouting, and taking the tiniest sips of her warm glass of sweet rosé. One of us got horribly drunk. Spoiler: it wasn't me. When I left that night I saw her snoring, open-mouthed, in her garden chair, while her kids roughhoused, spilling juice and Nik-Naks on the couches inside.

I looked at her body on that table. Her milky skin, her slack lips. Small navy blue veins snaked over her eyelids and the delicate parts of her arms.

Yes, she had been a bitch, but she didn't deserve this.

"WHAT IS THAT?" asked Morgan. "Do you know?"

She was looking at the symbol burned into Liz Durison's chest. An Anarchy sign turned upside-down.

"I've never seen it before," I said.

Morgan didn't break eye-contact. "I need you on this case."

I looked at her. "How do you know this is paranormal?"

I mean, I could tell that this was not a regular murder, but there was no practical proof. I didn't know which creature had done this to her, and I wouldn't know where to start. No bite marks, no claw-scratches—

"I could feel it," she said. Good grief, the woman can go a long time without blinking. Do they teach you how to do that in the police academy?

"What?" I asked. "What could you feel?"

Morgan bit her lip, as if the memory caused her discomfort. "When I went out into the garden, it was like there was a kind of... menace?... all around me. The stars disappeared, the breath went out of my lungs."

Now she had my attention.

"It's difficult to explain. Everything I looked at seemed evil. As if it had been tainted with some noxious energy. I thought it was in my head, obviously. But there was, like, this cold black mist that started pouring in."

Uh-oh. "Black mist?"

"I mean, it wasn't *real.* It wasn't really there. It was just a feeling. A terrible feeling that seeped straight into my body, into my bones. Made me feel—"

"Dead," I said, and she finally blinked.

"Yes," she said. "Cold. Hopeless. Like I'd never breathe again."

Yep, that sums up being dead pretty accurately.

We looked down at the rosé-swilling woman with the inverted Anarchy symbol—or whatever it was—branded into her skin. I bent over to get a closer look. It was a "V" breaking out of a perfect circle. Suddenly the species of the killer became obvious to me. Black mist, Morgan said, and a "V"?

"Will you take the case?" Morgan asked.

I couldn't take my eyes off the symbol. My wand was vibrating on my hip.

"I didn't want to ask you," she said. "Not really. It's too dangerous. But—"

She didn't finish her sentence. She didn't have to.

But what choice do we have?

I was two months late on rent and my fridge at home was emptier than a turkey cage at Christmas. Of course I'd take the case. If I had to be completely honest, I'd take the case even if there was no pay-day. Because I was pretty sure a vampire was responsible for this; I could sense it on my skin. I could smell it. And I was ready to kill every last one of them.

CHAPTER 5
THE WEREWOLF WAS NOT HAPPY

It was just past midnight when I got home, and I felt absolutely shattered. I hung my trench coat up on the hook at the front door and placed my helmet on the table in the entrance hall. I loped into my lounge, which was crowded with books and relics and the occasional ghostly specter. It felt so good to be back. It may be a haunted apartment, but it was my haunted apartment, and it was home. In the old days, wizards lived in remote places, in communion with nature. It's not so easy for an urban wizard, but I'm happy with my place, which is on the very top floor of a Jo'burg skyscraper, away from the human bustle of the city, and close to the stars. The enchanted elevator, called a Swift, takes only Touched species up past the fiftieth floor. The Untouched humans don't even know the top floors exist.

I needed a drink, a shower, and bed, in that order, and as soon as possible. While I was standing in front of the bookcase and thinking how exhausted I felt, my feet as heavy as concrete blocks, a book fell off the shelf and slammed onto the floor.

The ghost—or whatever it is, we've never been formally introduced—has certain quirks, one of which is to welcome me home by rearranging my reading material, amongst other things. I picked up the book, an ancient red cloth hardcover with brittle, sunned pages and speckled edges, and slid it back in place.

"Hello to you, too," I said.

I MADE my way to the kitchen. The fridge was as bare as I had expected, and the liquor cabinet was looking worryingly empty, too. I really had let things slide. Running out of food is one thing, but running out of Ferra's home-distilled Cinnamon Whisky is unforgivable.

I splashed what was left of the bottle into a chipped tumbler and took it to my room. The bed was disconcertingly neatly made.

"I told you not to make my bed," I said to the empty walls, but I could feel that the ghost wasn't listening. One of his many talents is selective hearing. He likes to know when I get home safely, but after that he buggers off, where to is anyone's guess. I took a large sip of my drink and it blazed in my mouth and set my throat alight. I took another one, and this time it hurt less. The third sip started the slow, welcome burn down inside my body, a dynamite fuse, and made the disappointment and frustration of the day fade just a little.

It blurred the edges of my failure, softened the stone that had been sitting in my stomach since seeing the gurgling man in pink boxer shorts dyeing the brothel linen red. Maybe it was a good thing that there was no more whisky, I thought, setting the empty glass down on my chest of drawers. If I had a whole bottle I may have drunk it all, and that odiferous orc who calls himself a landlord would have walked in and found my dead body there, clutching the empty spice-fragrant bottle to my chest like an out-of-luck pirate.

The alcohol that was softening my dread-coated insides was also forcing down my eyelids. I was tempted to just lie down, fully-clothed, and give in to the delicious sleep it was pulling me into, but my skin felt gritty and I could smell my own stress-sweat glowing in a halo around me. I was so stinky that I would have given Uragh a run for his money. Believe me, that's saying something, and it's not the kind of statement I wanted to make. No way I could climb into that perfectly made bed looking and feeling like that, so I turned on the shower and stripped out of my underwear while I waited for the solar heater to kick in. Seeing my naked skin reminded me of Liz Durison's body, and I imagined what it looked like when Morgan found her, lying on that lawn of grass painted black by the starless night.

I pushed the image from my mind and stepped into the shower. It was not the time to re-live the violence of the day.

The warm water felt good on my sore muscles, and it seemed to ease my thoughts, too. I scrubbed myself, trying to wash away the evil I had seen; the cruelty. Of course, I would need something a little stronger than almond-milk bodywash to do that job.

As soon as I had lathered up, I heard my phone ringing, and I sighed and rolled my bloodshot eyes to the cloud of steam hovering on the ceiling.

I turned the shower off and climbed out of the glass cubicle, still covered with suds and dripping with water, and hunted for the thing, which I eventually found in the kitchen, where the tiles were cold beneath my bare feet. I swooped and caught it on its last ring.

"Hello?" I said. I didn't recognize the number, but that didn't mean it wasn't Morgan trying to get hold of me. "Hello?"

"I'm looking for a Jacquelyn Denna Knight," said a lofty voice. "Wizard?"

"You found her," I said, torn between wanting to know who the owner of the smug voice was, and telling him where to shove his witching-hour phone-call.

"Ms. Knight," he said, "I need your help."

Look, buddy, I thought, *I need a towel and a good night's sleep. So you can—*

"My name is Estelar Pavaris."

"Oh." I've never been one for name-dropping but when Estelar Pavaris, VIP Elf Esquire, owner of the Elf Press and Associated Magazines (and the biggest mansion in town) phones you in the middle of the night, you listen hard.

I cleared my throat. "What can I do for you, Mister Pavaris?"

"I have a situation," he said. "I heard you were the best at solving the particular... challenge I have."

Now that we were talking, I saw through his aloof tone and heard a slight wobble in his voice. He was worried about something. Really worried. I padded slowly back to my bedroom to fetch my bathrobe, which I wrapped around my still-dripping body.

"What problem is that?" I felt bad for the guy, and I didn't want to be indelicate, but I had a date with my pillow. I needed Pavaris, as rich and handsome and important as he was, to cut to the chase.

"I'd prefer to discuss it in person, if you don't mind, terribly?"

"Of course," I said. I didn't mind a meeting with Pavaris. From what I'd heard, business meetings with Estelar inevitably ended up with gold coins raining down on your face. Also, I was intrigued.

"Ten a.m.?" the elf ventured. "At the mansion?"

I caught sight of a lonely, slightly withered-looking apple on my dining room table. My stomach growled, pulling off a pretty convincing werewolf impersonation. I picked the apple up and was about to bite into it when I realized I'd be even more hungry in the morning when I woke up, so I stashed it in my robe pocket, instead. The werewolf was not happy.

"I'll be there," I said to Pavaris.

I ended the call and started looking for my pajamas. They weren't where I had left them, dirty and crumpled on the floor. I swore and opened my cupboard door and there they were: folded beautifully and waiting for me on the shelf.

"I told you not to fold my pajamas!" I yelled at the room, but there was no one there.

FINALLY, finally, I crept into bed and felt the cool cotton pillowcase against my cheek. My scratchy eyes drifted closed... and the doorbell rang.

"You have *got* to be kidding," I said, flinging off the duvet, jumping out of bed and barreling toward the door. It had to be Uragh. Who else would be ringing a doorbell at this uncivilized hour? Orcs don't care about civility. Orcs don't care about—

But when I wrenched the door open it wasn't a big, smelly orc, but a small waif of a boy with bright jade coins for eyes and grubby clothes that smelled like the city slums. A street urchin. I knew the smell all too well. A charming street urchin, but an urchin nonetheless.

I sighed, and sagged against the doorframe. "Bron. It's one o'clock in the bloody morning."

"I saw your light on," he said.

"I've had a long day," I said. "Scamper."

"I just came to ask you one thing."

"I don't have any food for you," I said, the apple burning a hole in my pocket.

"I didn't come for food," he said, looking slightly offended.

"I know what you came for."

"Please will you at least think about it?"

"You're just a child," I said. "How old are you, anyway? Ten?"

"Sixteen!" he said. "I'm practically an adult."

I laughed out loud, and started to close the door.

"Fourteen," he whispered. Still lying. He wasn't a day over twelve.

I opened it again, and sighed again. It was the longest day in the history of my life, and probably in the history of the world, ever, since the beginning of time.

"The answer is no, Bron. The answer was no yesterday, and it will be no tomorrow. So you can save us both some time by never asking again."

The boy looked disappointed, but there was a gleam in his eye that told me he'd be back the next day. He was nothing if not tenacious. He bowed, and turned to leave, ready to disappear into the darkness from whence he came. A night sprite.

"Bron," I said, and he whirled around. I threw the apple to him, and he caught it. "See you tomorrow."

CHAPTER 6
THE HIGHFIRE CROWN

I stood before the Pavaris mansion with my jaw hanging open. I had seen photographs of the place but the pictures on a screen hadn't done it justice. It was the size of a castle, expertly built, beautifully shaped, solid yet ethereal, crafted from rose and ivory marble and edged in gold. It was the magical version of the Taj Mahal, and it glowed with its inherent enchantments in the bright African sun. Pretty finches with feathers of fire lined the top of the gate and they hopped and chirred in greeting as the giant double door opened in on itself, revealing the lushest, most vibrant and well-manicured garden I had ever seen.

I wondered how much of the landscape was real, and how much was an illusion. As far as I knew, we didn't get finches in Jo'burg. That emerald carpet of a lawn would take a team of gardeners and an Olympic-sized pool of irrigation water a week to keep it looking that way. A conjuring spell would be a lot more affordable, not to mention the water saving benefit. Do elves even care about carbon footprints? Probably not. Maybe I don't give them enough credit, but I've never met an elf who cared about anything much more than his own self and—at a stretch—his family. As Ferra likes to say: *There's a reason there's an "elf" in "self"*. Sometimes she forgets the "S" altogether: if one of her twelve kids is demanding more than his share, she bangs her copper pots around and yells, *Stop being so elfish!*

I walked up the wide glittering stone path lined with dark green groundcover. The beds bloomed with frilly irises, purple spotted foxgloves and small white daisies, and the end of the walkway was announced by a pair of ornamental Kumquat standards heavy with fruit. I could smell the honey citrus blossoms in the air.

Two men with rifles over their shoulders suddenly appeared out of nowhere, and they didn't look pleased to see me even as I jumped in surprise. The pair had been there all along, blending in perfectly with the pink marble pillars on either side of the front door thanks to some sort of camouflage voodoo in their uniforms. I recovered quickly and lifted my chin at them, not smiling.

Then I heard vicious barking, and a pair of shiny diamond-collared dobermans raced around the corner. I quickly grabbed my wand, ready to throw up a shield, but the groundsman broke his invisibility camouflage, too, and I saw the dogs were on leashes. They made their way past us, the dogs straining to get at me all the while, keen to take a bite. Once they had passed, I took a breath and clipped my wand back in place.

"Ms. Knight," said the taller guard, returning my non-smile. "Mr. Pavaris is expecting you."

HE LET me into the cool vast interior, luxuriously decorated with oriental carpets and bronze sculptures and giant gold-framed portraits of other Very Important Elves. The guard led me up the sweeping staircase and into the library, which took my breath away. I tried to remain professional, but the sheer volume of books and the antique ladder on wheels thrilled me. The armed man regarded me with thorough disdain. I ignored him and began to study a row of books, and a business card on the shelf caught my eye.

LOCKTON INSURANCE.

I was about to pick it up when I heard my name being announced from behind me.

"Ms. Knight."

I recognized the smugness in his voice, and the desperation, and I turned to greet him.

Pavaris was tall and handsome, if not slightly older than I had imagined, and dressed in expensive ivory robes threaded with silver. He smiled and took my hands in his as if I was a long-lost, dearly beloved, relative.

"Welcome," he purred, and gestured toward the chaise longue in front of an arched window. "I am Estelar."

He pronounced his name as if he was the lead actor on a London stage. *Esta-laaaaaar.*

"Call me Jax," I said, hoping to relay in my tone that I wasn't there to be his leading lady. I wanted to get down to business and then get out of there. I had, as they say, other fish to fry.

He melted down onto the Chesterfield across from me and clapped his hands softly to the right of his slightly pointed ear. Two servants appeared out of nowhere. One snapped open a rose-gold brocade tablecloth with a flourish and laid it over the coffee table between us, and the other began setting down plates of tea-time treats. Soft white cucumber sandwiches with the crusts cut off, tiny carrot cupcakes impaled with miniature candy carrots, cardamom sugar cookies, rainbow macarons, and glistening petit fours.

Yet another servant appeared and poured us three different drinks: sweet peppermint tea in river-green glass tumblers, Ethiopian coffee in espresso cups, and snifters of ice-cold sparkling water with fresh slices of lime. If blatant displays of wealth impressed wizards, I would have been impressed. As it was, I was just curious to know what Pavaris was hiring me for, and why he felt the need to put on this show. I was a starving wizard from the bad part of town and he knew that. Why the flourishes? Why the lavish tablecloth? Why the French pastry? I didn't touch the food, even though the werewolf in my stomach was trying his best to claw his way out and onto the table.

Estelar noticed my restraint.

"You're wondering why I asked you to meet me," he said.

"I am."

"You're busy. You've got other cases. You want to get out of here."

I looked at him. His eyes were Pacific blue, and beguiling.

"You're the most talented wizard in the country."

"Not quite," I said.

He looked offended on my behalf. "Certainly the best in the city."

"I don't know about that," I lied.

"Your humility notwithstanding, you do come most highly recommended."

I stabbed a sandwich with my delicate gold fork. If the man was going to natter, I may as well have a snack.

"I understand," he purred, "that you're an extremely busy woman. But I need to hire you, and I want this case to be your sole focus."

"I can't do that," I said, wiping my mouth with a napkin that had been starched to within an inch of its life. "I accepted an important job last night, and it's not the kind of job that can wait."

A picture of Liz Durison's branded chest flashed in on me. The smell of her, too, which made me stop chewing and put the rest of my sandwich down. I dusted the crumbs from my fingers.

"I'll pay you double." Pavaris dabbed at his lips, too, as if trying to clean away the lowliness of talking about money at the tea table.

I noticed a hairline crack in my coffee cup. "What do you need?"

Pavaris put down his glass of tea, and his mouth twitched. He stood, and smoothed down the glimmering cream fabric of his robes. "Please," he said, "come with me."

THE ELF LED me to a small room in the center of the mansion. At the entrance stood a huge gilded birdcage covered in a fuchsia silk scarf, and in the middle of the room was a pedestal topped with a satin cushion.

Pavaris chewed his bottom lip and rubbed his forehead. There were lines on his skin I hadn't noticed before, and the drapes in the room looked sun-bleached and dusty.

"I don't know how they got in," he said. "I don't know how they took it. I'm the only one who can disable the security enchantment on this room."

I tore my gaze away from the empty satin cushion atop the pedestal and looked into his eyes again. More beseeching, now, than beguiling. I frowned at him.

He rubbed his forehead again, clearly agitated. "I'm the only one, do you understand?"

I did understand, and that's why I was confused. If you imagine a regular security system, with motion-sensitive beams and screeching alarms and a touch-pad to set and disable it, and you multiply the sensitivity and intelligence of the beams by a hundred and add a magical dimension to the password so that it changes every second and no one can bypass it, ever, apart from the caster of the spell, then you'll have an idea of an elf's safety enchantment.

"What did they steal?"

Pavaris took a moment to gather himself with some deep—and deeply unattractive—nasal breathing, then said with a hand on his chest, "My Crown."

"Your crown?"

"It's not just any crown," he said. "It's the HighFire Crown."

I searched the spinning rolodex in my head for the term. It sounded familiar.

"The HighFire Crown," said Estelar, "has been passed down from generation to generation in my family. A magical item of immeasurable value. Pale gold animated with white fire. Diamonds forged in the Baltic volcanoes, pearls from the depths of Atlantis."

Pavaris had missed his calling, I thought. He really should be on a stage somewhere. I had the feeling he was about to weep, and I didn't have the time or the inclination to watch him ugly-cry.

"Where were your guards?" I asked, hoping to snap him out of his soliloquy.

"Comatose," he said. "Victims of some potent sleeping spell. I would have guessed they were dead if they hadn't been snoring so thunderously. That's what woke me up. It sounded like someone was sawing the house down. They were alive, thank the Void, but not everyone was as fortunate."

His heavy-lidded eyes rested on the cage beside us. I pulled off the bright silk scarf and he flinched. On the bottom of the cage lay a large stiff bird, eyes closed, legs in the air like brittle winter sticks.

"Your security bird," I said.

"Pharos. Wonderful bird. May he rest in peace."

"Pavaris," I said. "He's not dead."

The elf looked up from wiping his eyes. "I beg your pardon?"

"He's not dead," I said again, and unclipped the door of the cage, sliding my hand in and picking the phoenix up off the shredded newspaper floor. I couldn't help but notice that the masthead on the newspaper was one of the Pavaris Publications that had folded last year. It seemed cruel to draw the comparison, but it seemed apt that it was covered in phoenix feces.

Pharos was a big guy, heavy in my hands, and Pavaris could be forgiven for thinking he was a goner with his dulled feathers and lolling navy tongue.

I nestled Pharos in my left hand, covered his breast with my right, and looked at him intently. I found the bird's heart and placed the pads of my fingers over the indigo plumes that covered it. I tried to focus on the emotion in the room: Pavaris's devastation, his bereavement, his sense of loss.

"*Contendis,*" I said, and we held our breath. The phoenix remained, for all intents and purposes, dead.

Estelar frowned at me. What kind of a cruel wizard was I, I imagined him thinking, coming in here and giving him false hope? I squeezed the bird a little tighter and decided to try again. This time I used my own feelings instead of the elf's: my ego, still smarting from yesterday, my hunger, my fear. The one advantage of having had a terrible childhood is that I can draw on the pain whenever I need it. It's always there, in the background, a ghostly ache of my heart. I thought of my parents and felt the sadness swell in my chest and I swirled it up, sent it along my arm, and directed it through my fingers and into the phoenix's chest.

"*Contendis,*" I said again.

At first nothing happened, but then the bird's eyes twitched, and I let out the breath I didn't know I had been holding. Pharos shook a wing out, and cycled madly in the air with his feet. I turned him over and he gripped my thumb, then shook out his other wing, and shivered. His dull feathers came alive with color and he nibbled at his chest, perhaps wondering why it felt odd.

Pavaris stuck out a slender finger. Pharos hopped onto his hand, nodding and chirping. It was the elf's turn to have his jaw hang open, and he looked at me as if I was an angel incarnate. I've never had an elf—or any man, for that matter —look at me like that. It's a feeling I could get used to. But even more pleasing was the fact that he was lost for words.

"It was a heart-pause spell," I said. Estelar knew what that meant. It's an easy spell to reverse if you catch it in time, but a couple more hours and the bird wouldn't have had an encore.

"Thank you?" Pavaris said. I'm not sure why it was a question, but it didn't matter. He agreed to pay me half my fee upfront and I left the opulent estate thinking that I knew exactly who had stolen the HighFire Crown.

CHAPTER 7
CRIMSON-TINTED GLASSES

I traipsed out of the Pavaris mansion feeling pretty good about things. Not only had I saved his phoenix and guessed who the thief of the HighFire Crown was, but I would soon have enough money in the bank to pay for two full months' rent, plus a bit of change for a bag of groceries. Life was good. Life was very good, I thought, as I walked along the smooth pavements in the lavish elf suburb, passing elves walking their glossy dogs with expensive jeweled collars and shining blond coats, and new mothers cooing into their designer prams that probably cost more than my entire apartment. Elves aren't that bad, now, are they? Although you wouldn't catch me sharing that particular notion with Ferra.

It was easy to feel at peace there in elf-land. The elves had created a kind of Shangri-La for themselves, buying up all the expensive property in the north of Johannesburg, bribing stubborn residents or forcing them out in other devious ways, and making it their own. The elf suburbs were huge gated communities guarded closely 24/7 by their appointed staff in black official-looking uniforms. Whoever stole the Crown had extreme talent of the magical variety, or had super cunning, and a serious case of the smarts.

Who am I kidding? I thought. To break through an elf security enchantment, you'd need all three.

Immediately outside the wealthy suburb, the roads became pot-holed and dirty, and weeds pushed their way up through the cracks in the sidewalk. This was more the neighborhood I was used to, and my shoulders relaxed. I didn't feel like an alien here, in my black outfit and burnished hair. A grid of shacks with corrugated iron for roofs glimmered in the late morning sun, and litter, caught in chicken-wire fences, swayed and snapped in the breeze. Kids in faded shirts ran and cheered and played while mothers hung up hand-washed laundry. It didn't take a genius to guess that one day soon, the people living in the hothouses would bloom out of their shacks and demand some of the land next door. I had felt uncomfortable with the sheer extravagance of the Pavaris mansion, but standing there watching the kids play in the shadows of all that imported marble and flashing gold made me feel positively ill. I didn't have much time to indulge in my self-righteous nausea, however, because a limousine the color of coal glided to a stop right next to me and three heavies jumped out the cabin and tried to wrangle me inside.

IN A HOT FLASH I was transported back in time to when I was nine and living on the gray streets in downtown Jo'burg. I had just used my burgeoning magic to slip a twenty-rand note out of a passerby's cream linen pocket, and I was dreaming of the bag of hot chips I was going to buy with it. I was too hungry to feel guilty. When I joined the small gang of street kids I was a traumatized little girl, lost in every way. They took me in and taught me their special brand of magic: quick and dirty spells that you could sneak into almost any scenario without being caught. The money in my hand was proof that I could look after myself. It made me feel clever and strong and independent, and less broken. It was everything to me.

There was a vendor on the corner who would give us his just-expired food if we didn't hang around and bother his paying customers. We used to call him Mr. Hot Dog because there was a funny painting on his shop-front of a vienna-man wearing a long bun, with a squiggle of tomato sauce running down his body. Mr. Hot Dog was having a slow week and didn't have any leftovers for us that day, so a couple of us hadn't eaten in a while. Those days on the streets were when I got to know my inner werewolf.

I CLUTCHED the precious cash in my small hand—black-nailed and grubby—and set my sight on Mr. Hot Dog's greasy service window, which was one of my favorite places in the world, especially then, in the cold of winter, because the hot kitchen air would billow out and keep me warm in the quick, stolen moments of walking past. No hanging around, though, to breathe in the old sunflower oil deep-fryer smell, or the aroma of swollen frankfurters in their warming drawer. No loitering to defrost blue fingers, or we wouldn't get our scraps. But this time I had money, and I'd be able to stand in the short queue and feel the steam on my face and my icy hands as I waited with the other paying customers. I knew Mr. Hot Dog would stuff my packet with as many extra fries as it could handle, without it splitting down the sides, so I'd be able to share them with my fellow Ferals without feeling much anguish. I thought of the spice and the vinegar, and I began to salivate.

I must have been ten steps away from the vendor when the thug grabbed me. He was wearing some kind of invisibility enchantment so when he picked me up by the scruff of my neck I felt like I was flying. I kicked and screamed and he slammed his hand over my mouth so hard that my teeth cut my lip, and I could taste the blood.

(So much blood in my memories; sometimes I feel as if my whole life has been tinted by blood—like crimson-tinted glasses.)

I kept writhing and kicking, and screaming into his hot, salty palm, which was as big as my face. He growled at me to keep quiet, but I had other plans.

"Monstras!" I shouted. It was a reveal-spell that the Ferals had taught me. The invisibility enchantment rustled and fell off the man like a slippery blanket. I looked at his wide, determined face, and screamed right into it, blood spraying his cheek.

"Help!" I yelled. "Help!" but my words were muffled, and, even if they weren't, I already knew from experience that people didn't stop to help children in rags, even when they're in trouble. If I had been wearing a pretty dress, and my hair was washed and braided, my skin scrubbed, maybe strangers would have stopped the man, demanded he let me go, but I was not a cherished child. Not anymore.

The twenty-rand note fluttered to the floor.

A bronze-colored SUV pulled up, and the passenger door was flung open. The kidnapper hurled me inside as if I were a rugby ball, then slid in and slammed the door.

"Go!" he instructed the driver behind the smoked-glass screen, and looked around at the pavement we had just left, checking for potential witnesses, or anyone who may have wanted to stop us. Seeing no immediate threats, he pulled out what looked like a white pen and jabbed me in the arm with it. I squealed as the needle bit into me, and then the pain quickly faded. I thought it must be an injection, a sedative, but then I saw him look at the display window on the device. He seemed satisfied, and spoke into his phone.

"Got her," he said, looking again at the reading on the pen. "Yes, I'm sure. Her Magus is a ten."

Then he sat back, grunted, and started wiping my blood off his face with a blue handkerchief. The car took off with a squeal of tires and joined the fast-moving traffic out of the city center. I never saw the Ferals, or Mr. Hot Dog, again.

The flashback had temporarily blinded me, but I soon snapped back to reality, back to the ominous coal-colored limo and the three savages who were trying their damnedest to wrestle me inside.

No way, I thought. *Not again.*

"Let me go!" I screamed, and I bit one of the hands that was forcing me down. It was a mistake. Orcs taste terrible. I tried to kick the other one, tried to reach for my wand—my crossbow was still jammed—but they blasted me with their brute strength and foul breath till I all but fainted into the interior of the car. Apparently magical bulletproof coats don't provide that much protection against three oafs who insist on kidnapping you. Stories about wizard-trafficking echoed in my head, and I felt a new surge of strength. I refused to be a victim. I shouted and forced my hand free, grabbed my wand from my utility belt, and held it up to the orc sitting on the car seat across from me, cool as a cucumber. And by that I mean greenish, with unsightly bumps on her skin. A pickle wearing lipstick.

"Effectus advers—"

The orc leaned forward and smacked the wand out of my hand before I had time to complete the incantation. I fell down onto all fours and searched the floor of the limo. Luckily, my wand didn't seem to like the idea of being relinquished to the Orc Mafia, so it flew into my hand as soon as it sensed my grabbing palm.

. . .

"*Effectus*—" I whirled toward her on my knees, but it was no good. This time she pursed her lips at me, as if I were a recalcitrant child, and dealt me a killer right hook to the jaw.

I fell back, dropping the wand again, seeing stars and holding my face where she had hit me.

"You think you're the only one who can do quick and dirty?" she asked. "You're wrong."

She nodded at the bodyguards to close the doors, and they did so. I scrambled off the floor and back onto the seat. The cabin was cool, and quiet.

"What do you want from me?" I asked, massaging my cheek that was sparking with pain.

I didn't take the punch too personally. Orcs prefer to communicate with their fists; it's a cultural thing. They're not big on words, they don't need to be. Why have a debate with someone when you can just punch them in the face? I stared at the woman and bunched my fingers into a white-knuckled fist. If that's how this conversation was going to go, I was ready.

"I need your help," she said, and I guffawed, sore jaw and all.

"This is an unusual way to ask for help," I said. It hurt.

She leaned forward and down, exposing an unflattering amount of orc cleavage, and picked up my wand. She held it in her clammy hands on her lap. I could practically hear the thing crying.

"Most people are polite about it, you know?" I said. "They say please instead of fracturing your face."

Her face remained stony. "Please," she said, and then, as an afterthought, "my husband is in danger."

I read the inscription on the salad-plate-sized medallion that hung on a gold chain around her neck. SHAGAR, it said, confirming my worst suspicions. This pickle-face wasn't just mafia, she was Mrs. Godfather.

"*Faex*," I swore, just under my breath. "You're Shagar Khargol."

She seemed pleased. Finally, I was going to treat her with the respect she deserved. Instead, I dashed for the door. It was locked. Even if I had managed to magic it open somehow I'd have the brutes outside to deal with.

"Look," I said. "I'm flattered, really. That you'd ask me. But I've actually got two other cases that I'm working on right now and—"

The orc tensed. She was getting annoyed, and if I wasn't careful I'd be spitting out teeth after this briefing-slash-abduction.

"The reason I didn't say *please*," the orc said, "is because I'm not *asking* you to work on this case."

The Orc Mafia don't ask for favors. You either do what they say, or you sleep with the fishes. I knew that if I refused the wife of Don Vito Khargol, the notorious Orc Godfather, I'd be in a whole world of pain. My aching jaw would be nothing but a pleasant memory.

I swallowed my smart-arse reply, and instead said, "Tell me about your husband."

CHAPTER 8

THE GODFATHER

S ugar Shagar (or Mrs. Godfather, as some orcs call her) was known for her unwavering dedication to her husband, her meatball linguine, and her ovaries of solid steel. I had never met the woman prior to her right-hooking me in the face, but as I sat there across from her, in her husband's especially comfortable air-conditioned limousine, I felt my nerves chewing me up from the inside like a school of nervous piranhas.

I have a rule that has served me well in the past, and that is to never accept a job from fae, goblins or orcs. Fae are on the warm side of evil, and wildly unpredictable. Goblins are the most treacherous of all magical species, and orcs... well, they say you should never get on the good side of an orc (getting on the bad side isn't such a big deal, because you'll just be dead). The Orc Mafia, on the other hand, is far more dangerous.

I looked into Shagar Khargol's watery eyes. They were a warning: they were the color of the mud at the bottom of the lake they'd dump my lifeless body into. And that's if my corpse was lucky enough to make it to a large body of water instead of just being unloaded into a burning inner-city dumpster. I looked into those chilled marshy eyes and began sweating.

"Why do you think he's in danger?" My throat was so dry, the question came out quaky.

"I have eyes and ears all over the SubRealm," Shagar said. "I know things you'd never guess at."

I wondered, then, if she was in such a good position to receive orc intel, why she was bringing me in.

"He doesn't listen to me," she said. "He thinks he's invincible."

(From what I had heard, he was right.)

"He thinks he'll be The Godfather forever."

As far as I knew, Don Vito "Or'Capone" Khargol was highly respected, and the most feared orc on the subcontinent. It would take immense balls—or stupidity—to attempt to knock him off his perch. I certainly hadn't heard of any kind of political conspiracy; I was going into this completely blind.

I had to press her. "What have you heard?"

Shagar looked out of the tinted window and absent-mindedly tapped on my wand in her lap. I wanted to ask her to stop, but was afraid of another blow to my glowing skull.

I wiped my clammy hands on my pants. "Why would anyone want to kill The Godfather?"

Don Vito holds the entire orc community together. He's tough, but fair, and he dispenses justice when he believes it necessary. Call it kangaroo court, or call it karma. If you have it coming in the orc world, it will get you. It'll probably arrive five minutes early and sock you where it hurts. It's the orc way. Without a Godfather, though, the status quo will be shredded. There'll be blood on the streets, and not in a good way. I needed to find out why Don Vito was in danger, and not just because Sugar Shagar was asking—*telling*—me to. Usually I don't take kindly to giant lipstick-wearing pickles giving me instructions, but if I didn't find out what was shaking the grapevine in the SubRealm, then we'd may as well all start picking out our favorite flaming dumpsters.

The limo dropped me off outside my building, which was at the same time a favor and a warning. Shagar had managed to tell me absolutely nothing in the half hour I was her prisoner in the luxury sedan, but the message was clear: *Find out who wants The Godfather dead, Or Else, and... we know where you live.*

I trudged toward the entrance of my building, greeting the local drug dealer on the corner, and my trench coat felt heavy on my shoulders. Things had really been looking up, this morning, but now I felt like a bee stuck in its own honey. Worst of all, just before I pulled open the door, I saw in my peripheral vision a man standing halfway up the block, his hands in the pockets of his jacket, his gaze firmly on my back. I turned my head toward him so quickly I almost gave myself whiplash, but by then he was gone. I grasped for the wand that Shagar had returned to me, and felt reassured by the smooth silver against my skin, then walked in and slammed the door behind me.

I was tired and felt like taking the Swift up to my apartment, but I hadn't done any training that day so I knew my muscles needed a bit of a workout if I wanted to stay parkour-fit. I jogged up the steps, all eleventy million of them, and when I reached the top floor my legs felt like they would never work again. I jellied my way to my front door and slid my key into the lock, but something was wrong. Something smelled off. The key wouldn't go all the way in, and it wouldn't turn. With shaking hands I looked over my shoulder, then forced it, and the key snapped off in the lock.

"*Es stercus!*" I cursed.

Did this have to happen today? Really? Today?

And then I realized what that rotten-egg-in-vinegar smell was. Uragh had been there, and he had changed the freaking lock, and added a few extra of his own, made, presumably, out of orc steel, which is pretty much unbreakable. That's when I saw my landlord's note on the floor, a scrawled message on the back of a bulk fishpaste packaging card. "TOO MONTHS," it said (I think). "OUT."

CHAPTER 9
MAGICKAL POISONES AND HOW TO CATCH A SERIAL KILLER

O f course, a locked door has never stopped me before, so I put my hand over the mechanism and sent some fire its way.

"*Ignem Exquiris,*" I chanted, and the heat from my palm softened the metal just enough so that when I pushed my bodyweight against the timber it opened with an annoyed click. The steel was still glowing when I got inside and kicked it closed again, and the smell of charred wood floated in the air. The upside was that I had just broken into my own apartment. The downside was that I wouldn't be able to lock the front door anymore.

The carpet had been vacuumed, and my dirty clothes from the day before had somehow crawled, on their own accord, into my laundry hamper. On schedule, the red hardcover fell off the bookshelf and slammed onto the floor.

"Hello, Ghost," I said, picking it up, dusting it off, and easing it back into place, a snug fit between *Magickal Poisones* and *How To Catch a Serial Killer.*

I sat down at my rickety pine kitchen table and tapped the toe of my boot against its matchstick leg. On the top of the table lay my jammed crossbow. I had to think. I had to eat something and fix my crossbow and think. Morgan would be asking for an update on the Liz Durison case, and Pavaris had already left a long and detailed message on my phone about how he needed his Crown back yesterday. After thinking he had hung up, he dropped his phone and starting weeping. Then there was Sugar Shagar, who was anything but sweet, but her case was probably the most urgent of the three. No, she wasn't going to pay me, but I'd rather be homeless than dead.

It's not like I didn't see the urgency in Estelar's case: it was clear that the HighFire Crown was much more powerful than he was letting on. I suspected the Crown was the whole reason the Pavaris fortune existed. It was the magical item that was holding up the whole building, the whole empire, and, though difficult to believe, I suspected it was also holding up Estelar's face, too. I had watched him age right in front of me that morning. At first I thought I was imagining it, but there were creases on his skin when I left that were definitely not there when he first took my hands in his. His hair turned from blond to ash-blond. The change was subtle, but I have an eye for detail, and I pay special attention when a client offers to pay double my usual fee. Whenever that happens I get very suspicious indeed.

The mansion was pristine when I arrived, but things began to come undone. I noticed how threadbare the oriental carpet was in the entrance hall on my way out, while an hour before it had appeared brand new. The huge crystal chandelier in the entrance sparkled less. Then there was the crack in my coffee cup, and the sun-bleached curtains. When I walked past the bed of irises again, after saying goodbye, they had wilted, and the petals had turned gray.

I couldn't shake the feeling that I was missing something. Maybe it was because of the illusory grounds and his theatrical personality, or maybe deep down, I just didn't trust elves, but something was awry, and I was going to get to the bottom of it.

I unclipped my wand and pointed it at my crossbow. I thought of how it had let me down at a crucial moment at The Jupiter Drawing Room, and I felt the flush of shame on my cheeks as I remembered my failure to kill the satin-skirted vampire with blood-stained lips. I breathed in the wood-smoke scented air and turned it into loathing inside my chest. I hated feeling shame, I hated failure, and I passionately and unreservedly hated vampires. The anger swirled in my chest like a black tornado, and I pulled it up and pushed it out toward my impotent weapon.

"*Curas Vulnum,*" I said, and a stream of current flowed out of the tip of the wand and forged a glowing strip on the barrel of the bow. I thought it looked like it was doing a good job (although, to be fair, I know very little about the mechanics of crossbows. I just like how you can pull a trigger and have an arrow shooting straight into a vampire's cold and desiccated heart). When the current faded and the weapon stopped glowing, I picked it up, blew off the imaginary filings, and checked the cams and the cables. They seemed to be in good shape. Looking through the scope, I aimed at the bookshelf, at a reading lamp, at a scruffy old wingback I found at the local charity shop for two hundred bucks. It had a throw cushion on it, a threadbare one with a screen-printed picture of the Mona Lisa which I've never liked. I took aim, and I fired.

The whooshing of the arrow out of the flight groove and across the room was music to my ears. The projectile found its target beautifully, and pinned Mona to the chair with a spear in her left eye.

"Yes," I hissed, and fist-pumped.

Usually I wasn't good at repairing things, with or without magic, so the victory was especially sweet. But then I heard a cry of someone in pain, and it was coming from the chair. I did a double-take. I looked at Mona Lisa, dropped the crossbow on the table, and raced over. No, it wasn't Mona Lisa who was crying (obviously). It was someone else. Someone invisible.

Oh my god, had I just shot my ghost?

"Ghost?" I said. I really needed to get him a name. That's if I hadn't just killed him, of course. "Ghost?"

There was another groan, and I looked around the place like a mad woman. Where was he? Can you really shoot a specter? Then the groan turned into a chuckle, and faded away.

I pursed my lips. "Very funny."

Just my luck to get haunted by a spirit with a stupid sense of humor. I wrenched the arrow out of the cushion—waste not, want not—but then there was another whooshing sound and a new arrow struck the wall just above me with a sharp clack and a crumble of plaster. A cool wind forced me down to the ground while the crossbow shot wildly around the room and my heart pounded against the floor. Only when it ran out of arrows did the cold weighted blanket slide off me, allowing me to stand up and survey the damage. There were eleven arrows embedded in my furniture and walls.

I guess I'm not very good at repairing things, after all. I wanted to say thank you to the ghost for saving my life, but I could tell that he was already gone, and the room felt bare and lonely.

CHAPTER 10

GET YOUR GLAMOUR ON

I t was time to get my glamour on.

I needed orc intel, and the only way that was going to happen was if I infiltrated the ogres in their own playground: the stinky subterranean SubRealm. Magical creatures prefer to keep to themselves. It's an age-old preference to be with those who look (and smell) like you. It's not like I wouldn't be welcome in the SubRealm, but I'm pretty sure the orcs would clam up faster than oysters at a seafood buffet. No, I had to go in as one of them. It wouldn't be pleasant, but, as Directress Copperfield used to say, nothing in life worth doing is easy. Hopefully there'd be no traitorous crossbows in the crowd.

For someone like Morgan, glamour would mean stilettos, London-bus red lipstick, and gold sequins. For me, it means the opposite: I had to really dress down to fit in there, in the sewers. I don't have mirrors in my apartment (too many evil energies can use them as windows, or doors), so I stood in front of my silver toaster, instead, and practiced my Orc Face.

The Glamour potion was a shimmering purple liquid in a small glass bottle, sealed with navy blue wax. I had been saving it for a special occasion and I guessed going under-cover to save my life qualified as that. It was old now, and I hoped it still worked. Ferra had given it to me as a gift a couple of years ago and it had remained in my medicine cabinet, untouched, since then. One of the problems with these bespoke potions is that, unlike chicken soup from Woolworths, they don't come with expiry dates. Would its vintage make it more, or less, potent? Or, more worryingly, would it make its effects unpredictable? Not worth thinking about, really, as there was nothing I could do but risk it.

I scratched in a kitchen drawer for a paring knife and sliced off the top of the wax, then uncorked it with my teeth. It made a popping sound. Before I lost my nerve I took a small sip. It was cloyingly sweet, and then dastardly bitter, and then it snapped all over my tongue like Pop Rocks. I closed my eyes and tried to think of the prettiest orc I knew. Not surprisingly, my mind remained blank. Then I tried to think of Sugar Shagar's face. Her clammy blue-cheese skin and Death Marsh eyes.

I felt my face changing shape. My forehead bulged, my chin erupted. My lips swelled up like animal balloons. The baggy hoody I was wearing stretched along with my body, but not enough to accommodate my new bust and biceps, turning it into a crop top.

I opened my puffy eyes. The Glamour potion had worked, perhaps a little too well for my liking. I stared at my warped reflection in the toaster, moving my chin from side to side with a kind of grimace on my face that was no act. The new rolls on my neck had swallowed up my vampire-bite tattoo, and I had that characteristic orc camembert sheen on my cheeks. The worst thing was that I could see my own facial features in the orc glamour-mask, my big glass-green eyes, the shape of my lips. I smiled, showing my teeth, just out of curiosity, and was immediately sorry that I had done so. My mouth was like a field of mossy tombstones. I breathed into my palm, and my breath was... well, let's just say that I was sure I would fit right in.

THERE ARE secret entrances to the SubRealm all over Jo'burg City. It works kind of like the London Underground, except the people are friendlier. You have to know where the doorways are, and the spell to get in, but apart from that it's as easy as pie. Portal Magic isn't my strength, but it doesn't matter when you know the SubRealm password. The potion's effects had mostly subsided, and I was happy with the trial. I still wasn't a hundred percent human-looking so I pulled on my cap and sunglasses and left my apartment building just as the sun was painting the skyscrapers pink and orange, and headed toward the closest entrance I knew, greeting the neighborhood drug dealer as I went. If she noticed that I had put on weight and my fingers were the size of frankfurters, she didn't let on.

I was planning on a leisurely walk, but then I saw that man again, the one who liked standing with his hands in his pockets like a superhero with nothing to do, the late afternoon light streaming all over him like a spotlight. And this time he was moving forward, following me.

My evening stroll turned into a run as I ducked into the narrow alleyway to my right, then slipped into the next road, behind a construction site banner. A worker yelled at me that I wasn't allowed to be there and I showed him my rather large middle finger and kept running, deeply regretting my earlier date with the stairs; my calves and lungs were still burning from that little workout. I reached the round manhole in Simmonds Street and lifted the lid, straining my shoulder and reminding me that I needed to get back to my weight training, or I'd lose my edge. I climbed down the slimy rungs and slid the lid back in place, overhead, with a satisfying clang, and hoped the stalker hadn't seen me get swallowed up by the SubRealm.

Once I got to the bottom of the hole I caught my breath, downed the rest of the potion, and checked it by running my fat fingers over my mask. It was big, and ugly, and perfect. Then I mumbled the orc password—*Knorghad*—and the door opened up for me. Orc magic isn't very sophisticated, thankfully, so breaking in is easy for a wily wizard like me. I tried not to choke on the fumes that assaulted me as I walked through the old sewerage pipe. The SubRealm runs like an ants' nest below the whole city: massive and convoluted. It's a network of thousands of different pipes and levels and old mine-shaft tunnels. I stopped a smart-tram and jumped in, and rode it all the way to the Gold Reef Quarter, where the tunnels are veined with gold. The goblins (and the dwarves) hated the orcs for squatting in the mineral-rich ground there. *Finders Keepers*, the orcs had snuffled, and fair play to them.

There was shouting up ahead, and the tram slowed down as if afraid. Did the vessel know something I didn't? I urged it to keep going, but it stopped altogether, so I climbed out and ended up having my leisurely evening stroll, after all. The shouting got louder, and I could smell not just old sewerage now, but the distinctive odor of orc B.O. Thank the Void I was allowed to grimace. It would help me to fit in.

THE REEF IS A MASSIVE CAVE; a hall cored out of the earth for communal games and get-togethers. Think of a German beer fest underground, and you'll know what it's like. Men singing drunken lyrics while they smash their tankards together hard enough to shatter them. Buxom waitresses carting timber boards packed with fried food and pretzels. Faded flags hanging from the soil ceiling and the walls.

I was expecting the air of festivity, but the excited shouting was new to me. Something else was going on. I ordered a Troll Lager and took the dripping mug toward the commotion at the back of the hall. It was tricky, drinking with the glamour on, and I managed to dribble the first sip down the front of my crop top.

Smooth.

I edged closer, and saw men yelling and hopping about, throwing money at the bookies' table. I muscled my way through the crowd to see what the buzz was about, and was at once sorry that I had. In the middle of the crowd, in a large steel cage, were a pair of magical creatures, and the handlers were trying to bait them.

"Fight!" shouted an old orc right next to me—a hundred years old in the shade, with the crumbling teeth to prove it —making me jump and spill more of my beer. There were kids in the crowd, too, and one small boy was hoisted onto his father's shoulders and made to cheer.

"Fight! Fight!" the others were shouting.

One of the creatures, a giant pearlescent rainbow-hooded cobra, swirled up from his coil and showed his opponent his fangs. The other animal, a three-eyed lynx, backed up against the back of the cage and hissed in fear.

Oh, no, I thought. *Oh, no no no.*

I felt my mask blanch, and I backed away, out of the crazed crowd. I had enough on my plate without having to become a volunteer to the supernatural SPCA. I prayed silently that the animals would show more intelligence than their audience, and just refuse to fight, but somehow I knew the orcs weren't going to let that happen. Shaken, and trying to figure out what to do, I sat down at one of the beer hall tables and gulped down my lager.

Think, I thought to myself. *Think.* (Although, in my experience, telling yourself to think is never a very helpful exercise.)

The young orc skinhead sitting across from me looked me up and down with approval, and clicked his fingers in the air for another round.

"Ergh," he grunted, in greeting.

"Ergh," I replied in my best orc voice. I drummed my sausage-fingers on the table, tapped my foot. What the hell was I going to do, now? I was supposed to be there to gather intel on The Godfather, but I couldn't get the picture of the terrified animals out of my head. The waitress arrived with a tray of drinks, and my new friend slammed a fresh tankard in front of me.

"Orgh," I said, thanking him, and we smashed our glasses together and drank. I heard the cage-fighting crowd in the background and it made me feel hot and jittery inside.

"Zargulg," he said, hitting his barrel chest as a way of introduction. My mind raced. I hadn't thought of an orc name for myself as part of my cover. Instead I just smiled at him with my mossy tombstones, and he seemed pleased. He was wearing a dirty blue vest with an arty print of Elvish Presley on the front. More importantly, he had a tattoo on his shoulder that I recognized: it was the Hammerskin insignia. I should have guessed from his shiny scalp: Zargulg was a member of the rival gang to the Khargol familia.

"Tell me," I said, trying my best monosyllabic conversation. "What word on Or'Capone?"

He narrowed his eyes at me. "No word."

"In trouble," I said, and the orc blinked at me. The lynx hissed and snarled in the cage behind us, making the hairs on the back of my neck stand up.

"Making trouble," said Zargulg.

I leaned in. "What?"

"Black Magic," he said.

Black Magic? I was confused. Orcs usually stayed well away from Black Magic.

He saw me frown, and said: "Black Magic Market."

The impatient gamblers started rumbling and chanting together, "Fight! Fight! Fight!"

Ah. That made more sense.

If Don Vito was elbowing his way into the Black Magic Market then his life could very well be in danger. Being a murderous mafia boss and nefarious criminal was one thing, but dabbling in substances prohibited by the Council was a whole other enchilada. A very dangerous enchilada. We're talking about a tortilla that can explode in your face. A Death Taco. Why was I thinking about Mexican food? Because I was starving, and my new boyfriend just had a plate full of piping hot samoosas put in front of him. He offered me one—*"Orgh?"*—but I declined. You can never trust an orc samoosa.

Something happened in the cage. I turned away from Zargulg to look, but I couldn't see anything through the excited crowd. I heard a cheer go up, and my heart sank. I could no longer ignore what was happening to those crated animals. I had to do something, and I was pretty sure it would land me in a heap of trouble. I drained my beer, banged the table, and burped loudly to show my appreciation and gratitude. Zargulg seemed pleased. When I stood up, he caught my baseball-mitt-sized hand and squeezed it. He wanted me to stay. Actually, I could see by the glint in his eyes that he wanted a lot more than a drinking partner, and I suppressed the shiver that strummed my spine.

"I'll be right back," I assured him, and he smiled. It was not a pretty sight.

I LEFT the tables of beer-swilling orcs with their oily bar snacks and drunken singing, and made my way back to the animal cage-fighting crowd. I stumbled a little but caught myself in time. Walking with feet the size of cinderblock bricks was not as easy as it looked, especially after drinking two orc-sized, troll-strength lagers on an empty stomach. I approached the braying audience and insinuated myself back into the boisterous gathering. Their bodies were sweaty and smelled like sauerkraut and salami, and I got shoved and stomped on as I forced my way forward, past the cheering toothless granny orcs and the greasy men and yelling children. Finally, I reached the front of the crowd and could see the animal cages again. The lynx was bleeding, and snarling in fear, and the cobra's cape was shredded. I could smell urine and blood. Behind them there was a queue of more caged animals, fodder for the night's entertainment. One of the animal handlers poked a sharpened stick through the cage and stuck it into the lynx's back, trying to get it to attack the snake. The wild cat growled at him, its three eyes wide with panic. I didn't have to call up any emotion, it was already all there in my chest. I focused my gaze on the door of the main fighting cage, which was closed with a simple latch. I couldn't whip out my wand there, in front of the orcs, so instead my hand crept up to the pentacle ring around my neck and squeezed it. I stared at the latch and thought, as loudly as I could: *Destroy. Destroy. Rumpis!*

I had expected the latch to crumble, or to just fall off, but the anger I was feeling was obviously fiercer than I had realized, and it blew the whole side of the cage off, sending hot wire and sparks into the shocked crowd. Orcs shrieked, shielding their children, and the cobra and the lynx didn't need to be told twice to disappear. They both darted out of the cage and into the scattering crowd before the handlers could do anything about it. Taking advantage of the chaos, I looked over at the other cages that were lined up behind the fighting ring. There were seven of them, all prisons to various creatures awaiting a painful death, and I blasted them open, too. A pink, glittering alligator strutted out, followed by a squawking Arctikomodo dragon—the kind that breathe ice instead of fire—an albino ferret, and a silver bat. It called to mind that song... something about a parcel in a pear tree? I could hear the melody in my head but I couldn't get a handle on the lyrics. I forced myself to focus. I had to get out of there. I was feeling tipsy and my thoughts seemed strange and unpredictable.

A parsnip in a pear tree?

The animals all scampered and slithered and batted their wings away from the broken cages and into the Reef hall, scaring the orcs as they went. But where would they go? Where would they hide? How would they escape?

"*Faex*," I swore. I hadn't freed them, I had just given them a larger prison. That's when I felt a hand the size of a Christmas ham grab my ass and pull me toward him. Zargulg. He winked at me and pulled me close, and I almost passed out. Orc breath! It's hard to describe. Think disposable nappies and garlic, and add a dash of maggoty fish. That would be an improvement on how they smelled. In fact, I wouldn't be surprised if they used a similar combination as a breath freshener. Eau de Onion Salmonella Peux-Peux.

Oh my god, what was wrong with me? Was I drunk?

The hall started swirling around me. Troll Lager was strong, but usually I can hold my liquor as well as any of the orcs that surrounded me. Zargulg grunted in pleasure, and then I knew what had happened. The bastard had slipped something into my drink. Some kind of tasteless tranq-spell potion, some sleeping draught, and I had been too distracted by the sound of the animals to even notice.

"Whoah," I said, as I stumbled and almost fell. People rushed past us. The orc caught me as if I was swooning and he was my Prince Charming. My fury started building again. I thought I had used it all up on breaking open the cages but the fact that this slimy bastard had drugged me made me as angry as hell. But the potion was strong, and my arms fell to my sides, my face felt slack. No matter how vicious I was feeling, I wouldn't be able to do magic if I was paralytic. I started sliding to the floor, and the orc looked left and right and picked me up, ready to take me away. I started kicking and screaming, but it was all inside my head: my limbs just melted helplessly against him.

Filius Canis, I thought, but my lips were too numb to talk. *Es Mundus Excrementi.*

I felt my consciousness fading, as if the thoughts in my head were shrinking smaller and smaller and were about to disappear altogether.

No, I thought. I won't let this happen, but Zargulg had used enough tranquillizer potion to kill a small horse, and my thoughts turned to static and then faded out in a silent blip.

CHAPTER II

CONTENDIS

When I came to, down in the Reef hall in the SubRealm, Zargulg the orc had me in a dark corner away from the main chamber. It was close enough to hear the commotion, but far enough away so that he had enough privacy to assault me. The corner he pushed me into was dark and smelled of damp soil. His ham-hand groped at my crop top and then tried to pull my pants down, but I forced my eyes open and growled at him. It was his first warning.

He laughed, thought I was joking, and kept pulling at my pants, but my utility belt had other ideas.

Fiat Fulgur, I thought as loudly as I could—because my lips still weren't working—and my belt buckle buzzed with current. The orc jerked and grunted—*Argh?*—and his shocked hand flew up to his face. He looked at it, and me, puzzled, wondering how and why I was wearing a live-wire chastity belt.

"Leave me," I barked in my best orc tone, lips still numb. That was his second warning.

I started to walk away from him, off-balance and as dizzy as a hypnotized chicken, when he grabbed my hair and pulled me back toward his dark corner, and his hands went for me again, this time rougher, and more demanding. He forced his face into mine and tried to kiss me. The feeling of his hands on me, and his mouth so close to mine, made a wave of nausea rise in my throat. I groaned and buckled forward, spraying hot vomit all over his shoes. I vommed so hard that I thought I'd see my spleen on the floor. My whole body was one nasty cramp. He didn't let that stop him, and came for me again.

I didn't give him a third chance.

While I had been vomiting so violently, I had fumbled for my wand, and unclipped it. Now I held it in an unsteady hand. The gold veins in the walls and colorful banners swirled all around me, but now that the orc's poison was out of my system, my head was starting to clear.

"Fiat Fulgur!" I shouted. I was weak, and the lightning that shot out of my spell-stick wasn't as potent as I wanted it to be, but it did the job. It hit Zargulg square in the chest, setting his vest on fire and sending him flying backwards, into a catering table full of dirty dishes. The table snapped under him, and he fell to the floor under a crash of broken porcelain and glass. The smell of singed synthetic fabric and orc chest hair went up in a brown cloud.

Zargulg looked at me with a mad kind of fury. I saw it on his face, then, that he understood I was a wizard. When I put my hand up to my mouth to wipe it, I realized my glamour had slipped. My fingers were decidedly human-looking, no longer like bratwurst, and my face felt free. The tranquilizer he had fed me must have destroyed the effect of the glamour potion, and my Orc Face had decided to go on an early vacation.

I didn't stick around. I was out of that ominous corner before you could say Orc Vomit (which I could still taste in my mouth, thank you very much). I raced through the Reef hall, running over tables, knocking over food and jugs of beer, bowling over old men, waitresses, and the occasional child. Orcs stared at me as I raced toward the exit. They had come to the Reef hall for a night of entertainment, but now there were magical animals on the loose, some of them dangerous, and a fleeing wizard knocking over their drinks. Some of the more aggressive orcs stood, staring at me, and pushed their sleeves up, flexed their fists. The coin dropped: someone had used quick and dirty magic to free the animals and cause chaos, and I was clearly the troublemaker. Something told me they wouldn't hesitate to knock me out and throw my body in a cage with one of their tortured creatures. They began walking toward me, pushing over tables, not breaking eye contact. After the problems I had caused, they wouldn't allow me to escape without adequate punishment. My brain was cotton-wool, my limbs were still clumsy, but I knew that if I didn't get out of there—

Next thing I felt this bang on the back of my head. I saw stars, and as I fell forward in slow motion I noticed out of the corner of my eye the offending tankard shatter on the floor. I thought they were unbreakable. I was wrong. My wand went shooting out of my hand, and I went flying along the compacted soil floor, getting a complimentary mouthful of shoe-bottom dirt, while at the same time, grazing all the skin off my palms. It was as if someone had doused them with paraffin and lit a match. I ignored the pain—as much as it's possible to ignore your hands being set alight—and got up to keep going, but there was that meaty palm on my skin again, grabbing my ankle and pulling me down. I could smell Zargulg's singed hair. Behind him, a dozen more orcs advanced.

"No!" I shouted, more to myself than anyone else. I kicked him in the face and felt his nose break under my heel with a satisfying crunch. He yelled in anger, but he didn't let go. I tried to scramble forward, to grab my wand, but it was no use. My body was broken, and he was five times the size of me. He flipped me onto my back, as easily as if I was a ragdoll, and smiled down at me. My dizziness was back, courtesy of the bloody orc-glass tankard that had almost taken my head off, and I realized I didn't have it in me to fight. Not anymore. My body went limp on the hard, stony ground.

JUST THEN, the escaped albino ferret came scampering along, and with amazing aim and dexterity it flew up Zargulg's shirt—or what was left of it—and bit him on his barbecued nipple. Zargulg screamed in pain and fright, and tried to pull the animal off, but it had locked its little jaws.

"Aaaargh!" he yelled, clearly beside himself, pulling at the creature and screaming in pain every time he did so. I took the gap, scrambled to my wand, and picked it up in a move that would have made an NFL quarterback proud. The exit was fifty meters away, but instead of rushing for it I spun on my heel and pointed the wand at Zargulg, who was still scrabbling to get the creature off his chest. I knew I had no more destructive energy left, so I had to get creative. I whipped my wand in the air like a fly-fishing rod and aimed at the ferret.

"*Contendis,*" I said, and a wisp of smoke flew out of the tip of the wand and arced in the air, then dropped and curled around the ferret and pulled him off the orc... taking his nipple with him. Zargulg bellowed and tap-danced in pain while his greasy blood poured down his scorched chest. The magical ferret didn't fight my spell. He flew at me, I caught him, and smuggled him into my inner breast pocket.

I sprinted and kicked open the exit door, then slammed it closed behind me. I fell, exhausted, into the smart-tram, which seemed very relieved to see me, and shuttled me quickly toward fresh air. I clipped my wand to my utility belt and breathed a shuddering sigh of relief.

"Goblin City," I said to the tram. It slowed down, as if asking if I was sure. I nodded, and sparks of pain ignited the base of my skull. Ferret squeaked, but stayed buried in the warm, dark pocket. I patted my jacket, and decided to call him Gizmo.

My palms were shredded and dotted with blood, my muscles were aching. Gently, I rubbed my bruised scalp.

"Goblin City," I said again, relaxing into the tram. "There's someone there I need to see."

CHAPTER 12

OCEAN OF GOB

Goblin City is in the east of Johannesburg, in what used to be a popular amusement park, but was abandoned when a rollercoaster unaccountably left its rails, hurtling into the sky and then down again, killing over a dozen Untouched people. GO CITY was the perfect place for the goblins to set up shop. GobCom, the goblin committee, bought the dilapidated theme park for next to nothing (the humans didn't want it, saying it was cursed), painted an extra BLIN onto the billboard—so that it read GOBLIN CITY—and called it home. The goblin race went from being spread out all over the province, to having their own playground at the outskirts of the city. The child-friendly restaurants, toddler-sized bathrooms and kiddie rides were all ideal for a species their size. The fair-themed snacks were perfect for their sweet tooth, the tragic history of the rollercoaster accident and subsequent urban legends suited them, too, because it meant humans stayed out of their territory. Goblins hated it when humans came to visit, but I didn't give a damn. I needed to see an old enemy.

I spotted Nilve SaltySnap in the Popcorn Barn, where she was scooping up colorful buckets of popcorn for the pedestrians who passed by. Goblins are obsessed with popcorn, the saltier the better, which I always thought odd, because when I think of their green, slimy skin, it makes me think of slugs and snails, and everyone knows what happens when you pour salt on a snail. They also had these really pointy teeth, like dirty needles, and I could never understand the mechanics of them chewing air-popped corn. Anyway, to each their own, right? I certainly wasn't going to get in their way. Besides, I had just escaped a skinhead orc and the rest of his gang: I was sore, and tired, and I had more pressing matters to attend to.

"Hey!" chirped a random goblin from behind me. He jumped to tap me on the shoulder. "Hey!" he said again. "You're in my way."

Instead of batting the rude goblin, I stepped aside. Injuries notwithstanding, I was feeling quite magnanimous after having survived the evening and scored a pet ferret. I patted my pocket. I try to not take my beating heart for granted, but sometimes things happen to highlight my good luck.

"I'll take one," I said to Nilve SaltySnap when I reached the front of the queue.

Her face dropped. "Oh, no!" she said. "Not *you*."

I laughed. "I'll try to not take that personally."

"I wish you would," she said, spitting on the ground next to her.

God, the way these goblins spit.

The way they drool, it would put a hungry bulldog to shame. I'm always surprised that there's any dry land left in GC. Soon they'll have to climb into that huge fake ship in the Rides Section and sail somewhere new on their ocean of Gob.

"I'm not taking you to the hotel again," she said.

That's where they all slept: in beds and makeshift hammocks and on the floor and in the baths. A hotel that used to take two hundred tourists now houses over a thousand goblins.

I shuddered. "The last place I want to go is that hotel," I said. "Can I buy you coffee?"

Nilve narrowed her eyes at me. "Why are you being so nice?"

"I'm not being nice," I said. "I need something."

The goblin flinched. "No! I won't! I won't do that thing again!"

"Simmer down, Salty," I said. "All I need is some information."

Her eyes tracked from left to right, making sure no one was eavesdropping. "What will you give me?"

"I don't know," I said. "We can discuss it."

"Fine." She threw down her scoop.

"Not so fast," I said. "What about my popcorn?"

"You hate our popcorn," she said. "That's one of the reasons we don't trust you."

"It's not for me," I said, and opened my trench coat. The white ferret stuck his head out of the top of the pocket, perfectly on cue. "It's for Gizmo."

We settled down at a booth in the HobGob, one of three coffee shops in Goblin City, and I ordered two coffees, and a bowl of water for the ferret. It was a mistake. The coffee, I mean. Goblin coffee is sour, and disgusting, and fills you with a kind of existential dread that travels deep into your bones. My good mood evaporated in three sips, and I relinquished the remainder to Salty, who had no qualms in guzzling down my leftovers. Not even the sight of Gizmo eating his popcorn cheered me up.

Maybe the good mood was just a coping mechanism, after all. The trauma of the last few hours reared up and smacked me in the face. I leaned against the table top and my sinuses started to sting with tears. I breathed in and held them back. I wasn't about to cry into my empty crappuccino in the middle of a cursed amusement park infested with goblins. I would never live that down.

I looked around, taking in the calm, convivial atmosphere. It was a welcome change from the Reef hall. A black and white tiled floor, artwork of coffee and pastries on the walls. Goblin chefs and baristas worked at the back, and waiters and waitresses walked in endless circles from diners to the kitchen and back around again, their loop punctuated only by the banging of the flapping double doors. There was something very calming about it; almost mesmerizing. I think my face must have looked a bit blank, then, because it made Nilve curious. If I didn't know her so well, I would have said she seemed a little concerned.

"What the hell happened to you?" Nilve asked, licking the milk froth off her rubbery lips.

"You don't want to know," I said, shaking my head. I had to pull myself together. I needed intel, and I needed it fast.

Our waitress was back, snapping pink chewing gum and twirling a pen in her hair. She took out the small order notebook from the front pocket of her apron, and asked if we wanted anything else. Nilve ordered a third coffee, and asked for a menu. "You're paying, right?"

I thought of my depleted bank account. Pavaris still hadn't made payment. "Right," I said.

She ordered three plates of pancakes and a lime milkshake. I stared at her over the yellow formica tabletop until the food arrived. She poured maple syrup over the first tower of flapjacks and got to work. You can say what you like about the slimeballs, but they certainly are efficient eaters. I kept staring as she licked the syrup off the first plate, and attacked the next.

"What?" she said, and grinned, showing me every one of her dirty needles.

"I'm in trouble."

"I can tell." SaltySnap spoke with her mouth full of food, spraying me with pancake crumbs. I dusted them off my coat, and kept talking.

"Someone wants Or'Capone dead, and I need to know who that is."

Salty's eyes practically doubled in size. "No one wants him dead," she said.

THERE'S an old joke that goes like this:

Q: How do you know when a goblin is lying?

A: Her lips are moving.

THEY'RE DUPLICITOUS BASTARDS, goblins, and as dodgy as an email from Lagos. But if you're a paranormal private-eye who is any good at your job, you'll know how to use this to your advantage.

"So," I said, crossing my arms. "This 'no-one'. Who is he? What's his problem with the Don?"

"No one, no one," said Nilve, slurping the alarmingly bright-green milkshake. "No one has a problem with the Don. No one is planning a hit on him."

"When?" I demanded. "When are they not going to kill him?"

"Maybe tomorrow," said the goblin, moving on to her third plate of food. "But definitely not tonight at nine p.m."

So it wasn't an empty conspiracy theory. Someone really was planning on taking Don Vito out. I looked at the time on my phone. It was just past seven.

"This is not good news," I said. "Also, if you eat all those pancakes you're going to get serious indigestion."

"What do you care, Wizard?" she spat at me. "Goblin is as goblin does."

"Tell me who's behind it," I said.

"No one is behind it," said Nilve.

"Damn it, Salty," I grabbed her slimy wrist and she shrieked. Gizmo bolted back into my pocket. "Don't you understand? If Don Vito dies, the whole Realm goes to hell. Do you think you'll be sitting here drinking that toxic-looking lime milkshake if that happens?"

Nilve stopped slurping and whimpered.

"No! Because this whole place will be bulldozed. Your popcorn barn? Your bumper cars? Your cute little toddler-sized tables? Burnt. To. The. Ground. You get me?"

Nilve glared at me, and then her wrist, which I finally let go. I lowered my voice to what I hoped was a dangerous whisper.

"If a gang of evil orcs, or fae, or goblins, whoever they are, are planning a *coup*, you need to let me know who they are, so that I can stop them before it's too late. Because if the Khargols are killed, the Realm gets turned upside-down. The mafia will gun down anyone they suspect of collaborating. And without The Godfather's iron fist, the orcs will think they can bloody do what they like, and there'll be more fires than the Council will be able to put out. And if the goblins have anything to do with the hit—and I mean *anything*—the mob will not hesitate to bomb the hell out of this place. You know how orcs feel about the Don, and you know how they feel about treacherous goblins. I'm talking civil war, Salty. You can kiss your hotel and your miniature train rides and all of this goodbye."

SaltySnap sat up straight. "Not happening," she said.

"Who'll be pulling the trigger tonight?"

"Not goblins," she said, having the grace to look ashamed. "Certainly not goblins."

"Which goblins?" I demanded. "Can we stop them?"

She shook her head and looked forlornly into her empty glass. "Not goblins. And definitely not tonight at nine p.m."

Okay, so that's all she knows about that. Probably.

I needed to go, but I also needed to get paid by the Pavaris Estate.

"Is there anything else you'd like to tell me?"

She clamped her lips shut. It was a micro-movement, but it happened. She may as well have shouted across the crowded restaurant.

"Anything? Nilve?"

"Nope," she said. "Nopity-nope-nope."

"What is it?"

She started whistling innocently and twiddled her thumbs.

"Holy Hex, I knew it," I said. "I bloody *knew it*. You know who took the HighFire Crown."

AT FIRST I was baffled at the crime that took place at the Pavaris mansion. The sleeping spells that the guards were put under were typical of fae magic, while the phoenix's heart-pause was a classic dwarf spell. Getting around the elf's security enchantment, though, was impossible for anyone but Estelar. And then it came to me. You wouldn't need to break the enchantment if you used Portal Magic to transport yourself directly inside the center of the building. The Void knows Pavaris had enough mirrors around to make that happen. And it just so happened that I was sitting across from the smartest goblin I knew, and her specialty? Portal Magic.

I had suspected goblins all along, because only they have the audacity, the greed, and the cunning to pull off a crime like that. Goblins loved gold and magical items, and the High-

Fire Crown was both of those things. But as dishonest as Nilve was, she wasn't the thief... I didn't think. But it sounded like she knew who was.

"Tell me," I said. "Please."

"Give me your ferret," she said. "Quid Pro Quo."

I shook my head. "No way. Not giving you my ferret."

"It's beautiful," she said, licking her lips. "I want it."

"Salty. The ferret stays with me."

"It's a shame," she said. "I may have had something to tell you about that Crown."

My temples throbbed with frustration. My anger got the better of me and I used my arms to sweep all the plates and glasses onto the floor with a crash that echoed through the coffee shop. The goblins around us stopped and stared. Why did I have to deal with this schlock? All I wanted to do was kill vampires. Is that so hard? No. No, it's not. Unless you have to deal with vain, nagging elves and endangered mafia bosses and sneaky goblins like Nilve. It was no use. I knew I wouldn't get anything more out of her. I made sure Gizmo was tucked in safely, then stood up and left the table. The waitress watched me leave, blowing a big bubble with her gum. It popped.

"Hey!" Nilve shouted. "Hey, Wizard! You forgot to pay the bill!"

"I'll settle the bill when I'm paid for finding the Crown," I said over my shoulder, and walked out of the coffee shop. The rollercoaster rushed along its tracks, its passengers laughing and shrieking. Goblins streamed past me as I made my way out of Goblin City, passing residents clutching candy floss and red toffee apples and mini-donuts drenched in melted chocolate. The games arcade beeped and sang its cheerful tunes, and the outside lights turned on with a bang. I checked the time again. Estelar would have to wait. I had to warn The Godfather.

CHAPTER 13
THE MASQUERADE

I f I had thought that the day before had been the longest day of my life, today was shaping up to be a decade longer. All I wanted to do was go home and climb into bed, but I had to warn Don Vito Khargol, and I couldn't waste any more time. I used the frustration I was feeling with a certain devious goblin I knew; one with a penchant for maple syrup pancakes and thinly veiled lies, and I used a conjuring spell to get my motorbike over to the entrance of Goblin City. Usually conjuring objects takes a lot of magical energy, but Ferra had helped me out with a nifty solution. I like to think of Ferra as my surrogate mother, but also the magical dwarf version of Q (as in, Q from *James Bond* movies). She's always got something new to show me, some high-tech invention with a touch of enchantment. When I had complained to her that I was rubbish at Portal Magic, she made me a summoning ring for my motorbike. Because they're magically linked, all I need to do is touch the talisman and think of my bike, and it appears in a cloud of black glitter. It saves my energy reserves (and my fuel bill). If I was any good at Portal Magic I would have just stepped right out of GC and into the Orc District in Illovo, but it was not to be. Besides, I had a lot to think about, and the fifteen-minute ride on my bike would settle my nerves. I bashed on my helmet and kicked the bike into action. It thrummed beautifully beneath me as I took off toward the highway.

People in Johannesburg are forever saying how cosmopolitan the city is, how we're so lucky to have such a melting pot of skin colors, languages, and cultures. But what most humans who aren't touched by magic don't know is that there are thousands of magical creatures living amongst them. We call it the Masquerade, and the illusion is to be protected at all costs. Basically all that means is that the muggles—I mean, the Untouched—don't have a cooking clue, and we need to keep it that way. Morgan is one of the few Normals who know the truth. The Scorpions are forever negotiating that razor edge of solving paranormal crime while revealing as little as possible to the everyday civilian. If you've watched *Men in Black*, you'll have an idea of what they do. Switch out some slimy aliens for vicious vampires, and you've got the Scorpion Special Ops. If they do a good job—and they usually do—the Untouched will continue believing that they are the only humanoids on the planet. Ha! Can you imagine that? Can you imagine a world without magic? It must be like living in black and white, with blinkers on. Color-blind and narrow-sighted, and depressing as hell. Regular humans think that it's "science" that keeps their crops green and their planes from falling out of the air. Look, I never said they were very bright.

What humans don't know is that there is a vast source of magic out there, of energy, that can be tapped into for good and evil. They don't know that if the Void were to disappear overnight, there would be untold repercussions in the Untouched world. It's not that science isn't magic (it is), it's more that if there was no magic, there would be no science. And without advanced tech, well, we'd be without a lot of different branches of magic. Dwarves, like Ferra, are particularly good at harnessing science to augment their magic. I use something less technical. I was born with the ability to transform my emotion into sorcery. I find that pain is especially powerful. It's the major tenet which Blood Magic is based on: power from pain, preferably from someone else. But I've never been into the Dark Arts. I use my own suffering, instead.

I slowed my purring bike to a stop and parked just outside the strip of restaurants on Oxford Road. The trip had put Gizmo to sleep. I wondered how many magical creatures were mingling with clueless humans at that exact moment. We all have to do our bit to keep the Masquerade in place. The different species try their best to blend in: they use glamour potions when the need arises. They use secret entrances and have their own restaurants and shops. Wealthy orcs, who can afford to live somewhere other than the SubRealm, usually live in the suburbs close to the city. The Khargols live and work in Illovo, where they own an Italian restaurant which serves as a front for their various illegal dealings. They only serve orcs and other magical creatures, and if a regular human ever tries to get a table they are refused on the account of the restaurant being full, a chimera they cast every evening when they open for business. Their family home stretches three stories up from *Cucina Or'Capone,* despite them not having any children, a bone of contention in their marriage... at least according to the SubRealm gossip rags.

I tucked my helmet away and locked the bike with a security spell. When I saw a reflection of a woman's face in the shiny fuel tank of my bike, I drew in a sharp breath and spun around, wand at the ready. There was a swish of fabric in flight, and I tried to spot her in the thick, dark night. I had recognized the face: of course I had. It was the vampire from The Jupiter Drawing Room. She knew my scent now, and was determined to hunt me down. I breathed in the black night.

I'm ready for you, you monster, I thought. *Come and get me.*

She was perching somewhere on one of the building ledges, I was sure. She had lost the element of surprise, so she would wait and watch some more, until the time was right. I stood there for a whole minute, playing bait, but she didn't come back. That worried me, because a vampire with even a smidgeon of emotional intelligence is far more dangerous than one of those stupid vamps who just follow their appetites blindly. You know that EQ psych test with the kids and the marshmallows, right? Well, I was the marshmallow on display—a pretty tempting one, if I don't say so myself—but she didn't fall for it. That wasn't good news.

I CLIPPED my wand back into place and entered the seemingly crowded Italian restaurant. As soon as I made it through the door I was able to see through the Khargols' enchantment, and there were in fact only three tables occupied, while from outside it had looked packed to the rafters and cozy with laughing and music and candlelight. The *maître d'* tried to stop me, but I opened my trench and flashed my wand at him. He stepped back with a bow, letting me continue into the kitchen, where a sad-looking orc was stirring a vat of singing clams. I greeted him with a quick wave and made my way to the office at the back. Shagar must have told the security guards to expect me, because when they saw me coming they nodded and knocked on Don Vito's door, then opened it and ushered me in.

The huge room looked more like a man-cave than a mafia HQ, emphasis on the *cave*. A huge screen on the wall showed an orc boxing match, set to silent. There was a foosball table in the middle of the room, and The Godfather sat in an expensive leather chair at his desk, near the orc-sized gas fireplace, which was set to low. He was smoking a Cuban cigar while he counted money at the huge mahogany table, polished to within an inch of its life.

"Ergh," I said, and he stopped what he was doing and looked up at me in slow motion. His hands were knuckle-dusters of gold and diamond rings, and they glinted in the low light of the cave.

"Ergh," he said, not looking especially pleased to see me. He leaned forward and pressed a buzzer on his desk, and I wondered if he was going to get his heavies to throw me out. Instead, I heard heels clattering down the stairs, and Sugar Shagar arrived wearing an apron splattered with what I guessed was either her latest victim's arterial spray, or napoletana sauce.

"You doing here?" she asked, wiping her hands on a tea towel. I wondered what it must be like being married to a woman with Death Marsh eyes. Not that Vito's were any friendlier. I wondered how many people they had killed between them.

"Warning," I said. I tapped my wrist where my watch would have been, if I had ever owned one. "Trouble. Nine o'clock."

"Argh," grunted The Godfather, and swatted his hand at me in a dismissive way. Shagar looked up at the gold-rimmed clock on the wall. It was seven-thirty. She frowned and wrung her hands.

"Vito," she said. "You hear? They're coming!"

The Godfather grunted, and picked up a pen-knife from his desk. He started cleaning his nails with the blade.

"See?" she said to me. "He doesn't listen!"

I saw.

"Tell him, Gnarg," she said to one of the couches in the room. I heard a cartridge of a gun being smacked into place, and I jumped. I hadn't seen him sitting there, in the dark. It was the Don's personal bodyguard.

"I'm ready," said Gnarg. Despite having a name that sounded like a cat choking on a hairball, Gnarg was always ready.

People joked about Gnarg, and the way he stuck to The Don like a shadow-fish. They were inseparable. Gnarg took his job Very Seriously. People joked that Gnarg probably slept in the same bed with Mr. and Mrs. Khargol. With his eyes open.

"Your gun won't matter, Gnarg!" she shouted, the blue veins in her face bulging. "You can't protect him."

"I protect him," said the bodyguard, snapping the safety off his rather large weapon.

Don Vito looked at his wife. "See? Gnarg. No problem."

He licked the pad on his middle finger and continued to count his money.

"I'm being serious," I said. "I have good intel that they are planning to arrive at nine p.m."

"What?" whispered Sugar, her frankfurter-hands flying up to her mouth.

"So, if I were you," I said, "I'd disappear. Take a holiday. Go and visit one of your private islands. At least till this has blown over."

The Godfather laughed. "Run?" he said, then the smile disappeared. "The Godfather doesn't run."

"Don't think of it as running. Think of it as a well-earned vacation."

"The Godfather doesn't go *on vacation*." His mouth twisted when he said it, as if taking time off was a ridiculous concept. What he didn't realize was that if he didn't take my advice he'd be on a permanent vacation. *Faex*, I was exhausted. What I wouldn't do for a week on one of the Khargol isles. Apparently they own a dozen of them somewhere in the Pacific. I thought of the crystal ocean, Jack Johnson drifting on the warm breeze, and Piña Coladas. Then I remembered where I was and pulled myself together.

"I don't think you appreciate the gravity of the situation." I took a step forward to assert the authority I knew I didn't have. "You need to get out of here."

Vito slammed his knuckleduster jewelry on the desk, making me jump.

"Girl Wizards," he sneered, "don't tell Don Vito what to do."

"First of all," I said. "I'm not a Girl Wizard. I don't even know what a Girl Wizard is."

"Ha," he said.

"And I'm not telling you what to do. Your wife hired me to—"

Sugar swore. The Godfather looked at her, fury in his frown.

Oops. I hadn't realized that was classified information.

He stood up, clenching and unclenching his fists at his sides. "You call this girl?" Yellow sparks of violence flashed in his eyes.

Shagar clasped her hands together and whipped her hair from side to side like a B-grade actress in a Spanish soap opera. "Vito! Vito! They want you dead. I need to protect my man!"

"I have my protection!" he shouted, gesturing at Gnarg, who grunted. "I don't need a *girl* to protect me."

I'd had enough. "Suit yourself," I said, and turned to leave.

"No!" shouted Shagar. "Please!"

"If he wants to get himself killed, that's his prerogative." I was tired, hungry, sore, and I definitely wasn't going to stick around for an assassination courtesy of a gang of needle-toothed goblins.

"If he won't leave," I said to Sugar, "then you should. Go somewhere safe."

"Never," she said, jaw muscles tensing. "I'll never leave my Don."

The display of her devotion and unwavering loyalty seemed to take the edge off Vito's anger, and he sat down again. I still had the feeling that Shagar might have a black eye the next day, but only if the man survived the night, which I was pretty sure he wasn't going to. I felt for my wand and prepared to leave. There was nothing else I could do.

"Fuori," he said to me, smacking his hand in my direction as if I were an annoying fly, but the gesture was unnecessary. I was already on my way out.

I THOUGHT OF GOING HOME, but I remembered how cold and lonely my apartment had seemed when I had been there, earlier. The scrawled eviction notice, the spontaneous arrow-firing incident, and the now unlockable door added to my unease, especially with that creepy stalker around.

There was only one place I wanted to go: my home away from home, Ferra's place.

Actually, now that I was thinking about it, it was nothing like home. It wasn't haunted, for one, plus it was cozy, had plenty of cinnamon whisky, and as much warm, home-cooked food as I could eat. It also happened to be owned by the only person who could fix my crossbow so that I could trust it to not try to kill me again. I jumped on my bike and headed over to the Copper Cog.

CHAPTER 14

THE COPPER COG & ALE

When Ferra saw me, her face lit up with the same warm glow of the vintage lanterns that blazed in her glimmering steampunk-themed pub, and she squeezed me so hard that I thought I heard a rib crack. The pub was warm, heated by a blazing fire in the center of the flagstone floor, fed by huge hunks of timber, and each table had its own miniature floating fire in the center. Ferra was in her usual working attire: Dwarf-sized denim dungarees and a viking helmet, and her Scot-red hair plaited into pigtails. She had saved every penny she could for years, working as the head matron at The Copper-field Institute, and when she had enough capital saved up she resigned and built this place: *The Copper Cog and Ale*, which did a roaring trade every day of the week and twice on Sundays.

Clocks ticked cheerfully on the exposed brick walls and shiny copper piping vaulted overhead. The pub was large, but cozy, and there was always a table free for new guests. Dwarves are able to conjure up extra tables and rooms on demand, which is really handy if you own a restaurant. All magical creatures are allowed entrance, but elves know to stay away. The atmosphere is fantastic, the food is mouth-watering, and the home-brewed beer is even better.

I sat down at the bar Ferra was working behind, slicing lemons with one hand and pulling a dark stout with the other.

"It's been years!" she said.

I laughed. "It's been less than a week."

"I was talking Dwarf Years," said Ferra. "It's been too long. You don't visit your dwarf-mother anymore."

"Werewolves couldn't keep me away," I said. "How are you?"

"All the better for seeing you." Her eyes were bright nutmegs flecked with gold.

When we met at the Institute, Ferra kind of took me under her wing and I've been there ever since. She was tender-hearted to all the orphans, but we had a special connection. She's been my surrogate mom ever since. You'd think that running a successful business and having twelve children of her own would mean that she'd no longer have time for me, especially now that I'd grown up, but Ferra's heart behaved kind of like her magical restaurant—there always seemed to be room for more.

"Hand it over," she said, wiggling her citrus-scented fingers at me. I was confused for a moment, and then I remembered my crossbow. I unclipped it and placed it on the counter, and Ferra pushed the cutting board aside and picked up the weapon, inspecting it closely with one eye open.

"Hmm," she said.

"Not good?" I asked. Of course, I knew the answer.

"No good." She ran her hand along the damaged shaft. "I take it you tried to fix it?"

I nodded, embarrassed. A wizard really ought to be able to repair her own crossbow.

"EiLEEN!" she yelled, and one of her kids came running. "Put this down in my workshop, will you?" The young dwarf took the thing and scampered. No one made Ferra speak twice.

"Thank you."

"I haven't done anything yet," she said, and winked. "And look at the state of you."

I looked down at my worse-for-wear clothes and my grazed palms.

"And you're too skinny," she said, pushing a stray strand of red hair out of her face, blush-cheeked with the heat of the kitchen and her ability to multitask to the max. Right then she was crushing ice with a steel mallet while taking a long and complicated order from an orc in a tuxedo. I had, quite frankly, had enough of orcs for the day, so I turned my back and checked on Gizmo. The ferret seemed settled enough, so I put him on the bolted copper counter and gave him a pentacle-pretzel to snack on.

"And who's this, now?" Ferra asked. "I thought you didn't *do* pets."

Ferra always punched me on the arm when I said I wasn't interested in getting a pet; she was forever taking in strays, and had more animals than children. She said it would make my apartment less lonely (she doesn't know about Ghost), but the truth is that I can barely look after myself, never mind a creature that would depend on me for care. I can barely keep a pot plant alive. The one on my windowsill is forever wilting, making me feel guilty. And the plight of my cupboards... suffice to say that even the cockroaches in my kitchen had died of starvation. Thinking about the sad state of my refrigerator made my stomach growl, and before I knew it, there was a huge plate of steaming food in front of me: golden-skinned chicken, roasted to perfection, crispy potatoes, spiced burnt-butter pumpkin, and creamed feta spinach. I breathed in the aroma as if it was the last meal I'd ever eat.

"Eat up, Jinx," she said, using my favorite nickname. "There's plenty more where that came from. And apple and rhubarb crumble for dessert." Then she put a large pint of Copper Cog Ale in my hand. *Deodamnatus*, I love that dwarf.

"He saved my life," I said through a mouthful of gravy-smothered potato, gesturing at the ferret. "His name is Gizmo."

"Well," Ferra wiped her hands on a cloth. "What a handy creature to have around." She filled a bottle-top with some saffron-infused apple cider and put in on the counter for the ferret to drink.

Raucous singing erupted from a far corner, then shouting for more ale. Ferra rolled her eyes toward the giant Da Vinci-esque vellum airship that floated on the ceiling.

"Those goblins," she sighed. "They'll be the death of me."

I looked over and saw a party of a dozen drunk goblins. "Celebrating something?"

"Must be."

"They'll be sorry tomorrow," I said, picking up the chicken drumstick and sinking my teeth into the crispy salted skin. Sometimes Ferra's food was so delicious it made me feel like crying. "Imagine the hangover headaches you get when your head is that size. You'll get your vengeance, then."

Ferra smiled at me. "Och. As long as they pay their bill they're not too much bother. They've practically been throwing gold coins into the air like peanuts."

"Really?" That was interesting. "Where are such no-good goblins getting that kind of money from?"

"Ask no questions, hear no lies," said Ferra, pulling up a

barstool and sitting down. "Now tell me why you look like you've just been dragged through the week backwards."

I took a long sip of the beer, and the cool liquid was balm to my throat. Gizmo seemed to like his drink, too.

"Any idea what magical albino ferrets do?" I asked. "Apart from saving Girl Wizards' lives and eating barbecued nipples?"

Ferra frowned at me. "Er, what now?"

"Never mind," I said, putting my cutlery together in the middle of the plate. "It's a long story."

"I love long stories," said Ferra. "Especially if they involve barbecued nipples."

"I'll fill you in next time." I could feel my eyelids starting to close. The warmth of the place, the feeling of safety, the comforting food... it was all I could do to stay upright and not slide down onto the flagstones to take a nap. I needed sleep, but there were things I needed more than rest. My phone had five messages from Pavaris, all bemoaning his declining health and crumbling mansion. Morgan had asked for a meeting, and my landlord had sent a text that just read *OUT*. I wondered if I'd get back to my apartment and find everything tossed out of the window. I hoped not; it was a long way down.

"You want to know what ferrets do?" said the dwarf. "It's in the name. Think verb, not noun."

Now it was my turn to frown. "Ferret? Like, rummage?"

"You've got it. Delve. Dig. Discover. From the Latin *Furo:* thief."

"Oh," I said, looking at the creature with more admiration than before. "Well. That could come in handy, indeed."

"Watch this," said Ferra. "Gizmo? Gizmo." The ferret looked up from his half-eaten pretzel and blinked at Ferra, who I think he was a little bit in love with, after the gift of her saffron cider.

"Gizmo, find the key to my cellar."

The ferret didn't hesitate. He shot off the counter and disappeared into the storeroom beyond. Ferra looked up at the clock on the wall: a masterpiece of bronze panels and black rivets. It was eight-thirty-six p.m., which made my anxiety spike and straightened my spine. No one else seemed to be taking The Godfather's death threat very seriously. Maybe I'm a bit off my rocker to put so much credence in the opposite of what a sneaky Goblin told me over a lime milkshake. Still, it gnawed at me.

"Can I have my bill, please, Ferra? I need to run."

"Your money is no good here," she said (as she always does).

Gizmo came flying back: a white streak on the bar counter. He had the ring of a silver key in his mouth. The clock struck eight thirty-seven.

"Ah, bravo, little man," said Ferra, taking the key with a chuckle, and stroking the ferret. "Bravo." She topped up his makeshift cup as a reward. I blinked at him, and couldn't believe my luck. My new pet happened to be able to find lost things... and I happened to need a magical item found.

GIDDY, I excused myself and ran to the restroom. I splashed cold water on my face and looked at my reflection in the polished brass of the mirror. *You can do this,* I told myself. *Your luck has just turned.* When I got back to the bar, Gizmo was gone.

"Where's Gizmo?" I asked, hoping Ferra had sent him on another mission to the storeroom.

She looked up from sawing biltong for the snack bowls. "I thought he was with you."

"He's not," I said, my heart sinking.

Ferra put down her knife. "He followed you to the restroom."

I re-traced my steps, looking on chairs and under tables. The pub was so packed, he could have been anywhere.

"Gizmo?" I called, although I realized it was a bit early in our relationship for him to answer to his name. Out of the corner of my eye I saw a flash of white on the carpet across the room. There were too many patrons in the way to be able to see the floor properly, so I got on my hands and knees and started crawling, not caring what the other people thought of me. I saw another flash of white, and followed it, and ended up leopard-crawling underneath a big, low table. The diners were rowdy and I realized that it was the table of celebrating goblins. All of a sudden Gizmo was right there, in front of me, with a mischievous look on his face. I was so relieved I reached out to hug him, which was difficult in the circumstances, so instead I squeezed him against my cheek.

And I made my eyes big and disappointed-looking—how else do you let a magical ferret know that he's in trouble with his new momma?—but then I overheard some of the goblin conversation and it all clicked into place. It turned out that Gizmo wasn't just good at finding objects, he could find information, too.

"...silly elf..."

"...past his prime, now, that's for sure..."

"Elf on the shelf!"

Drunken roars of laughter. I froze. They were talking about Estelar.

"...well, it's safe now..."

"...no one would guess where it is. Very clever move."

"Very clever goblins."

There was a spate of maniacal laughing, smug and a little insane. My nose twitched. The carpet smelled like stale beer and goblin socks, and it was unpleasantly damp underneath me. I was hoping the dampness was spilled ale, and not spit.

"Poor Pavaris," said one of them, then hiccupped loudly.

"I don't think those two words have ever been used in the same sentence before."

More giggling and banging of glasses on the table as they called for another round.

Where is it? Where was the Crown? I wish I knew a spell to improve my hearing. Or my telepathy.

"I think we'd better settle up after this one. I'm out of gold."

"Don't worry," said one of them. "Qwynkle will pay for it with his rather large paycheck."

"Rather largshe ish right," slurred another.

Paycheck from whom? If they still have the Crown, if they hadn't yet fenced it, why would they get paid?

"Qwynkle, Qwynkle, little sta-a-a-a-a-arrrrr," sang the drunk one. "How I wonder where you arrrrrrrrre…"

Qwynkle? So he's in charge. Gizmo scuttled into my pocket.

"Like a diamond in a crrrro-o-o-o-wn… Watch out elf, you're going do-o-o-o-o-own."

Qwynkle's in charge, and this was his gang. I didn't want to be involved in anything a gang of goblins had their hand in, but it looked like I didn't have a choice.

"He said he'll meet us here at nine-thirty, after he's... iced the Italian cake."

My whole body turned cold. *Holy hex,* I thought. Forget about the Crown. Qwynkle was about to kill The Godfather.

CHAPTER 15

RED SINGING CLAM SAUCE

I knocked my head on the table trying to scramble out too quickly. The assassination plot was still in play, and I needed to stop it. I shouted goodbye to Ferra as I bolted out the door, Gizmo safe in my pocket. I jumped on my bike and revved it to red-line, and I hit the tarmac with a squeal of tires. It would usually take me ten minutes to get to *Cucina Or'Capone,* but I made it there in six. At one minute to nine o'clock my helmet was spinning on my handlebar, and I was inside the restaurant. I had stuffed Gizmo into the bike box with a quick apology and a slim slot to breathe through. I wasn't sure I'd make it out of the *cucina* alive.

Don Vito was sitting at the very front table inside the restaurant, facing the road, with Shagar on his left, and his bodyguard, Gnarg, on his right, and he didn't even look up when I burst in there. Didn't even twitch, despite it being thirty seconds before someone was going to turn him into pink Swiss cheese.

"Don Vito!" I said. "They're coming!"

I was seriously on edge, panting, sweating. I expected them to scatter and/or pull out their weapons. They did neither. The Godfather just kept slurping up his red singing clam sauce.

"Vito!" I shouted. "Please! You've got to go!"

Vito Khargol put down his fork and reached for his linen napkin. He wiped his mouth, then took a leisurely sip of his wine. I hoped the clam linguine was good, because it looked like it was going to be his last meal.

"Shagar?" I said. She just looked at me with her mouth clamped shut. Her eyes were bereft, her expression resigned. She knew it was coming, and there was nothing she could do.

That's when I heard the music approaching. Goblin Punk—The Kings of Klash—being blasted from a car that was driving slowly. Too slowly. Qwynkle and his henchmen were here.

GNARG PULLED out his revolver and snapped off the safety catch. Sugar lifted a glass of water to her lips, and I saw her hand trembling. The ice chinked against the sides.

"We're in no danger," Vito assured me. "We have everything under control."

Shagar shifted uncomfortably in her chair, and The Godfather picked up his fork again, winding the strands of pasta slowly around the tines. I smelled olive oil and oregano in the air.

The safety catch, the ice clinking, the pasta being wound around the fork, it was all in slow motion. The music was getting louder, but I could still hear my heart beating in my chest. I reached for my wand.

The car came into view: a midnight-blue sedan with evil toad-skinned goblins hanging out of each window, and two popping out of the sun-roof, all holding AK47s as nonchalantly as Somali pirates. The punk rhythm got louder still.

"Get down!" I shouted. "Get down!" (This was meant as an instruction to tuck and roll, not to dance).

The Khargols moved so slowly, as if the air had inexplicably turned to syrup. Gnarg grasped his gun and started shouting like *Rambo*, all guts and glory. He was the star in the movie inside his head. I ramped up the anger I was feeling at the gang and forced it into a fizzing firework inside my chest. I held my wand up to the large plate glass window that served as the façade to the restaurant. The music was building and building, and was about to pay off. I could feel the vibration in my boots and fingers as it built toward the crescendo, and as the song climaxed the goblins crossed our vision and began shooting. The first few bullets blew the glass front away and it crashed all over and onto us, sparkling silver, and the shards rained down onto the floor. The goblins kept their fingers on the triggers of their automatic rifles. Gnarg looked at his gun in horror; already out of bullets.

"*Clipeum Glaciei!*" I shouted, and a huge blast of water erupted from my wand and sprayed in between the assassins and the orcs, and it froze in the air with a satisfying crack. The room grew instantly chilled, and Sugar Shagar stared at me, mouth agape. I motioned for her to hit the deck. Of course, ice will only take a few bullets before shattering like the glass before it, but it bought the orcs a couple more seconds to drop under the table, which Gnarg eventually did, pulling Shagar with him, but Don Vito? That arrogant bastard. He just sat there like a duck with a target tattooed on his forehead. As the bullets began to break down the ice shield I tried to construct another one, but my wand was all out of frost. I think it was Vito's reaction that did it. Why try to save a life when it's clear he didn't want to be saved? Sometimes I wish my wand would be a little less intuitive and just listen to my commands. With the goblins almost out of direct sight I tried one more time to create a new shield, but it didn't work.

Someone in the gang sprung the trunk open, and out of the boot popped another goblin: a slimy jack-in-the-box with a grin and a fresh round of ammo, and with a hailstorm of bullets he destroyed what was left of my shield (and the restaurant). Shrapnel flew in all directions, forcing me to cover my face, and when the music finally started to recede I looked around wildly, through the smoke, and saw exactly what I had expected: The Godfather sat collapsed forward, into his pasta bowl. There was red everywhere. I looked down at my own chest, and saw the tell-tale burn marks of where the bullets had hit me, and bounced off my graphene trench.

Shagar hauled herself up off the floor, saw what had become of her husband, and started screaming in a way I hope I'll never hear again. Gnarg lifted Vito up and shook him, but his chest was ripped open, his body limp and unresponsive, and Gnarg went all *Rambo* again, but this time without bullets, just an awful kind of moaning and shouting. I had to get out of there. It was too much for me.

WALKING OUT, the world went silent. The repercussions of failing to protect The Godfather fell on me like snow-ash, one flake at a time, until I was covered in gray. The orcs would split into factions, now: those who wanted the power that had just been relinquished, and those who would seek justice for Don Vito's murder. There would be bloodshed in the various tribes. The orcs would declare war on the goblins. The goblins would declare war on everyone. The Council wouldn't be able to uphold the Masquerade, and the whole world would come crashing down. I couldn't let this happen. Everything was a stake. But what could I do?

Girl Wizard, I remember Vito saying, as if I was a child who had no hope in protecting him.

Well, I wasn't a child, and I had done my best, but he was a bloody fool, and now he lay face-down in his red-sauced pasta. Those clams aren't singing anymore.

I ambled along the sidewalk in my silent bubble of devastation, and, of course, because it had been that kind of day, when I got to the parking lot, I realized my bike had been stolen. In my rush to get inside to warn the Don, I'd forgotten to put my security enchantment on it, and some asshole had come along and helped himself. In this city, everything grows legs. House numbers, letter boxes, manhole covers, paving stones, pavement plants. Nothing is sacred, nothing is safe. My jaw started to ache, and I realized I was biting down hard, grinding my teeth with the sheer frustration of it all. Serves me right for thinking that my luck had turned, right? I almost laughed at the sheer ludicrousness of my situation, then I rubbed my face and tried to pull myself together. All I had to do was to summon my bike, and hope that Gizmo was safe during the trip. And I needed to start taking better care of the magical ferret. Losing him twice in one night was not very good pet-parenting by anyone's standards.

I stood there and breathed in deeply, pictured my bike, and touched my talisman. At first I thought the ring hadn't worked, but then I started to see the tell-tale sparkles in the air, the golden smoke, and my bike appeared in front of me. I was so relieved to see it, and stepped forward to check on Gizmo in the box, but then I stopped dead in my tracks. It wasn't just the motorbike I had summoned; the thief was beginning to appear, too. And that would have been okay, if it was just an ordinary criminal, but it wasn't.

She didn't steal the bike because she wanted a ride; she wanted something else entirely, something a lot more personal. It was the vampire from Madame Woolf's brothel, and she was here to finish me. She sat astride my bike and sniffed the night air between us, and I raised my wand.

CHAPTER 16
VAMPIRE SMOKE

The vampire hissed when she saw my wand. I expected her to fly off my bike and come straight for my throat, but instead she sat there, pleased with herself, a vampiric queen on a stolen throne. Her cape was as black as night, but a handsome shade of teal blue inside, a color I had never seen before on a vampire. As the stars sparkled above her I worried about Gizmo. If I died in this battle I hoped Ferra would take him in. I hoped he would find his way to her. I hoped he was alive in that box. She sat there, looking me up and down. Her name came to me then: *Desdemona*. We had some kind of telepathic connection. Just my luck.

She was there to kill me, so why was she hesitating? Suddenly I sensed another presence, and then another, as two shadows swept up out of the dark to stand behind her. She hadn't been hanging back... she'd been waiting for backup. I automatically felt for the crossbow on my back, but of course it wasn't there.

"Missing something, Wizard?" Desdemona asked. Her voice carried with it a coldness I could feel deep in my bones.

"Nothing I can't do without," I said, wand firmly in hand. The shadows took a step forward, into the beam of the orange streetlight, and I saw their faces, pale as sour milk, and the hatred rose inside me. They had been watching me, waiting for when I was at my most vulnerable, and they had found me at exactly the right time to do maximum damage.

"Why do you do it?" I asked her. There were plenty of synthetic blood products on the market, all kinds of flavors and brands. In the words of one of the latest commercials from Plate-let, *We've got every taste of blood you can dream of.*

Traditional tasting Metallic Velvet Red, warm, in a coffee cup, for the conservative folk.

Cherry sippy straws for vampire children.

Guarana-laced frappés for the hipster vamps.

Reconstituted in a protein shake for the health goths.

Scarlet espressos and red cappuccinos for the yuppie city slickers.

Of course, I knew why she did it. Because she was inherently evil, and nothing would change that. What was it inside some people that made them think it was okay to kill and torture? I'd never know, but what I did know for certain was that I was ending this vampire's life tonight. I had failed once, and I refused to let it happen again. I would not let her claim any more victims. I grasped the pentacle ring I wore around my neck, the one that used to belong to my father.

"Fiat Fulgur!" I shouted, and the energy I pulled from the Void swept through my body, mixed with my emotion, and bolted from my wand in a hot, bright current. Desdemona blocked the lightning with her forearm, but I could tell it hurt her. It knocked her off the bike, which fell on its side, and she rose into the air above it and hissed at me again, her cape flowing behind her. I had angered her, and she was going to make me regret it. She started walking on air toward me, showing her fangs.

"Fiat Fulgur!" I yelled again, but this time she was prepared for it. She dodged the electricity, which zapped a billboard behind her, scorching it. She kept advancing.

She swiped the next bolt, too, deflecting it in the direction of the streetlamp, melting the wires inside and blowing the bulb. I had never seen a vampire deflect magic like that. She was more powerful than I expected. Fire wasn't working. I had to change my tactics.

"Glacieum Exquiris!" I shouted, and this time ice shot out of my wand like a javelin and speared the vampire in the chest. Her whole body shunted backwards with the force of it and waves of ice radiated out from where it penetrated her, as if the residual magic in the icicle was freezing her body. Desdemona screamed and wrapped her hands around the frozen spear while the other vamps hissed their disapproval

at me. She was choking, and black blood lined her lips. With a roar of fury she dislodged the icicle and threw it on the ground, where it shattered into hundreds of pieces, reminding me of the earlier assassination of Don Vito. The memory brought back my anger at The Godfather and the Qwynkle's goblin gang, and I seized it in my chest and expelled it from my wand.

"Ventum Exquiris!" I yelled, and a strong wind stirred up between the buildings. A hurricane-force insta-storm that originated in my body and was now swirling in front of me, ready for my command.

Quick and dirty magic will always be my favorite kind, perhaps because of who taught it to me and how it helped me survive those tough years with the Ferals. But quick and dirty magic doesn't kill vampires. For that you need elemental magic, the more academic kind you learn at places like the Copperfield Institute. Fire. Ice. Wind.

I whipped up the tornado, feeding it more and more energy from the Void, till it was humming with potential destruction, then I cast it with all my force toward the enemy. There was no dodging a hurricane that size. It swallowed the vampire and her minions—along with a couple of cars parked behind them—twisted them like licorice, and spat them out on the tarmac. One of the vamps was thrown into a concrete paver, smashing his head open, and immediately turned to ash. One of the flying cars smashed into a storefront, and the security alarm started shrieking. The other vehicle, a yellow Mini, perched precariously on top of a large tree.

The cops would arrive soon. I needed to clean up and get out of there. I let the wind fade, and the Mini dropped out of the tree and onto the pavement below, and two of its doors sprang open. I went to hoist my bike up—it had been dragged fifty meters out and had the scratch-marks to prove it—and check on Gizmo, but as I opened the bike box I was struck on the back of the skull. I melted to the ground and hit my head again on the way down. Could feel gravel in my scalp as I lay there, spread-eagled on the road. Desdemona grew out of the tarmac in front of me like a black weed. There was a hole in her chest and the skin there was frozen blue. A major head-wound from her trip in the tornado poured glistening midnight blood down the side of her face and soaked her shoulder. She snarled at me, showing off her stained fangs.

I covered my neck. She could kill me, but there was no way I was going to let her taste my blood. Her own blood dripped and dripped, black on black, and I saw the moon and stars in it. I was dizzy—I guessed concussed—and wondered if my legs would ever work again. There was only one way to find out. I kicked Desdemona, connecting my boot-heels with her ankles, and she cried out and fell. Using a parkour floor-to-crouch bounce I was off the ground and on top of her before she even knew what was happening. I tried to see clearly through my dizziness but the stars were flaring all over my vision, and my head was pounding as if I had an angry gorilla trapped in my skull. I'd have to go by instinct.

My legs were pinning her arms down, and she thrashed beneath me and hissed.

"*Glaciem exquiris,*" I whispered. It needed to be subtle, this time, or I'd risk knocking myself back, off the vampire's body, and she'd be free again. Nothing happened.

Easy does it, I thought, trying to keep my thoughts together as Desdemona clawed at me with all her strength, her black fingernails shredding my pants and drawing blood from my burning thighs.

"*Glaciem exquiris,*" I whispered again, slightly louder, and I imagined just the smallest shard of ice, like I had seen on the floor or *Cucina Or'Capone*. Small, sharp. An ice arrowhead.

It appeared, perfectly formed, on the tip of my wand. Desdemona stopped flailing when she saw it, and her eyes grew wide. I remembered then in crystal detail the twin midnight whirlpools of her eyes the night before, and the dying man in pink boxer shorts on the bed, and it was all I needed to plunge the ice dagger into the side of her neck and rip it sideways, slicing her throat deeply, all the way through the cartilage of her windpipe. Her body lost its grip on me, and her arms fell slack at her sides. I stood up, off-balance, reeling, and relieved.

Being a vampire slayer has many obvious drawbacks, including getting your head bitten off by your target on any given night. But not me, not tonight. One of the handy things, however, is that you never have to guess if a vampire is truly dead or not. It's not like a slasher flick where the killer keeps coming back to life again and again for extra thrills.

Desdemona's body began to shrink; her skin started to shrivel. She became an old crone, then a leather-skinned skeleton, and then the remains spontaneously combusted and burned a pure blue flame until there was nothing left to feed the fire, and all that remained of the vicious creature was a small mound of ash, glittering with embers.

I felt so relieved then—and so light-headed because of the hits I had taken—that I crumbled right there, next to the warm ash. I needed to rest, just for a moment, before the squad cars arrived. I just wanted to see the back of my eyelids for a second. They say you shouldn't sleep on a concussion, but my brain seemed to be short-circuiting, and I didn't have a choice. My body lolled onto the hard ground that smelled of vampire smoke, and the light in my head went out.

But then I heard a hiss, and my eyes flew open. I didn't understand. I had seen Desdemona ash right in front of me. The cinders were still there, still hot enough to burn me if I reached out to grab them. And then I saw it was one of the vamps from earlier, one of Desdemona's minions, and he grabbed me by the back of my hair and dragged me over the ground toward one of the cars that had been collateral damage from the tornado. I struggled against him, but I couldn't move my arms—he had bound my wrists with some kind of wire—which made reaching my wand impossible. The vamp was taking me somewhere, and I had nothing left in my body to fight it.

CHAPTER 17
THE STALKER. THE SAVIOR.

In self-defense courses—I've taken every one in the city—they say that if you can help it at all, never let your attacker take you to a second location. Crime statistics will tell you that your chances of survival at a second location are vastly diminished. It's probably doubly true in cases when the attacker is a vampire. I knew that if I let the savage force me into that yellow car, I may as well enjoy my last breath, right there on the grimy, oil-stained road. Police car sirens wailed in the distance, which made him move faster. I felt his super strength hoist me up by my arm and my hair, my scalp on fire, and he was about to throw me into the battered vehicle when he stopped, and dropped me, instead, with a thud on the road.

A man with iron rods for biceps had appeared, and was holding the vamp by the scruff of his neck as if he were a defenseless kitten, scrabbling in the air, and then he threw the creature so hard and fast into the graffitied wall opposite that the sound of his bones cracking was like a rifle shot. Not yet content that the vamp was dead, the man—who I recognized now as the stalker from outside my apartment—crossed the road and approached the slack body. Then he looked both ways and pulled a gun out of his holster, and quickly fired a bullet into the vamp's head. His revolver had a silencer, so there was only a muffled rap of gunpowder exploding down the barrel and a quick flare of light, and the vampire began to shrivel and ash.

The man in the leather jacket—my mysterious stalker/savior—tucked his gun neatly back into his holster and walked toward me. I was in no condition to thank him, or even to say hello, because the minute I felt his arms around me, lifting me from the hard ground, my consciousness hazed away.

WHEN I WOKE UP, my body felt broken. I felt like I had run a marathon and then been beaten up, which is kind of what happened, I guess.

I blinked in the dim room, my eyes adjusting to the beginning of dawn light. Was I dreaming? It looked like I was home, in my bed, but that was impossible. It felt like my bed, smelled like my bed, but... how?

There was a bottle of water on my bedside table which I'm pretty sure I hadn't put there. I glugged it down in one go. Every muscle hurt. Damn, I was a mess. I was still wearing my torn clothes that smelled of stale blood and vampire ash (don't get me wrong, I love the smell of vampire ash, just not in my bed). I moved my legs, considering getting up to shower, but my body ached so much I thought better of it. The memories of the night before came rushing back, and I felt the icy fingers of dread grip my stomach. The Orc Godfather was dead. When the Realm woke up to this knowledge, it would be very bad news indeed. There would be accusations, dirty politics, plots of revenge. Orcs bombing Goblin City and goblins scheming hit after hit until their enemies were all in the ground. A *coup*, if we were lucky, and a civil war, if we were not. Humans and other creatures would get caught in the crossfire, and the Masquerade would fall. All hell would break loose, as if I didn't have a big enough headache already.

I heard an almost inaudible shuffle at the opposite side of the room. Ghost. He must have been worried when I missed my curfew last night.

"Ghost," I croaked. "You could have at least taken my clothes off."

There was silence, then a strange voice said: "I don't usually take women's clothes off. Not on a first date, anyway."

The voice was everything. It was the voice to shut up all other voices. Deep, sonorous, gentle, sophisticated. Was my ghost learning how to talk? And if so, who was he learning from? James Earl Jones?

I shot up in bed, looking for my specter, and saw *him* instead, and the trauma of last night tapped at my skull again. The stalker. The savior. The superhero with nothing better to do. The light was low, but I'd recognize that build anywhere.

I licked my chapped lips, voice still croaky. "What the hell are you doing here?"

"Checking to see if you're okay," he said.

I mean, I knew the stalker knew where I lived, but—

"I'm okay," I said. "You can go now."

"*Are* you okay?" he asked. "I was going to check for injuries, but I thought I'd wait till you woke up."

"How did you get in?"

"Your front door was unlocked."

I needed to get that door fixed, pronto. I had to make it a priority. I'd do it right after I found Pavaris's Crown and somehow miraculously prevented civil war in the Realm. And found Liz Durison's killer. And had something to eat.

I stared at the strange man, wondering who the hell he was, and what he wanted with me.

"So... you've just been sitting there, watching me sleep?"

"Yep."

"That's not creepy at all."

"I thought we'd moved past that," he said. "Since I saved your life."

"I didn't need saving," I said. "I had the situation under control."

"Really," he said. It wasn't a question.

I remembered my attacker trawling me along the tarmac by the hair while I struggled, wrists bound. He was about to put me into that yellow Mini. I didn't fancy my chances of staying alive if he'd succeeded. Now he was a lump of carbon. He was probably being swept up with the rest of the trash as we spoke.

"I liked how you ashed that female vampire," the man said. "Some pretty creative magic you have in your arsenal."

"You were there for that?" I asked. "And you only stepped in when I was half-dead and being dragged away?"

"Well," he shrugged. "As you said. You didn't need saving."

Of course, I didn't believe that. Everyone needs saving in this cruel world, present company (i.e. me) included. But was the man always this infuriating? It didn't matter, he'd be out of my life soon.

He looked amused. "Are you always this infuriating?" he asked.

What.

"I think it's time for you to leave," I said, covering my chest with my faded quilt, even though I was fully clothed.

He stood up and dusted off his jeans. "You're welcome."

"I had it under control," I said again.

He turned to leave. "Sure you did."

"I wanted the vampires alive. I had questions to ask them."

"Yeah, well," he said, shrugging. "The way I saw it was, either that vampire killed you, or I killed him. And I preferred the latter."

"Why?" I asked.

"You know what they say about vampires," he said.

I do know what they say about vampires; I say it all the time. "Yes," I said.

The only good vampire is a dead vampire.

He smiled, then, and began to head out, but I needed to know more.

"You've been following me," I said. "Why?"

He stopped and sighed in a long, weary breath, and scratched his cheek. "I'm afraid I'm not at liberty to tell."

I pushed him. "What are you after? I don't have the Crown, if that's what you're looking for."

"I'm not looking for the Crown," he said, and started to walk out the door. "I don't look for objects. I look for people."

"Well. You found me," I said. "Now what?"

"Now what, indeed," he said.

"You can't just leave!" I shouted at his back, and he waved without turning around, but then he stopped. "Oh, by the way, your bike is in your parking bay downstairs, and your weasel is sleeping on your couch."

"He's not a weasel!" I shouted. "He's a magical albino ferret!"

"You're welcome!" he said again, and closed the front door behind himself.

CHAPTER 18
THE MISSING WIZARD

My phone vibrated with an alert. It wasn't a message—although I seemed to have plenty of those, too—it was a new contact. *Darick* it said, and there was a phone number. So the stalker had a name.

"Darick," I said out loud, and the hairs on the back of my neck stood up. Was it just me, or did the name have a distinctly vampiric ring to it? But then I remembered him throwing that bloodthirsty vamp against the wall and shooting him in the head. The stress of the last few days was making me paranoid, that was all. I saved the number.

Unsettled, I checked the other messages. Pavaris, weeping, again, saying his arthritis was getting so bad he could hardly dial my number anymore. What could I say? I wouldn't be upset if that happened. The man wouldn't leave me alone. Then there was Morgan's voice, asking if we could go for drinks.

I don't want to put pressure on you, Jax, she said. *But you need to give me* something.

I checked the news for anything about the crime scene last night at *Cucina Or'Capone,* or the smashed cars outside, but there was nothing. Someone did a quick clean-up job before the cops got there, and it hadn't been me. I had apparently been knocked out and drooling over some stranger's superhero-sized shoulder. I was about to stop scrolling through my news feed when I saw a headline that caught my eye. It was from a thread with news from the Touched world.

Renowned Wizard, Ametrix Belore, missing in mysterious circumstances.

Ametrix Belore had been on his way to a Council meeting, the article said, when his car was found abandoned on the side of Sandton Drive. No other details had yet been established. That was very odd, I thought, a wizard just disappearing into thin air. Devoted husband, apparently, and loving father of twins. There was a picture of him, and he looked nice enough. I noticed the amulet around his neck: it was a Dragon's Eye stone, set in an intricate ring of gold. Ametrix was well-respected—or respected enough to be involved in meeting with the much-vaunted Council, so he didn't sound like the kind of man who would make himself disappear... although, you never did know. A feeling of foreboding bubbled in my stomach. Something about this felt familiar. I did a quick search on Forage for previous news articles concerning missing wizards, and the bubbling turned to full-on lava. Nine other wizards had been reported missing in the last month, and none of them had been found.

Right on cue, my phone rang, and I dropped it in fright. Luckily it was on my lap in bed so I didn't break the screen (again). The last time I repaired it things didn't turn out well.

I scooped it up with trembling fingers. "Hello?"

"Mrs. Knight?" said a young boy whose voice was just on the edge of cracking.

"Jax," I said. "Who is this?"

"J-Jax," said the boy. "I was wondering if... My sister and I have decided that—"

"I'm not taking any new cases on at the moment," I said, more harshly than I had intended.

"Oh." His disappointment thrummed through the line, a rope of emotion, as if to strangle me.

"Sorry," I said. "I've just got way too much on my plate at the moment."

"I—"

"I can give you a number of a colleague," I said.

"No," he said. "We want to hire you. No one else."

I moved the receiver away from my mouth and sighed, rubbed my eyes. I really couldn't afford to take on any more work. As it is I was failing at... 100% of my current cases.

"My mother," he said. "We don't know what to do—" and his voice broke in earnest, this time trying to stave off a sob.

And then I understood. The Belore twins. The missing wizard's kids. Of course they had called me. How could I say yes when I knew I couldn't devote a decent amount of time to the case? I kicked the wall. There was no way I could accept it. No way. Not gonna happen.

"All right," I said. "I'll do it."

I showered as quickly as I could and changed into leathers that were not full of holes made by vampires. I checked my fridge (still empty) and the locks on my front door (still broken), and then headed toward the twins. I may be failing at my own life, but maybe I could make a difference in theirs.

I ARRIVED at the Belore house with a stone in my throat. After all, I knew what it was like to lose a parent, and let's just say that I didn't have high hopes for Ametrix turning up alive. The twins met me at the gate to warn me.

"She's not herself," said the young boy, who had introduced himself as Eafaris over the phone.

"She's gone mad," said Pepin, his twin sister.

The poor kids, having to deal not only with a missing father, but a mother driven insane by grief.

"Show me," I said, and they led me inside.

"I wasn't going to show you," Eafaris said. "I didn't want you to be distracted."

"Let me worry about that," I said. "Do you have someone we can call?" I asked them, but they shook their heads in unison. "We've tried to call Aunt Bellatrix in Manhattan," Pepin said, "but she's not answering."

Hmm, I thought. I heard that there were things going down in the wizard circuit in Manhattan. I hoped she was safe, unlike her missing brother. There was a squeak from my pocket, and the twins looked at me quizzically. I took the ferret out and let them play with him while I went in to see their mother.

I OPENED the door to the missing wizard's study and saw Mrs. Belore—Francis—muttering to herself and her wand, and walking around in circles.

"*Res ac mortales,*" she chanted. "*Res ac mortales,*" but nothing happened.

"Francis?" I said gently. I felt terrible, intruding on such a personal moment. The woman was trying to conjure her husband back to her, but we both knew that the Void didn't work like that.

"Francis," I said again. "I'm Jacquelyn Knight. I'm here to help find Ametrix."

I may as well have been a sheet of wallpaper. She didn't look at me. I don't even think she heard me, so deep was her focus.

"*Res ac mortales*," she intoned, over and over again. "Come back to me, Trix," she said, silent tears pouring down her face. "Come back to me."

A magical harp stood in the corner of the room. I recognized it as a Morninglark harp, a very powerful magical tool. It could blight an entire season's crops with one specific melody, and it had over a thousand of those to choose from. It had white magic uses, too, more than black, but as with most magical items, it was known first and foremost for its dark power. It could be used to bless, and to curse, and it could also be used to force the truth out of someone. I've always wanted to see one, and I'd heard that the intricate carvings on the spine dance when you play it. I refrained from touching it, though. Ferra calls me tone-deaf, and that's when she's being kind. You wouldn't want to hear me sing an ad jingle, never mind play a deadly harp. A wizard's got to know her limitations.

I watched Francis Belore walk in her continuous circle, her casting ring. She was wearing a navy blue dress with dots on it, and her feet were bare. I reversed out the door, and closed it.

WE SETTLED IN THE LOUNGE, and Eafaris brought me a cup of red birch tea on a trembling saucer. They sat on the couch together and looked at me expectantly, two matching masks of desperation, and my heart went out to them.

"Is there anything you can tell me?" I said. "Any idea of what could have happened?"

"No," said Pepin.

"We've been racking our brains," said Eafaris. "But it was just an ordinary day."

I swallowed hard. This was too close to home. My breast-bone ached with the memory of my own parents, who were also taken on an ordinary day. Isn't that when most devastations happen?

"Someone's taken him," asked Eafaris. "Someone's taken him, haven't they?"

Pepin let out a sob, then covered her mouth. I blinked away the tears that stung my eyes.

What could I say? That everything would be okay? That I'd find their father and bring him home? I knew I couldn't.

Music began playing in the background; a beautiful, haunting melody.

"I promise that I'll do everything I can to find him," I said.

Pepin handed me an envelope with my name on it. I looked inside: it was crowded with cash.

"What's this?" I asked.

On the side-table stood two plundered piggy banks. My heart ached.

"Your pay."

"I haven't done anything, yet."

"Please," said Eafaris. His face was more solemn than any child's should ever be. "Just find him."

THERE WAS CRASH, and a shattering of glass. Both twins gasped and jumped up at the same time. We ran to the study, where their mother was. Eafaris stopped dead in his tracks when he saw her; Pepin, too. "Mom!" they shouted.

The Morninglark Harp was playing, and Francis, eyes closed, was dancing to the tune. A large Ming vase lay smashed on the ground, and the blood from her soles had smeared the floor with red.

CHAPTER 19
IMPALED ON A WHITE PICKET FENCE

I left the Belore house reluctantly, having quieted the harp, pulled the shards of porcelain out of Francis's bleeding feet, and bandaged them up. I bundled her into her bed and cast a protection spell around her, warning the kids to watch her, because it would only last twelve to twenty-four hours. I hated leaving them so distraught, hated taking Gizmo from their shaking palms, and saying goodbye to their pale faces, but I had a job to do. Technically, I had four jobs to do, and not enough time to do them, but today was not a day to get hung up on technicalities.

My first port of call was to find Qwynkle. If the Realm was going to go to hell, I needed to get that Crown back on the right side of magic. If it fell into the wrong hands, well... it didn't bear thinking about. I had a short window of time before the news spread about Don Vito's demise, and I meant to take advantage of it. Liz Durison's naked body flashed in on my mind, reminding me of what had started this whirlwind of the last couple of days.

Yes, Liz, I thought. *I'll get to you. Let me just deal with the world falling apart and then you'll have my full attention.*

I was about to climb on my motorbike when a charcoal-tinted limo appeared, and started following me. I recognized it instantly as the Khargol car.

Filius Canis! I thought. It was Sugar Shagar making good on her promise to kill me if things went south. I started sprinting away, and ducked down a service lane. The Belores lived in a quiet, pleasant, leafy suburb in Greenside. I imagined the orc mafia opening fire and gunning down the deck chairs and the pink flamingoes. I imagined Shagar telling her brutes to stand back while she personally impaled my head on one of the white picket fences. Instead, Gnarg popped up in front of me, right when I was about to parkour up the drainpipe of a timber-cladded house, and tackled me so hard that we were both airborne for a moment before crashing to the slasto pathway. He was around four times my size and weighed roughly the same as a male rhinoceros, so after his body slammed mine into the ground I was so winded I felt as if I would never be able to breathe again.

GNARG CARRIED ME, coughing and wheezing, to the limousine. It made me think of Mr. Hotdog all over again.

What was it about bad men dragging me into cars, lately?

He obviously wanted to kill me somewhere else, and not in this nice neighborhood, or he surely would have done it right there and then, in full view of the flamingoes. The car door opened, and Shagar admonished the bodyguard.

"Gnarg!" she said. "We said bring her in *gently.*"

Gnarg shrugged. He clearly thought he had been gentle. My lungs, on the other hand, would probably never be the same. But it wasn't that that niggled me.

We, she had said. *We* said bring her in gently.

Gnarg tipped me into the interior of the expensive car and then it suddenly made sense. There Sugar sat, and in her frankfurter fingers was another bunch of frankfurter fingers, and they were attached to a—very much alive—Don Vito. Her Death Marsh eyes twinkled at me.

"How?" I asked, breathlessly. I had seen The Godfather die. I had seen his chest ripped open by the AK47 bullets. Had Shagar hired someone to bring him back to life? If so, the consequences would be extremely serious. I backed away—as much as I could, anyway, into the plush upholstery.

"We wanted to thank you," said Shagar, and Vito grunted. I assumed that was his way of telling a *Girl Wizard* that he was grateful.

"How?" I said again, staring at the risen-from-the-dead orc, the worry climbing up my throat. "Magic?"

"No," said Shagar, shaking her head, her hair falling into her pickle face. She was wearing an extra bright shade of lipstick, which really showed off the green in her cheeks. She swept her hair away and smiled at me with all her teeth. I tried to not look too closely or risked fainting right there, in the cabin of their luxury sedan.

"After you warned Vito," she gushed, "he went upstairs and put on a bulletproof vest."

Shagar rubbed his hand in hers, and The Godfather grunted again.

"You're welcome," I said to him, reminding myself of Darick, and getting annoyed with him all over again.

"What's wrong?" asked Mrs. Godfather. "You're not happy he's alive?"

"Of course I am," I said, and I was. "But you could have told me earlier. I risked my life in there, trying to save your husband."

"Tell you?" she said.

"Yes, tell me," I snapped, still shocked by his living and breathing body an arm's-length away from me. "So that I wouldn't have worried so much. I've been thinking of the repercussions all morning. I thought we'd be in for civil war. And I thought you'd put my name on your personal hit-list."

"Wizard," she laughed. "Tell *you*? He didn't even tell *me*."

I hated the Don then, just a little. What if Vito's personal bodyguard had thrown himself in front of him to take the bullets? What if Shagar had? His outright arrogance, which I found infuriating before, made me absolutely furious now. My anger crowded the car, and I felt I had to get out of there, out of the toxic fumes that emanated from the Khargol family.

It wasn't just orc B.O. I could smell. It was smugness and dishonesty and selfishness, and I had to get out of there. I opened the door to get out, and Gnarg put his baseball mitt of a hand on my shoulder, warning me to stay inside. Welcome fresh air streamed into the cabin.

"Why the deceit, then?" I asked, sitting back, crossing my arms in front of me. "Why the act? Sitting at the most vulnerable table and facing the street, knowing that gang was coming. And why didn't you duck when they started shooting?"

Don Vito cleared his throat. "We needed to see who it was."

"There's no point in hiding," said Shagar, "if they'll just come for us again. We refuse to live in fear. We needed to know who was behind it, so we could stop them once and for all."

"Now, they think I'm dead," said The Godfather. "Now they let their guard down, and we strike."

"Those goblins are dead meat," said Shagar, not without relish.

"No," I said.

"What?"

"I need them alive."

"Don't be ridiculous," Sugar said.

"They have something I'm looking for."

Vito grunted. "We'll buy you another one."

"You don't understand."

"No," said Shagar. "*You* don't understand. That goblin needs to die. And so does his whole dirty gang."

"Give me twenty-four hours," I said. "Please."

Don Vito pursed his lips at me.

"Please," I said again. "I risked my own life to help you. The least you can do is give me a few hours!"

"You have two," he said, and motioned with an impatient palm that I was free to go. I climbed out of the car and started walking toward my motorbike.

SHAGAR RAN AFTER ME. "We have something for you."

"I don't want it." I wanted nothing more to do with these people.

"Protection," she said.

I stopped, and turned around. "Protection?"

"Our men will watch over you. Make sure you come to no harm. As payment for saving Vito's life."

I wanted less orcs in my life, not more. But if it meant I got to live, I suppose I'd have to get used to a few dark-suited ogres following me around. Just till the cases were solved and I was out of danger.

"There's something else." She pulled her handbag around to her swollen front: a silly, dainty thing that looked doll-sized on her generous frame. "That gang leader. That goblin."

"Yes?" I was listening hard. "Qwynkle."

She looked surprised that I knew his name, but tore her eyes off me to search in her bag. I surreptitiously looked at her stomach while she concentrated on digging in her ridiculously small handbag. Was her belly bigger than before? It was hard to tell.

"Can you imagine," she said, "if the great Or'Capone was killed by a goblin with such a stupid name?"

I could see she wanted to laugh, and thought better of it, but her amusement was clear on her bright red lips. I thought it was an odd thing to say, but I also know from personal experience that cheating death makes you feel decidedly giddy.

"You need something from this Qwynkle?" she asked.

I thought of the rowdy goblins I had overheard at *The Copper Cog*, singing that drunken song, implying that Qwynkle had Estelar Pavaris's Crown.

"Yes," I said. "He has something I need."

"Sugar!" yelled her husband from the limo.

She flinched, her smile vanished, and carried on rooting in her bag.

"Suga-a-a-ar!" he roared.

Deodamnatus, would she just get on with it? I felt like I was growing old right there in front of her.

"The men," she said. "Vito's men. They're on their way to kill Qwynkle."

"But Vito agreed to give me two hours!"

"And he will. I'll make sure of that. But this means that I know where he is. You can find him."

I suddenly felt very suspicious. Why was she being so helpful?

She finally fished out the thing she was looking for in her bag, and handed it to me.

"This is what one of our informers gave us half an hour ago."

It was a scrap of paper with hurriedly written details on it.

KWINKLE

THE DOME

. . .

"He works as a janitor at the Dome," she said.

A janitor? That didn't seem to fit the idea I had of him.

"The Dome?" I frowned at her. "Are you sure?"

I wondered who had tipped them off, and realized then how connected Shagar really was.

"He's not just a gang leader," she said. "He's a thief who needs somewhere to store his loot."

The Dome was a large exhibition hall that floated in a small pocket realm above the industria in Northriding. Untouched humans couldn't see it, which made it a perfect place to house the Elves' Magic Display, a huge collection of replicas of famous magical items that would otherwise never been seen. The public had never quite decided if the expo was to educate the masses or just to show off the elves' wealth, but there it was, floating in the sky, and you could visit it for a hundred bucks a ticket.

No one would guess where it is, said one of those drunken goblins last night. *Very clever move. Very clever goblins.* I snatched the note from Sugar's hand and started to run.

CHAPTER 20
RUMPIS

I ran and leapt on to my bike, leaving the Khargols in my dust. I needed to get to the Dome before they decided to go back on their word and kill the leader of the goblin gang before I had time to find Estelar's Crown. I accelerated, my trench coat winging behind me.

"Tint visor," I said, and the helmet's screen darkened, taking the edge off the glare. I tried not to let my mind run away with me, tried to focus on the ride, but seeing Don Vito alive when I was so sure he had been dead had definitely rattled me. And I kept hearing that stupid sloshed goblin at *The Copper Cog* singing *Qwynkle, Qwynkle*. I couldn't shake it out of my head so I asked my helmet to play some music, instead. It wanted to play jazz, I wanted Afro-Marabi, so we settled on some slow rock. You're definitely living a charmed life when your smart helmet argues about your choice in music.

Once we were out of the wizard suburbs, the road to the Dome was wide and straight, and not too busy for a Friday morning. It felt good to zoom along, my bike humming comfortingly beneath me as I prepared myself mentally to steal back the HighFire Crown. The sky was a hopeful shade of blue, with just the faintest brush of cirrus. Today was the day I would return to Estelar what rightfully belonged to him, and we'd all be able to breathe a sigh of relief.

I SWITCHED off the engine in the underground parking basement of the Dome, and this time I didn't forget my security spell. I ran up the wide, white marble steps and went straight to the counter to buy a ticket. The price had doubled.

"Two hundred bucks?" I said to the elf. "Seriously?"

The receptionist looked down her perfectly straight nose at me and pushed her expensive-looking tortoiseshell frames into place. "Seriously," she said. Behind her was a three-paneled screen of 3D videos about the various artefacts on display.

I handed her my credit card, which she took with just the tips of her fingers, as if I had passed her a bed-bug infested sock instead of a piece of plastic that had slim to no chance of working. We waited in silence, the elf tapping her perfectly manicured nails on the white marble counter. I stared at the intricate art on them. My nails were lucky if they got scrubbed by a nailbrush once a week, never mind the mini-Picasso treatment.

"Declined," she said, and picked up a large pair of brass scissors. Before I could stop her, she snipped the card in half. "Sorry," she sniffed (she wasn't). "Bank's orders."

I gritted my teeth and tried to think of another way in. Bloody elves. I could make myself invisible, but I'm sure their security would still pick me up, trying to sneak through. Then I remembered the envelope of cash in my pocket. I hauled it out and counted out two handsome blue hundred-rand bills.

The elf blinked her extreme lashes at me, plucked the notes from my hand, and forced her lips into a smile.

"Welcome to the Display," she said, and the machine spat out a ticket. She tore it off and passed it to me, along with a brochure and a map of the place. Not that I needed it. I had Gizmo.

I wasn't looking for Qwynkle. I had no interest in ever seeing him again. My plan was to go straight for the Crown. After my brief conversation with Sugar I was pretty sure that the gang leader was stealing magical items from elves' houses and swapping them out with these replicas. It was the perfect hiding place for the real plunder: in plain sight (if you happened to have two hundred bucks to burn). A cunning plan, perfect for goblins, and I could have kicked myself for not thinking of it sooner.

I walked along the first wall of the display and found the items fascinating, despite my climbing anxiety. The Dome interior was white from floor to ceiling, and the replicas were encased in floating glass boxes of various sizes. Some of the articles were exhibited in-situ: a wax model of a beautiful faerie with a mermaid tail, wearing an alice-band made of sea-shells that allowed her to travel through water or land. There was a cat collar made from vampire fangs on a rather startled-looking ceramic cat, and a model of an old, wizened wizard replete with purple robe and tall, pointy hat, holding an old book, and a staff that looked as ancient as he was. Funny, how everyone thinks of wizards as ancient male hermits. His white beard was so long it almost touched the floor. I'm glad I didn't have to deal with that; it would be super impractical in my occupation.

In the next glass box was a Skeleton Portal Key, which I would have loved to have, and the one after that had Elf Sneaking Boots that allowed you to travel virtually undetected. There was a beautifully engraved Equillar—a dagger used to cut through magical enchantments—and a ten-thousand-year-old witch's wand, made from a dragon's wing-bone. A magical hand mirror that made the viewer look exactly how they wish to be seen, and an amulet of fire: Pale Flames. The information card didn't say what magic the amulet held. In this unpredictable world, I guess some things are best kept secret.

I forced myself forward, but couldn't help looking at the treasures, wondering which were real, and which were replicas. A Lick of Leaping Silver: a finely balanced sword. A lizard-scale shield. Shadow Armor. A potent healing potion the color of the river pebbles. A blade of Sea Gold which could cut through anything with the force of an ocean wave. I could have studied the things for hours, but the clock was ticking.

I took Gizmo out of my pocket and realized I hadn't fed him all day. I was clearly not good at this pet-parenting thing. I felt bad and patted him and told him I'd buy him a packet of overpriced peanuts from the Dome's vending machine on the way out. I put him back inside his cozy nook and decided to look for the thing myself. How difficult could it be? I had a map and a—

And just like that, just like... well, magic... there it was, right in front me. Encased in its glass cube, and on a satin pillow with golden tassels that looked identical to the one on Pavaris's pedestal. I looked from side to side to see who else was watching. A handful of viewers walked past. An orc couple with a pram passed by. I purposefully looked away from the baby inside. Orc babies are incredibly ugly, and always make me think of an old joke about a bus and a monkey and make me laugh out loud, but now was not the time. I needed to be as invisible as possible. A group of teenaged elves ambled past feigning interest, followed by some Touched humans with nothing better to do. I narrowed my eyes, trying to inspect it, trying to ascertain if it was the real thing, but honestly, what I know about diamonds and gems is scary. Could I test it somehow? If I was able to channel its energy I would be able to find out if it was legit. A goblin pushed a mop bucket on wheels past me. I started, thinking it might be Qwynkle, but it was a female goblin with a limp, so I calmed down to a mild panic. Of course, a place like this would have more than one goblin on their staff. Elves don't sweep floors or clean toilets.

I INSPECTED THE CROWN, which was really quite bewitching with its gold flames and precious pearls. I tried to communicate with it somehow, tried to absorb some of its unique magic, but my energy was bouncing off the glass, which seemed to have some kind of enchantment on it. Another goblin walked past with his hands behind his back. He was wearing a gray business suit, and spectacles, and I waited for him to go before I carried on staring at the Crown in what I'm sure was a highly suspicious way. In my mind, there was no way to tell if the thing was real or not, so I'd have to just risk it, and run. Another goblin appeared: this one was wearing shades, a Hawaiian shirt, and a backpack, as if he'd just walked off the plane from Maui. I had to work fast. I surreptitiously unclipped my wand from my belt. If I wanted to get away with this, I'd have to be nimble. I ran through the relevant spells in my head, and my heart started thrumming. Another goblin popped up, a blond-wigged one in a summer dress, and I wondered if I was being paranoid (again) or if the gobs really were multiplying like wet gremlins right in front of my eyes.

Nope, not being paranoid.

There was another one in my peripheral vision, wearing a slate-colored janitor's uniform with the Dome insignia on the front, and he was watching me. Qwynkle. Must be. Someone had alerted him, probably that first goblin who had been pushing that mop around. Told him that there was a *Girl Wizard* in here, meaning to cause trouble. Without looking at them directly, I could count six or seven goblins now, all in clumsy costumes, seemingly ready to spring. Then a big crowd of Japanese orcs arrived and started taking awkward selfies with the ceramic cat. They streamed in like a huge, noisy bank of water, blocking out Qwynkle's view of me, although the other goblins still had me in their sights. The snotty elf receptionist strode in, worry etched in her otherwise perfectly Botoxed skin, and asked the orcs to not take photos or touch the items on display. One of the tourists grabbed the old wizard's staff from the display and began pretending to zap his mates with its magic. Another climbed up onto the Fae stand and pretended to kiss her while taking pics with his selfie-stick. The receptionist pranced around, trying to contain the situation, but they ignored her. I guess she didn't know how to grunt in Japanese.

I had a small window, and had to act fast.

"*Rumpis!*" I said to the glass case containing the HighFire Crown, and a large crack appeared on the front pane. The goblins quickened their pace, striding toward me. "*Rumpis!*" I said again, and this time the whole front part shattered, but stayed in place: a huge silver spiderweb. Bloody elf enchantments.

Fortunately, I had expected something like that, and I had another spell up my sleeve. Admittedly, it wasn't one I was very good at, but desperate times, etc., etc.

"*Nebulam,*" I said, and the display unit went up in a mantle of white smoke. This pleased me—I hadn't thought it would work so well—perhaps the *Rumpis* spell had damaged the enchantment as well as the glass. I didn't waste any time in grabbing the Crown and shoving it under my trench coat and into my infinity pocket. I whispered to it, then belted up my coat as quickly as I could.

"Thief!" screamed the goblin in the summer dress.

"Thief!" shouted the one with the sunglasses and backpack.

Security guards came running, their hands gripping the handcuffs hanging from their hips. I put my hands up. The Japanese orcs pointed their cameras at me and started flashing. Qwynkle was nowhere to be seen.

CHAPTER 21
EMPTY PEDESTAL

The orc security guards backed me into a corner and took out their pistols.

"My hands are up," I reminded them. I know how trigger-happy orcs can be, and I wasn't in the mood to be Killed by Clumsiness.

The goblins stood behind them, drooling at me. Literally.

"Open coat," said Dumbledee. I did.

"Ergh," said Dumbledum, looking at where the vaporized display case had been, now just an empty pedestal. He scratched his head. "Where Crown?"

I shot my arms out like an arrow in the direction of the goblin in the tropical island get-up. "He took it!"

Hawaiian shirt looked shocked. "No!" he said, shaking his head. "The wizard took it!" and pointed his creeping slug of a finger back in my direction.

"Who are you going to believe?" I asked. "A wizard with a clean record"—which wasn't the exact truth—"or a treacherous goblin in a Hawaiian shirt?"

The orcs' eyebrows shot up in unison. They saw my point.

"Search," said Dumbledee, and Dumbledum stomped over to the horrified goblin.

"No!" he shouted again, hugging his bag in his hands and reversing away from us. "No search!"

I don't know what he had in that bag, but the goblin's reaction to being frisked was all the reason the security guards needed to decide on the spot that he was guilty. When the goblin turned to run, Dumbledum smacked him down like a pro-wrestler, and the tourists all started cheering. I capitalized on the general confusion and snaked through the clapping crowd and out of the front entrance, where the guard posts and the reception desk were both conveniently empty.

OUT IN THE CRISP AIR, I mentally high-fived myself. The sun was shining, I wasn't in a gray room being strip-searched by orcs, and I had the HighFire Crown in my pocket. I took it out and turned it around in my hands, seeing nothing but my own palms. The invisibility spell would only last a few more minutes. I started jogging toward the parking basement. I was within ten meters of my motorbike when something shot out and tripped me, making me fly forward and crash to the ground. I smacked my face on the concrete slab, cracking a tooth and sending a blue current of pain up into my brain, blinding me for a full ten seconds. I was on my hands and knees on the concrete floor, blood in my mouth, sparks in my head. Worst of all, the still-invisible Crown had gone clattering out in front of me. A needle in a haystack would have been easier to find.

"WIZARD," said a mean voice behind me.

I turned and sat up, but there was no one there.

"You think you're the only one who can sling an invisibility spell?" he asked, and then the air dappled, like a heat-shimmer, and a particular ugly goblin janitor appeared.

"Qwynkle," I said, spitting out blood.

"I believe you have something of mine," he said.

"It doesn't belong to you any more than it belongs to me."

He licked his rubbery lips and blinked in a rather annoyed way. "Look, wizard," he said, with his hands behind his back. "You don't understand what's happening here."

"Then educate me," I said, crawling an inch backwards, feeling for the invisible Crown.

"A goblin? Educate a wizard?" He laughed. "Wouldn't that be something."

"Cut the smartass act, Qwynkle. I know that you gunned down The Godfather last night."

"Ah," the goblin said. "That was you. I wondered who put that ice shield up. Too clever for an orc bodyguard."

"Not clever enough," I said.

"Why were you protecting him?" he demanded. "Protecting someone as evil as him?"

"You know why. Because with Don Vito dead, the Realm will be thrown into chaos. I wonder if you thought of that when you accepted the bounty."

"Gold is gold," said Qwynkle.

I scrunched up my face up at him. "Said like a true goblin."

"Easy for you to be judgmental."

"What's that supposed to mean?"

I moved back a fraction more, my fingers searching for the Crown. I needed to keep the conversation going until I found it.

"Wizards, elves, dwarves. All born into money and privilege."

"If you saw my bank account you'd disagree," I said.

Qwynkle looked disgusted and spat on the concrete floor. "You're so steeped in it you don't even see it."

He had a point. No one would give a goblin a white-collar job, no matter how qualified he or she was. Which was probably short-sighted given how clever and cunning they were. They would make great lawyers and accountants.

"Look," I said. "As much as I'm enjoying this conversation, I need to go." I quickly glanced around behind me, hoping to catch sight of it, but it was still invisible.

He watched me, amused. "Are you looking for this?" he asked, moving his hands from behind his back, and revealing the Crown.

When I saw it I froze. "How?" I said.

"Candy from a baby," he said. "I stuck my leg out, you fell particularly hard. Stars in your eyes. I sometimes have that effect on people."

I clenched my teeth. "Give it to me, goblin."

He cackled, and the menacing sound echoed in the parking basement. "Give it to you," he laughed, holding his potbelly with his free hand. "Good one. I do like a wizard with a sense of humor."

My anger boiled inside my chest. I whipped my wand from my belt and pointed it at him.

He stopped laughing. "Now, now, let's not be hasty."

"You give that Crown to me right now," I said, "Or I'll destroy you. The only thing that'll be left of you is a greasy mark on the ground where you're standing."

"My, my, she's a feisty one," Qwynkle said, eyes glinting.

"Goblin. This is your last chance." My emotion was swelling in my chest, ripe to be expelled in the goblin's direction. He held the Crown in front of his heart.

"Be careful, now. You don't want to damage Pavaris's lucky charm."

He had called my bluff. He knew I couldn't risk attacking him while he held the Crown. I lowered my wand.

Qwynkle smiled and put two fingers to his lips and whistled hard. Goblins stepped out from behind corners, columns, and cars. There was a dozen of them, at least, all in their ridiculous costumes. The one in the summer dress's blond wig was on skew, and she reminded me of E.T. The only one who was missing was Hawaiian Shirt, who I guess was currently being interrogated by Dumbledee and Dumbledum. I still wanted to know what was in his bag.

"Goblins," he said in an authoritative tone, as if he were addressing a Toastmasters Club instead of a gang of slimy criminals in a parking basement. "I'm going to take the Crown, and the wizard is going to try to stop me. While I take care of this," he said, clutching it tightly, "I would like it if you took care of her."

He bowed his head at me, and spun on his heel.

"Don't you dare!" I shouted at his back, lifting my wand again. The gang of slimeballs started advancing on me again like they had inside the exhibition hall, but this time there were no orc security guards to turn on them.

There was malice in their big, bloodshot eyes as they approached. They bared their dirty needles.

"Stay where you are!" I yelled, but they kept coming. Closer, closer, till I felt the fear high in my throat. The adrenaline rushed through my body, giving me a clear shot of energy. I parkoured onto the roof a nearby car, out of the goblins' reach. They ran at the car—a sporty SUV—and tried to climb it, but their slithery skin made them slip and slide, and they couldn't gain traction.

They had stolen from Pavaris, they had gunned down a mafia boss, and now they were about to kill me. Gizmo squeaked in my pocket, probably wondering where his over-priced peanuts were. It made me think of when I first found him, which gave me an idea.

"Qwynkle!" I shouted, and he turned around. I locked my eyes on the Crown.

"Why are you still breathing?" he asked.

I used my wand like a fly-fishing rod again, like I had in the Reef hall, pulling it back behind me and then whirling its magic in Qwynkle's direction in a neat, glowing arc. "*Contendis!*" I yelled, and the wisp of smoke flew through the air and hooked the Crown. By the time Qwynkle knew what was happening, I had whipped it back, and the Crown came flying toward me. It landed perfectly in my hands. I tucked it back into my pocket. This time I wasn't going to let it go.

The goblin in the gray business suit had managed to get a foothold on one of the tires, and he hoisted himself up onto the bonnet. I pointed my wand at him.

"*Fiat Fulgur!*" I shouted, and the anxiety in my stomach moved up inside my body and rushed through my silver wand, sending a bolt of lightning at him. He cried out when it hit him, let go of the windshield, and tumbled, rolling off the car and down to the ground. I felt sticky hands grab me from behind, and I spun around. Blondie. Another goblin had managed to climb up too. I couldn't fight them both with magic at the same time, so instead I grabbed their oversized heads and smashed them together as hard as I could. They shrieked in fright and pain, and fell off.

"Next?" I said, breathing hard.

It was meant as a rhetorical question, really, but a new wave of goblins came forward and started scrabbling up on the car. *It's okay,* I told myself. *It's okay.* If I can handle three of them, I can handle thirteen. Using my trusty lightning spell, I knocked the new guys off one by one, before they were able to get up to my level. I was about to feel triumphant when I looked at Qwynkle, who now held a gun in his hand.

"It's time to stop playing games," he said. "Give it to me."

"Over my dead body," I sneered, and jumped down on the opposite side of the car, using it as cover between him and I. I hurriedly took Gizmo out of my pocket and put him on top of the rear left tire. He'd be safer hiding in there than with me, doing battle. I heard footsteps approach: the gang members who I hadn't yet picked off. They were using garbage-can lids as makeshift shields to deflect the fire spell. I had to think of something else.

"*Impedio!*" I yelled, and the two that had just sneaked past the fender froze in mid-lurch. I wheeled around the other side of the SUV and struck another three attackers with the same spell. They would only be frozen in time for a few minutes, so I had to get moving. Of course, there was still Qwynkle and his little pistol to deal with.

I stepped out from behind the car to face him. He had a determined look on his face and he raised his gun slightly. The ground was littered with the writhing bodies of his gang.

"*Impedio!*" I shouted, and ice-blue light streamed out of my wand in his direction, ready to paralyze him, but he side-stepped the flow of magic and hid behind one of the concrete columns. I started striding toward him. My anger was building, and I wanted to make sure that when I was finished with him, he'd be out of action for a long time. Goblins can hold a grudge forever, and there was no way I was going to be looking over my shoulder for the rest of my life. I held my wand out, ready to strike, when I saw the barrel of his gun sneak around the corner. It happened so quickly I hardly had time to duck my head behind my bullet-proof arms, but I managed just in time to deflect three of his missiles that were clearly meant for my face.

Then I got really mad. I lost control of my emotions, which means I lost control of my power. Magic shot out of my wand without me uttering a word, and a cable of destructive energy flew into the column that the goblin was hiding behind, blasting it away. Qwynkle leapt to the next one, firing a shot at me while he was airborne, getting me in the shoulder with a hot pop next to my ear, and I destroyed that column, too, and the next, and the next.

When I got hold of some sense, I stopped using my wand and woke up to what was happening. Qwynkle had circled me without me realizing what he was doing. Without the support of the concrete columns, the ceiling above us cracked, as if it were a lake frozen over with ice, and we were about to fall in. I stopped dead, understanding what I had done, but it was too late. With a rumble like the earth was ending, the ceiling crumbled and fell and covered us in an avalanche of concrete blocks and debris. I was crushed, and I couldn't breathe.

CHAPTER 22
MAGICAL ALBINO HEART

I couldn't breathe, couldn't move. The dark weight was crushing me. Concrete dust blinded me, but it's not like I would have been able to see anything, anyway. I was buried under ten feet of rubble. I was going to die at the hands of a Greedy Goblin, and my own bloody temper. All in all, I thought, as my lungs screamed for air, it was not an ideal situation. My only consolation was that Qwynkle was probably dead or dying, too.

I tried to move my arms, and then my legs, but no dice. I attempted to wrest some oxygen from the air around me but just managed to get a mouthful of grit. Warm liquid ran down my neck, and my head, still tender from the beating it took the day before, was pounding like a sugared-up orc toddler on a bongo drum. If I didn't claw my way out of there, and make it snappy, I was done for. I was literally heading toward fossil territory, and fast.

The bright side of dying, of course, is that my lungs would stop aching, my body would stop hurting. But I wasn't going to let that happen. Turns out I'm a sucker for punishment.

I tried to move my arms again, and this time there was slight mobility; in my legs, too. Perhaps I was in shock, before, but now I could move a couple millimeters. I gathered the little strength I had and kept trying, fighting against the cold, hard wreckage that was keeping me buried. A millimeter, a millimeter, a millimeter, and then an inch. I was rocking and rolling my body in fractions of fractions, knowing that every gain, no matter how small, would push me closer to survival. In my head I was in the dark ocean and kicking my way up to the surface, slow and steady. I climbed another inch, and then another. My face reached a pocket of air and I breathed, and screamed, and breathed some more. Another inch meant that I could see a fissure of light above me, and it gave me the strength I needed to keep going, or I would suffocate. I kept my eyes on the prize. Soon the lightning-bolt shaped crack in the sky became a small hole. Someone was up there.

"Help!" I screamed, using the precious air I had in my lungs to alert someone. "Help!" I was hoping against hope that it was a decent person trying to dig me out and not a vile goblin trying to hammer the last nail in my coffin.

And then I saw his face. Gizmo.

Gizmo had found me. He was sniffing the rubble and pawing at it, trying to get to me. He wouldn't be able to uncover me —he was just too small compared to the huge concrete rocks that kept me in the ground—but he knew where I was. He could show someone. He could be my white flag, my beacon. I kept swimming.

Ten minutes later there was the whine of a siren. An ambulance if I was lucky, the Dome's security alarm if I was not. I kicked and elbowed and rocked my ribcage, and focused on Gizmo, above, who was still digging, bless his magical albino heart. The vehicle arrived via the portal tunnel, and screeched to a stop near us. I heard doors being opened and slammed. Gizmo stopped digging and drew up to his full height in order to signal my position.

It took three orcs to dig me out, and when they laid me on the stretcher I was gray from head to toe, apart from the white of my eyes (and my magnificent pet ferret). They shoved an oxygen mask over my face and tapped my arm to bring up a vein. Saline. Tramadol. Antibiotics. The youngest of the orcs gently pulled a foil blanket around me, reminding me of Morgan and Liz Durison, embroidering my sense of survival euphoria with a dark edge of guilt. The paramedics wondered out loud how I could have survived the ordeal. I suspected it was a lucky combination of my graphene coat and the Crown.

Holy Hex! I sat up on the stretcher. *The Crown!*

The orcs grunted at me to stay still while they re-checked my vitals. I swatted them away. I was living, I was breathing, and I had the HighFire Crown. In that moment, that's all that mattered.

I felt in my pocket for it and when my fingers touched the magical item I immediately felt like weeping with relief. I pulled it out and looked at it, and my stomach cramped with an intense feeling of dread. The good news was that I was still in possession of Estelar's Crown. The bad news was that it was broken into three pieces.

CHAPTER 23
BOTTLE OF BLITZ

I made my way home slowly and thoughtfully. I was happy to be alive, but utterly shattered. I had so many balls in the air, ready to smash to the ground. How would I tell Pavaris about his destroyed Crown? Plus it was late afternoon, and I hadn't yet done anything to find Ametrix Belore. The memory of the twins sitting together on the couch in their house while their mother shredded her soles next door haunted me. And I really had to see Morgan to explain why I hadn't made any progress on the Scorpion case. I made a mental note to set up drinks with her for later that night. I took a deep breath and kept walking. Sometimes, that's all you need to do. One step in front of the other, and you'll get there eventually.

When I greeted the neighborhood drug dealer she took my IV-punctured arm, startling me. She was wearing the same as always: a kind of post-apocalyptic outfit with a big, black hood that covered her snow-white hair. She took off her Fong Kong Ray Bans and I saw her eyes for the first time: one quinine blue, and the other, overcast.

"Hey," she said, lifting her ebony chin at me.

"Hey," I said. I was covered in concrete dust, and my head was still bleeding, so I must have been a curious sight to behold, although she didn't seem to notice.

"I just wanted to let you know," she said, sliding her shades back in place so that I could see my reflection in them. I had a lot of questions, but one thing was for sure: I certainly wasn't at risk of winning Miss Universe.

The drug dealer was still holding my arm.

"What?" I asked.

"That man. Who was following you."

"Ha," I joked. "Which one?"

But she didn't laugh. "The one with the voice."

"Oh, yes," I said. "Him. The stalker."

Darick.

"He's been hanging around. Asking questions about you."

I stopped smiling. "Questions? Like what?"

"Where you go, during the day. When you come back. What job you do."

"Damn," I said. "I was hoping it would be more, like, what's my favorite bottle of blitz."

"Yes," she said. "That would have been better."

I laughed, and started to move away, but she didn't let go.

"You need to be careful," she said, her mismatched eyes arresting mine. "You're a Magus ten."

I remembered the Council rep who had kidnapped me off the street and taken a sample with his white medical pen. He had said I was a ten.

"I know," I said. It's a risky predicament, to have blood running in your veins that is as potent as magic gets. It's not something I'd want printed on a t-shirt. Trading Magus is totally verboten by the Council, but that doesn't stop some of the Black Magic Market creeps from dealing in it.

"Do you sell wizard blood?" I asked.

"No," the drug dealer said. "No way."

"Too dangerous for you?" I asked.

"Too dangerous for the Realm."

She was about to say something else, but changed her mind. I wrenched my arm away and entered my apartment building.

I caught the Swift up to my place, hoping that Uragh hadn't tossed out all my stuff and boarded up the entrance with old tomato crates and rusty nails. When I pushed open the door, everything seemed to be in place. Perhaps Ghost had spooked him. I took Gizmo out of my pocket and put him on the kitchen counter. Poured myself a glass of water, downed it, then drank another, and splashed some into an old tarnished silver eggcup for Gizmo.

"We'll go out soon to get you some food," I said to him. With the money in the envelope from the Belore twins I'd be able to buy some groceries. "What's your favorite food?"

He wiped his whiskers and nodded.

"You can show me when we go shopping," I said. Not that I had time to browse the local minimart, with Ametrix Belore still missing. Maybe we'd grab something from a takeaway place on our way to find him.

I slumped down into the second-hand chair with the arrow-hole in it and closed my eyes. I just needed five minutes rest. After a week like I had experienced, I needed time out.

"I almost died today," I said to the empty room.

The ferret scuttled down off the kitchen counter and came to sit on my lap. I stroked him.

"Gizmo saved my life." I said. "Again."

He snuggled up to me, nuzzling the dusty coat I had been too tired to take off at the door.

"Gizmo, do you know what I think?" I whispered. "I think we should get an ouija board. Then maybe when I talk to Ghost, he'll talk back."

The red hardcover book fell off the bookshelf with a snap.

"Ah," I smiled. "There you are."

IN THE SHOWER I watched as the water swirling down the drain turned from old-blood-brown, to gray, to clear. My head wound seemed to not be as serious as I had feared, and I looked up into the old lime-scaled shower nozzle and thanked the Void. Investigating paranormal crime was tricky enough without having stars in your head.

The clothes I had meant to throw away from the vampire fight the night before were mended and laundered and waiting on my bed for me. I picked up the pants and inspected them; they were better than new. I pressed the shirt up to my nose and inhaled the scent of laundry detergent. I zipped back in time to when I was a little girl, standing in our family kitchen.

SUNSHINE STREAMING THROUGH THE WINDOWS, the kettle singing for tea. Mom slicing fresh white bread with a shiny crust. Dad coming in from collecting the washing off the line outside, and playfully lobbing a clean sock at me. It landed on my head, and as

I tried to grab it, I missed, and it dropped down to the floor. I looked up at him, and we both giggled.

I HELD the shirt to my aching chest, and my sinuses stung.

"Thank you, Ghost," I said.

CHAPTER 24

DIAMOND-COLLARED DOBERMANS

We picked up some fish and chips from a food truck in Parkhurst, and I learnt that Gizmo loves vinegar and pick-pocketing. The ferret presented me with a fifty-buck note to pay for the food, and I had to return it to the rather grumpy-looking woman with a floral head scarf he had stolen it from.

"He skipped his ethics class in Polecat College," I said, but she didn't smile. What was it with this city, lately? Johannesburg was having a serious sense of humor failure.

"Don't do that again," I said to him, flashing my disappointed-momma eyes. "Stealing is wrong. You've been hanging around with too many goblins."

Thinking of the goblins made me clutch my trench coat tightly around me. The Crown, which I had very carefully repaired, was in my pocket and ready to hand back to Estelar. I had spent an hour on it, being as thorough as possible with my healing incantation, using my wand as a magical blowtorch. I only slipped once—and burnt a pearl that probably cost more than my entire apartment building—because bloody Bron rang my doorbell again. I told him to scamper.

I know my record of successfully repairing things is shoddy at best, but I did the best I could.

We left the food truck—and the lady who was still sending metaphorical daggers our way—and headed in the direction of Elfland. I felt as if I was carrying a million dollars under my arm, but in reality the Crown was probably worth more than that. Any doubt that I had in my mind that it was a replica fell away when I started noticing changes in my apartment as I repaired it. The Crown was only there for a few hours, but the charity-shop chair looked brand new, the dying plant on my windowsill perked up, and I started to feel super healthy: energized and strong. I could see how Pavaris became dependent on its power.

I RANG the doorbell at the Pavaris mansion, but there was no answer. When I tried to call him, he didn't pick up. I stood outside the giant walls of the estate and wondered what to do. There were a couple of marble statues that I could climb to get myself over the wall, but then what? A shadow moved beside me, and I remembered how his guards used some kind of camouflage voodoo. I turned toward the movement, ready to greet them, but I was wrong.

The scent of copper crimson, the one I know so well, tinted the air. A cape swished, and I saw a hint of teal in the moonlight. I groped for my wand, and promised myself I would never go anywhere without my crossbow again.

Now, usually I would want to kill a vampire every day of the week and twice on Sundays, but right then all I wanted to do was give the HighFire Crown, which was burning a hole in my infinity pocket, to Estelar, and be done with the whole Pavaris case.

Wizard, said the vampire, although he didn't say it out loud. It was more like a thought, in his voice, in my own head. I couldn't see him in the dusk light.

Give me the Crown.

"What crown?" I said, pushing the doorbell over and over, hoping the guards would come. My heart was racing.

Give me the Crown, he said again. *Jacquelyn Denna Knight.*

He was trying to mesmerize me. Trying to get into my head.

THE ELF DOESN'T DESERVE *it.*

It is too powerful for him.

Let us agree on a deal that is favorable to both of us.

HE HAD A POINT, I thought. Estelar probably didn't deserve it. All he used it for was to keep his stock from tumbling, maintain his mansion of mirrors and swan around in luxury robes. It could be put to much better use.

The elves are selfish, said the vampire, which made me think of Ferra.

They're greedy. They keep all their stagnant wealth to themselves.

The vampire was right. I shouldn't give it back to Pavaris.

If you gave it to me, I'd make sure its power was revered.

"Okay, vampire," I said. "You may be good at mesmerizing, but you're not *that* good."

I parkoured up the statue nearest to me and launched myself onto the top of the wall. I slipped and fell, but grabbed the ledge just in time not to fall all the way down into the front garden. There was rushing and barking, and then I remembered Pavaris's guard dogs. Handsome black shiny dobermans that would eat a wily wizard for dinner. They jumped up at me and growled, trying to sink their teeth into my ankles. My breath caught in my throat and I kicked at them, and in doing so I dropped my wand. Luckily, the dogs didn't notice, or they would have thought it was a game, and everyone knows that a wizard's wand is never the same if diamond-collared dobermans play fetch with it.

"Shoo!" I said. "Get lost!" but they didn't see a desperate woman hanging there, they saw payday. They saw a nice lean pork chop.

Finally, the vampire showed himself. He stood on the ledge so close to my clutching fingers that I was sure he'd step on them with his expensive Italian brogues and let me fall as fodder to the hounds.

"Give me the Crown," he said out loud. He had blood on his smart white shirt.

"It's a little tricky for me right now," I said. "Give me a hand up?"

He snarled. "You'll give me the Crown?"

"I'll think about it."

"You wizards," he hissed. "You're all the same."

"What's that supposed to mean?"

It wasn't the ideal time for a philosophical debate, but I had nowhere better to go. When I looked back at the dogs I could practically see the reflection of a juicy roast cartoon chicken in their shiny black eyes.

"You think you're superior to us," he said.

The muscles in my arms were burning, my hands were slipping. "We *are* superior to you."

"You think your magic is superior to ours."

"Well," I said, and would have shrugged if I were able. "If the shoe fits."

He hissed at me, and stomped on one of my hands. I yelled in pain, but I didn't let go. I'd rather take my chances with an Italian brogue over a couple of hungry hell hounds any day.

"Well," he said. "Soon you'll see that we have always been the superior race."

"Ha," I said. *Over my dead body.*

I don't know if he heard me think that, or if he had just had enough of the conversation, but suddenly my knuckles crunched under his shoe and I was tumbling down into the garden. The dogs lurched at me, sharp teeth flashing.

I GRABBED my father's pentacle ring on my necklace, felt the panic rise, and shouted "*Volas!*" Just as the dogs came within biting distance, snapping their jaws, their paws left the ground and they began floating up and away from me. I lay sprawled on the ground, with my hand outstretched toward them, light surging from my wrist. I didn't want to hurt them. It wasn't their fault they were trained to tear random strangers limb from limb. I kept the dogs in the air, but they were heavy, and I knew I wouldn't be able to hold them for much longer. They started falling, cycling through the evening air, whining and crying in confusion.

"*Volas!*" I said again, to prop up the first spell, and they stopped descending, but not for long. That's when I saw the two security guards, lying dead on the lawn of patchy grass. The fright I got when I saw them dispersed the spell again and I quickly used what strength I had left to shift the dogs in the direction of the giant empty swimming pool.. Once they had landed safely I jumped up on my feet, looking for the vampire. He was no longer on the top of the wall.

After catching my breath I began to look around, and was stunned by how neglected the front garden looked. The lawn, previously bright green and healthy looking, was patchy with yellow and brown, and the flowers were shriveled. It was as if the garden had succumbed to a vicious bout of black frost. The formerly perfect pathway was cracked and the roots of the kumquat trees were mulched with their own rotten fruit. I didn't even want to know what the interior of the mansion looked like, but with Pavaris not answering the door, it looked like I wouldn't have a choice.

"Thank you," the vampire whispered into my ear. He was right behind me, and I swiveled to face him. He smiled, showing his fangs. "I didn't know how to deal with those pesky dogs, and now I don't have to."

I narrowed my eyes at him, feeling the familiar heat of hatred rising inside my body. I had to kill him before he stole the Crown and... well, I didn't even want to think about how vampires would be able to use the item's magical power for evil. It couldn't happen. I wouldn't let it happen. I didn't often sling my Death Spell; it's extremely dangerous. Many wizards have lost their lives using it. I hoped I wouldn't be one of them.

"Obeis diem supremum, tempus est tibi, nunc def—!" I shouted, but he slapped his hand over my mouth before the phrase was out, and the magic didn't take. I tried to peel his fingers

away from my lips but he was much stronger than me. I, however, had more to lose, so I kneed him in the balls.

He hissed and crouched down, freeing my mouth to try again. But the Death Spell takes time to incant, a luxury I didn't have.

"*Clipeum ignis!*" I shouted, holding the pentacle ring and forcing my hand out at the vampire. My fire shield leapt up between us: it was golden, and glorious, and it singed my eyebrows a little.

"*Ventum exquiris!*" I yelled, and a gale of wind rushed over us, forcing the fire of my shield into a horizontal hurricane of destructive energy that barreled toward him, and hit him in his stomach. His cape caught fire with vivid flames, and he screamed in anguish. The dogs went nuts.

He tore off his cape and threw it on the ground. His skin was blistered, his hair burnt off, but he was still standing. The dogs were snarling and growling and bashing themselves against the walls of the drained pool.

"*Volas,*" I said, and the broiled vampire started floating in front of me. He started kicking and whimpering, as the guard dogs had done, and I moved him through the air with my magic toward the pool.

"No!" he shouted, when he realized what I was doing. "No!"

He was lighter than the dogs, and it was easy to tip him into the pool. I closed my ears when they got hold of him as I couldn't bear the sound. Still, I heard some of the tearing of flesh and crunching of bone, and it made me want to vomit into the dead plants. What was also making me feel sick was the realization that the vampires were after Pavaris's Crown.

The very recently deceased vampire was right about one thing: I couldn't give it back to Estelar. Returning it to Pavaris would be like signing his death warrant; these reckless vampires wouldn't hesitate to snap his neck for it. And he wouldn't be the only fatality. I fetched my wand from the garden bed, then stopped to catch my breath, and tried to swallow the acid bubbling up my throat. Giving Estelar his Crown back would be too dangerous for him, and if it landed up in the wrong hands it would be disastrous for the rest of the Realm.

CHAPTER 25

DEAD LEAF

The Pavaris mansion was just an echo of what it used to be.

I stepped over the corpses of the bodyguards and forced my way through the giant front double-doors. I paused in the entrance hall, taking in the devastation the absence of the Crown had wrought. The carpet I had observed last time as looking a little threadbare on my way out was now just a square of fibrous dust and dirty tassels. The sculptures had crumbled onto the floor, and the magnificent sweeping stairway was cracked, the handrail broken into pieces.

"Mr. Pavaris?" I called.

Thank the Void for those dogs keeping the vampire out of here, or he'd surely be dead. If he wasn't already.

"Estelar?"

I had a flashback to when I met the elf, when he was still rather spritely, and he had introduced himself as *Estela-a-ar*. That's when he still had some hope, I guess. Enough to buoy his spirits before the house started to fall in on itself. I climbed the wrecked steps, looking at the framed portraits of his relatives. Their eyes were shot through with red veins, their hairlines had receded. The gold of the frames was tarnished and dull. Every step I took increased my feeling of dread. My gut instinct was telling me to run, to get out of there before the destructive force ambushed me. But then I remembered I had the Crown, and that gave me the courage to keep going.

"Pavaris?" I called. There was a chirruping and squawking, and I remembered Pharos the phoenix. I followed the sound to his cage, but it was empty, and there was bird mess on the porcelain tiles in the passage. When I found the guard bird I was happy to see that he looked perfectly well, perched on the dummy butler in what I guessed was Estelar's bedroom.

"Hello, there," I said. "Where's the elf?"

Elf on the Shelf, the goblins had joked.

Pharos scratched at his neck with his beak, then showed me his wingspan. He had the most beautiful flame-colored feathers.

"Has he been feeding you?" I asked, regretting for the second time that I had not had the opportunity to buy those over-priced peanuts at the Dome. I had checked on Gizmo before going in; he was still sleeping soundly in my pocket after his vinegar-chip dinner, and I promised myself I'd buy him some greens on the way home. Or whatever it was that ferrets were supposed to eat; I'd Google it and get some.

That's when I heard Pavaris weeping. It was a strange sound, as if he were in some kind of chamber. I followed the sound to what I thought had been a guest bedroom, but now revealed itself as a huge spa room, with a giant hot-jet bath on bronze ball-in-claw feet, a double shower, a steam room with a mosaic floor, and some kind of capsule the size and shape of a jacuzzi, where the weeping was coming from. Feeling like I was intruding, I entered the room, cleared my throat loudly, and knocked on the lid of the device.

"Pavaris?" I said. "Pavaris? It's me, Jax."

He just kept crying. It was a piteous sound, and I couldn't stand it any longer. I wrenched open the lid, and there he was, golden goggles on, levitating on the surface of the black water in the flotation tank. I flicked his arm, and he startled. He flailed, accidentally took a sip of water, spat it out, then stood up and suctioned his goggles to his forehead.

"Jacquelyn!" he cried, flinging his arms wide. "You've come back to me!"

It appeared he thought we were back on the stage, and I was a prodigal wizard who had finally returned for a joyous reunion. Only when I passed him a hand towel did he remember he was naked, and quickly covered up.

"You found it!" he said. "You found my Crown!"

I was sorry to see how much he had aged since I had seen him just a few days before. Even when wet, his hair was white and his face was as lined and beaten as a dragon's wing. His teeth still looked beautiful, which cheered me up, until I noticed the tube of denture adhesive on the basin ledge.

"Oh, Estelar," I said, shaking my head. "I'm so sorry."

THE REALIZATION TOOK a while to sink in. I watched his face as it took effect, and I felt even worse. His eyes, ringed with goggle suction marks, went from hopeful, to dispirited, to enraged.

"How dare you?" he whispered to me.

"I've done everything I can," I said. At least that part was true.

"You came highly recommended!" he said. "They said you could find anything. Anyone!"

"There have been some complications," I said.

"Complications!" he shouted, and his voice broke a little. "I paid you double!"

Actually, his payment had never come through, but I wasn't going to bring that up now. Especially given the man was standing, dripping, in front of me, and I could see his scrawny white butt reflected over and over again in the millions of mirrors he had in there.

"I'm really sorry," I said again. "But I haven't given up."

Or, rather, the vampires haven't given up on getting it in their evil clutches, and I'd defend it with my life. But he didn't need to know that.

His eyes became small and intense: cobalt laser beams that burnt into me. "Your career is over," he said in a low voice. "I will tell every elf I know how you have let me down. I'll broadcast it in every magazine, and every news site and media property I own. I'll destroy your reputation."

Here I was, trying to save the elf's life, and he wanted to destroy my career. As they say, no good deed goes unpunished.

"Believe me, you've got bigger problems," I said, gesturing at the house around us.

"Cheap shot," he sneered.

"No," I said. "I know you don't want to hear this, but you need to get out of here. It's dangerous."

I couldn't bring myself to tell him about his security guards, or his dogs, but he had to know. "You're not safe here. You need to check your front garden," I said, and then, as an afterthought: "After you put some clothes on."

I didn't know what else to say, so I started to leave.

He hurried after me in his micro-towel. "You'll never work in this city again!"

Ha. If I had a hundred bucks every time I heard that, I thought, *I'd be able to hang up my wand.*

Estelar, still shouting, tried to follow me, but he slipped on his wet spa room floor and fell. I really hoped he hadn't broken his hip. I made my way down the passage, waved bye to Pharos, and almost tripped on a rug that had started curling up at the edges, like a dead leaf.

I ran down the stairs and out the door, and as I stepped out into the cool evening air there was a deafening smash behind me. I spun around and got a lungful of dust that hit me in a rolling wave. The massive crystal chandelier had smashed to the ground where I had just been standing, missing me by mere seconds. I imagined myself lying there, dead, crushed by crystal in a crumbling house.

CHAPTER 26

GRAVEYARD GATECRASHING

The explosive sound of the chandelier woke Gizmo up, and I remembered my promise to buy him something healthy to eat. I also remembered my promise to Morgan, and the Belore twins, and felt temporarily paralyzed. The HighFire Crown wasn't doing me any favors, either, virtually glowing in my pocket with the knowledge that I was suddenly a target for the entire city's vampire population.

I felt as if I had a flashing arrow sign pointing down at me, saying something like *'EAT ME'* or *'GET YOUR IMMOR-TALITY HERE'*. It was not a comfortable feeling.

We rode on the outskirts of the city as night fell. I've always preferred night-time to day; the relief of the coolness it brings after a scorching afternoon, and sometimes a thunderstorm. I've always loved the moon and the stars... at least, as far back as I can remember. On Summer nights in the inner city we'd find flat roofs to lie on and watch the sky and talk about what we wanted from life, what we'd do, who we'd become. Sometimes I wonder what happened to the other Ferals. Wondered if they were happy now, if they'd reached the dreams they had for themselves.

For a moment I felt hopeless, directionless, but then Gizmo's head popped out of my trench coat and pointed very determinedly west. I slowed down and peeled off at the next fork in the road, and Gizmo directed me through a suburb, and onto a main road, which was busy with cars on their way home from work or perhaps out for the night, seeing it was a Friday. Maybe one day I'll be one of those regular kinds of people who work 9 - 5 and socialize on weekends, but I doubt it. Once we were off the main road, which was well lit, we headed down an avenue with only minimal streetlights, and I shivered with the sudden cold in the air, and the dark.

"Where are you taking me?" I asked Gizmo. It was already almost eight o'clock and I had plenty to do without going on an impromptu sightseeing tour in the dark, but the ferret had proven to dig up things useful to me before, so I decided to follow his nose.

I instructed my helmet to turn on its night vision, and when we got to the end of the road I saw it was a dead end. Gizmo hadn't been wrong before, and I was desperate to find something, so I parked the bike and killed the engine. A small penlight I produced from an interior pocket was the first thing I tried to light my path, but the battery quickly gave out and the beam faded. I shook it and knocked it against my hand, but no dice. Sighing, I belted my coat as tightly as I could and held out my wand.

"*Illumino,*" I whispered, and the tip of the silver wand started to glow, lighting the path before me. We came to a huge wrought iron gate which was shut with a padlock the size of my head. I stepped back to read what it said.

OBSIDIAN HILL CEMETERY

Ah, well, I thought, as I melted the lock and pushed open the heavy iron door, *it won't be the first time I've gatecrashed a graveyard.*

I put Gizmo onto the floor of leaf mold and fragrant pine needles, and we entered the cemetery, slowly at first, but as the ferret caught wind of something he started to bolt, and I had to run after him, jumping over rocks and tombstones and heavy fallen branches.

"Wait!" I called to him, when it felt like we were running further and further into a darkness we wouldn't be able to escape. He kept going, though, kept pulling me through the forest until I felt I couldn't run anymore. It had to be an enchanted forest; there's no way a tract of land this large had been left alone by developers. They'd be in there with their bulldozers and architects' plans and builders, turning the final resting place of the forgotten into luxury suites and solarscrapers. No, this land wasn't up for grabs. I could feel it under my feet; it felt different. The soil, the air. Things happen in this forest, I thought. Evil things.

To underscore my point, I walked straight through a colossal spiderweb. I felt it on my bare cheeks just a moment too late, and it wrapped around my face and my body as if it had a life of its own, and lifted me into the air. I gasped and grappled, trying to tear it off my mouth, off my eyes. The silk was strong and sticky, and it threatened to suffocate me. The more I struggled, the more it wrapped around me.

"*Ignem Exquiris,*" I said, but the spell came out muffled. The spider silk was in my mouth, and growing. I realized the threads were alive, and would be down my throat, tying me in knots from the inside, if I didn't do something fast. The outside strands threatened to pierce my exposed skin, shooting through my neck and stitching my hands and cheeks.

I had to stop panicking, stop moving. Easier said than done, when a spiderweb is threatening to embroider you to death.

I breathed though my nose, which was still free, and stopped struggling. I closed my eyes and swayed in the cocoon that was trying to suffocate me.

Easy does it. Easy does it, I told myself. The only way out of here was to focus intently on a mental incantation. If you don't say a spell out loud, and you don't use your wand, it's a lot more difficult to give the momentum it needs to function. I had to go deep inside myself and find the thing I could use to make this magic work. I tried to stop hyperventilating, tried to slow my heart to a normal pace. The silk was getting tighter and thicker around my body, and the threads trying to travel down my throat were making me choke.

Trust the Void, I said. *Trust yourself. You can do this.*

I reeled my mind back to the time I was in the garden with my mother. I must have been four, or five. We were planting vegetable seeds for the summer. Some of the memories I have of my parents are hazy, nebulous. Sometimes I'm not even sure if they really happened or if I made them up on the cold nights on the street: small deceits to keep me warm. But some of the memories are so clear that it was like a film in my mind, and every detail is sharp, and scented.

Mom was showing me the correct depth of the hole we'd drop the seed into. Shallower for the smaller seeds, and deeper for the butternut squashes and orange pumpkins. She was wearing her gardening clothes: a soil-smeared apron and rubber clogs. The sunshine made her hair look like a golden halo around her face, and I remember looking up at her and thinking: this person is everything, everything, everything.

A WEEK *later the seeds had not yet germinated, and I became impatient. Couldn't she just magic them into growing? I demanded. Mom got down on her knees on the grass and said:* Sometimes it's better to let things take their natural course. Besides, the longer they take to grow, the sweeter they'll be. *And I wondered then how long I would take to grow, and if I would ever be good enough to deserve her. Because for as long as I could remember I had this feeling inside of me, this darkness. I wanted to tell her, then, in the garden, in the sunshine, where it felt safe, but I didn't know how to put it into words. Instead I sulked and stabbed the soil with my trowel.*

Mom seemed so filled with goodness. Dad was strong and kind and gentle. Would I ever be good enough for them? A part of me knew the answer was no.

FATE HAD COME ALONG and answered that question a few years later, and life had never been the same. I still missed them so much it made my chest glow with pain. But I wouldn't let Fate decide my destiny now, and I certainly wasn't going to let nature take its course, because I was pretty sure that course would be in the form of a monster-sized spider eating me for dinner. I let the shimmering pain I felt in my breastbone when I thought of that day in the garden, and how many days like that I had lost, radiate out of my body, and I channeled it through both hands, even though they were bound by my sides. I welcomed the Void energy and used every molecule of my flesh to focus the current into a white-hot edge, then I pushed it out and away.

Ignem Exquiris, I thought as clearly as I could, and lasers of fire streamed out of my hands and sliced through the spider silk shroud, cutting it open and dropping me with a muffled thud onto the forest floor soft with humus and damp soil.

CHAPTER 27
MONSTRAS

"Gizmo!" I shouted, walking in the direction I thought he had gone before I had stumbled into the spider's trap. "Gizmo!"

I turned the light on my wand back on, and kept walking. I was sure I could walk forever in this wood and still not get anywhere, as if it were some kind of treed infinity loop, but with lethal obstacles. Was it the magic of the mischievous fae? Maybe, but it didn't matter. All that mattered to me right then was to find my ferret and get out of there. I kept imagining the huge spider was after us.

I walked and called and walked and called for what felt like hours. The adrenaline was wearing off and I started shaking. It was a combination of post-shock nerves, and the chill factor of the cold fog that streamed into the wood like a smoke machine at a 90s rock concert.

I tripped over something; a small rock, or a branch, and fell onto the carpet of pine needles. My legs weren't working anymore. I needed to rest. As I sat there for a few moments catching my breath, I noticed that the tombstone nearest to me was glowing in the moonlight. A little white animal appeared on the top.

"Gizmo!"

I practically shouted his name, I was so relieved to see him. He cleaned his whiskers and nodded at me. I really needed to find a way to stop him from disappearing. Maybe get him one of those dachshund harnesses on a leash, like Morgan has for Pincher. But then I realized that restraining a magical albino ferret would be the opposite of clever, especially when his superpower seemed to be finding things I needed. I looked at the tombstone again. There was no name inscribed; the gravestone was blank.

Who gets buried here? I wondered. *In a bewitched forest with boobytraps?*

Gizmo nodded at me again.

"What?" I asked him.

He jumped down next to me and started to dig.

"You're kidding," I said. "You want me to dig up an ancient grave in a haunted forest?"

Call me crazy, but that didn't sound like a great idea. Gizmo kept digging.

An exhaustion overcame me. I didn't have the energy to shift six feet of soil, never mind deal with the consequences of doing so. Gizmo didn't seem to share my reservations, and I couldn't let the ferret do all the work, himself, so I sighed and took off my coat. I placed my glowing torch on top of the tombstone so we'd be able to see what we were doing, pushed up my sleeves, picked up a rock, and started trenching.

We dug together, only stopping to rest our arms. Even though I was bone-tired I just kept going. I didn't want to stay in the graveyard for a second longer than necessary. As it was, when we stopped to catch our breath, owls hooted, wolves howled, and shadows scurried in the distance. Fear rustled in my ears and on my skin. It was enough to keep me digging. The pine-scented fog rolled over us, and it was so thick that for a few moments we could only see each other's white silhouettes, and it was as if we were ghosts.

The work was easier than I expected. Good news, because I was exhausted. Bad news, because it meant that the grave had very recently been dug up. The earth smelled of compost and eucalyptus, and within twenty minutes I hit on something hard, and the fog cleared. It was a timber box. Not a coffin, not quite. More like a no-frills chest; something you pick up at a charity shop for a couple of hundred bucks. I scraped away the rest of the sand on the lid and then sat back with a stomach-hardening sense of foreboding.

We sat there in the moonlight, looking at the box.

"What am I going to find in there, Gizmo?" I asked, but I already knew the answer. The ferret nodded again, probably wondering why I wasn't opening it after all we had done to unearth it. There was more movement in the forest beyond. Every fiber of my being wanted to cover it up again and get out of there, but I knew that wasn't an option. I had to gather my strength and my courage and open the trunk.

It was nailed shut, and I didn't have a hammer or a jigsaw blade, so I used my wand, instead. I was going to destroy the lid with a *Rumpis* spell, but I worried that I might demolish the contents, too, so I decided on a different incantation: to reveal, instead of destroy.

"*Monstras!*" I said, and the dark dread inside me surged out of the spellstick and wrenched the nails out of the lid. "*Monstras!*" I said again, and this time the lid flew off the case and landed a few meters away. Rats squeaked and jumped out of the box and scattered into the darkness around us, joining the other scuttling shadows.

THE SMELL HIT me before I had time to look inside, and I gagged. Decay, dead flesh. The stench swam up my nostrils before I could turn away and I gagged again. I had to step aside to inhale some fresh air so that I didn't get sick. I swallowed hard and edged toward the box again. There were still three rats inside, not wanting to give up their claim on their all-you-can-eat buffet dinner.

"Shoo!" I said, chasing the stubborn city rodents with my glowing wand. "Get out!"

How did they even get in there? I wondered. And then I realized they were lured into the box on purpose, to speed up the decomposition of the body that had been stuffed into the chest. Someone had gone to a lot of trouble to hide this particular corpse.

I needed to turn the body over so that I could see its face. It was a man twice my weight, so it wasn't going to be easy. When I touched him my fingers sprang back in revulsion. His clothes and limbs were abraded by rats' teeth, and his skin had an awful wax pallor about it. I steeled myself and shoved my arms down through his armpits and lifted him up, onto his back. A churn of maggots fell onto me and I yelled and dusted them off. But I couldn't stop the vomit this time, not after seeing his face. I stepped away and sprayed the forest floor with my gastric juice. The cramp squeezed my insides like a sponge, and, hunched over, I vomited again.

"FILIUS CANIS," I swore, wiping my mouth with the back of my hand. "Gandalf never had to deal with this kind of mess."

I sat down and stared at the corpse's corroded face. Gizmo bounded toward me and cuddled into my lap.

"Good job, Gizmo," I said, stroking him. "Good job."

CHAPTER 28
JUGULAR HOOK

I had guessed correctly, but I wasn't prepared for the emotion it had made me feel. Perhaps "feel" isn't an adequate word. More like: it pounded me in the stomach and set fire to my heart.

The dead body buried in the haunted graveyard belonged to the twins' missing father, Ametrix Belore. Seeing the wizard's corpse lying there sent me tumbling back in time to That Day; to the worst day of my life. The day that turned everything upside-down.

I was seven years old. I had been playing at the neighbor's house all day—there had been a birthday party and a jumping castle, and Cheese Curls and a vanilla and strawberry cake—and I had stayed later than all the other kids, helping my friend—the birthday boy—unwrap his gifts and tidy up his room. The sun started to set, and his mother walked me back to our house, to the pedestrian gate, which I had a key for. I thanked her and she ruffled my hair.

"Anytime, kiddo. You're a gem."

She pulled the gate closed and gave me a final wave, and I walked up the simple path edged with daisies.

Something was different. Something was wrong. I knew it before I even entered the house. That was the first time I smelled that scent. The one I know so well, now. The smell that fills me with dread and dangerous thoughts.

Crimson copper.

I called for my parents and looked in the kitchen for them, in the garden, in the study, but they didn't answer. Their bedroom door was closed. I knocked on it.

"Mom?" I said. "Dad?"

Still no answer.

I stood there for a while, not sure what to do. Perhaps they were sleeping. I tried the handle, but the door was locked.

"Mom?"

Starting to get worried, I dropped my party pack on the carpet and wrapped my fingers around the doorknob. The metallic blood smell was much stronger now, and I knew for sure something was wrong. I had never melted a lock before. Mom and Dad had told me that I was only to do it in an emergency. I wasn't sure if it was an emergency, but it felt like one.

"Ignem Exquiris," I said, and the heat from my hand softened the metal of the lock just enough for me to push the door open.

No child should have to see what I saw when I opened that door. My parents lay there, lifeless, on their bed, their skin as pale as paper. There were red blooms on their pillows where their wounds had stained the cotton. I didn't understand. My mind raced and stumbled. I couldn't make sense of what I was seeing. I stepped closer, took my mother's cold hand, searched her face for some kind of answer. She had two dark holes in her neck, a thin line joining them. Dad had the same.

Inside I was panicking, but on the outside I was too shocked to cry or scream or do anything but stand there and look at their near-transparent skin.

Later I would learn snippets of information from the Ferals that I'd use as puzzle pieces to put the story together. I'd learn about city bleed farms run by vamps, about drug dealers and homeless people and prostitutes who'd be nabbed and bled for days before dying, then discarded in dumpsters, and their blood sold in straws on the Black Magic Market. The victims were always those on the fringe of society; those who would not be easily missed, so I don't know how my parents became targets.

The brazenness of the attack was also unusual: most bleed farms took place in abandoned buildings and drug dens over extended periods of time, but this crime was committed in broad daylight, in a friendly suburb, in our own house, while people were next door, singing and eating cake. Details that bother me to this day because I've never worked out why it happened to my parents.

Finally, the panic inside my body exploded to the outside, too, and I started to move. I took my mother's precious silver wand from her hand, and my dad's pentacle ring from his finger. I would need all the help I could get, I realized, my organs as heavy as lead, because from now on I was alone in the world. And it was a dangerous world.

I looked for the last time into my mom's startled Pacific blue eyes, which were staring at the ceiling, unblinking, and I closed the lids. A sob rose in my throat, but I swallowed it down. Now was the time to be strong. I closed my Dad's eyes, too, and that's when I saw the vampire standing in the corner of the room.

He had been there all along, watching me, as still as glass. His face was a mask of evil, his hair black as tar. A jagged scar ran up from his left eye, past his hairline and into his scalp. An hour passed in that split-second. An hour of us standing there, regarding each other, deciding on what to do next. An hour of me being within touching distance of my forever-sleeping parents who had loved me fiercely and without wavering, and their cold-blooded killer. A lifetime of love that was lost to me forever. Neither of us moved in that split-second, but then my body snapped into action and I bolted out of the room.

I'll never know if the vampire tried to follow me. I ran out of the house so fast I'm sure the garden gnomes' heads were spinning. I ran and ran, down the street, out of the suburb. I ran till I couldn't run anymore, and I stole onto a bus and hid under the seat until I felt I could run some more. I ended up in the city, and a few weeks later I found the Ferals (or the Ferals found me). I still have nightmares—of course I do

—bad dreams about that vampire standing there in the corner, watching me, watching me, watching me. Vivid flashbacks of my parents lying there, dead, and that evil, icy gaze on my back.

SEEING Ametrix Belore's face destroyed by hungry rats was one thing, but observing the injury to his neck was shattering. It was the same wound as my parents had. Two distinct, deep holes, joined by a line. It's the telltale mark of a jugular hook: the medical fang-shaped stent that vamps use to bleed their victims. Seeing the wound again, in the neck of a good wizard—the twins' father, Francis's husband—just smashed me to the ground. I sobbed so hard I could hardly breathe. I cried for what felt like eons, till I was completely empty of tears, till my ribcage ached and then became numb. Until I was void of everything.

I felt as if I had emptied myself totally in that cemetery. I vomited, I wept, I lay on the cold soil until it leached all the warmth from my body. I had nothing left. I had to get to Eafaris and Pepin and tell them and Francis what I had found, but I didn't know how I would be able to face them. I stood up, slowly, my limbs stiff and sore, dusted the soil from my arms and hands, and pulled on my trench coat. I went to stand over Ametrix's body, and I ripped the Dragon's Eye amulet from around his neck and pocketed it.

"Come on, Gizmo," I said, but the ferret had other plans. He had run to the next gravestone, a couple of meters away, which was also blank. Then he ran to the next, and the next. It was as if I began to levitate, then, like my spirit left my body and floated up to give me a bird's-eye view of the graveyard. We were surrounded by a ring of blank tombstones, and as the glow of my wand grew brighter, it revealed at least a dozen more freshly dug graves.

CHAPTER 29
FILIUS CANIS

When we escaped the Obsidian Hill Cemetery I felt like a different person, and not in a good way. The experience had taken everything out of me. I was a husk.

I checked my phone and saw that it was eight p.m., exactly the time we had entered the enchanted forest, so all those hours and hours in there didn't really exist—or did they? I had soil under my nails and my body felt broken from the fighting and the digging and the reliving of memories that had haunted me for as long as I could remember. I felt for Ametrix's amulet in my pocket. It was still there. It was like the Obsidian was contained in some kind of pocket of sub-reality. A small parallel realm where you could get away with spiders the size of cars and hiding murdered wizards. It would take a lot of magical energy to host that kind of thing, and that knowledge just added to my sense of foreboding.

If the vampires had that kind of energy to spare, what was going on? Where were they getting it from? They were clearly gaining a great deal of strength, quickly, and that terrified me. I needed to tell the Council before it was too late. But it was a Friday night, and I had no way of contacting them until Monday, and Monday seemed a very long time away.

I climbed onto my bike, slowly, gingerly, and set off to meet Morgan. She had sent me a message with a location pin earlier, saying: *I am buying you all the drinks tonight. ALL THE DRINKS. Get your ass here PRONTO.*

I recognized the bar. We had met there before. It was a kind of cutting edge place with blue neon lights everywhere and plenty of dark corners. Abstract art on the walls that made you feel drunk before you ordered your first extortionately priced cocktail, of which they had hundreds to choose from. It was an offer I couldn't refuse, especially after the evening I had just experienced. I rushed home to shower, change, and greet Ghost—who seemed happy to see me—then I Ubered to the bar.

WHEN I GOT there I had the feeling someone was following me. I felt for my wand, was happy to find it clipped securely onto my utility belt, and hurried inside. Morgan was tucked into a booth and deep in conversation with a guy that looked like he belonged in an Old Spice ad. I didn't want to interrupt them, but when she saw me she told him to get lost, but not before winking at him and passing him her card.

She stood up and pressed me deep into her embrace. The woman knows how to hug.

"No cinnamon whisky here, I'm afraid," she said. "It's a muggle bar."

When Morgan has a bit to drink she calls Untouched people muggles and it always makes me laugh. But not tonight. I was still thinking about Obsidian Hill.

"Two more beers," I said to the waiter, looking at Morgan's half-empty pint glass.

"And tequila!" said Morgan. "Bring a bottle!"

The waiter perked up.

"Don't you dare," I said. "Two shots, with lime and sugar. *Not* a bottle."

We sat down and looked at each other across the table. I felt like I had aged a hundred years since we had last seen each other at the city morgue, two nights before.

"You've been avoiding me," said Morgan.

"I haven't," I said. "I promise."

"Don't you lie to me, Jacquelyn Denna Knight."

"I wouldn't," I said. "You know that."

She nodded slowly. "I do know that."

The waiter brought our pints, and laid the small glasses of tequila in the middle of the table. I thanked him. I didn't even want to know what those tiny glasses of spirit of questionable quality cost. We chinked our glasses together, shooting the tequila, sucking the lime, and chasing it with our dark stouts.

"I know I've been... difficult to get hold of," I said.

Morgan laughed. "That's putting it mildly."

"I'm sorry. The past forty-eight hours have been insane."

"Tell me everything," said Morgan.

I sighed. "That would take all night." Morgan gestured for me to go on. I rinsed my empty tot glass and filled it up with water for Gizmo. I put the ferret on the table and he gulped it down and asked for more.

Morgan stared at us. "I thought you didn't *do* pets?"

"Gizmo is not a *pet*," I said. "He's a magical albino ferret."

"Well," she laughed. "That explains everything."

I STARTED from the beginning and told Morgan (almost) everything, from the foiled attempt to kill the vicious vampire at the Jupiter Drawing Room to the case of the HighFire Crown to the attempted assassination of Or'Capone. I told her about the stalker-slash-superhero who had saved my life and the goblin gang who had almost ended it. I didn't tell her about finding Ametrix Belore's dead body in the parallel pocket realm of the Obsidian Hill Cemetary. It was still too fresh in my mind, and I didn't want to risk another flashback. Plus, we were eating cheeseburgers, and it was hardly dinner conversation.

When I told her about being attacked at the Pavaris mansion she sat back and just watched me talk, her mouth hanging open. We were on our third round by that time, and I hoped I wasn't slurring. Morgan didn't seem to mind. She asked me lots of questions and I answered what I could. Gizmo fell asleep on the table so I bundled him back into my pocket. It felt so good to just get everything out, and I thanked my lucky stars for Morgan. She acts like a hard-ass but really she's the best friend anyone could ask for. It was so lovely and comforting sitting there with my best friend, eating and drinking and chatting. But I couldn't help feeling guilty.

"And I know," I said to her, "that all this doesn't excuse the fact that I haven't found anything on Liz Durison's killer."

"Uh," Morgan said. "It kinda does."

"No," I shook my head. "I made a commitment to you and your squad and I'm definitely on the case. Er … *I will be* on the case," I said. The ghost of rosé-swilling Durison wouldn't let me off the hook if I tried. Imagine the look she'd give me now, three pints in. Good ol' Liz. In a way I was starting to feel like we were friends. I caught sight of that neon-backed mirror behind Morgan, and my reflection sparkled back at me.

Yep, it was definitely time to cut myself off. One more drink and I'd be dancing on tables, and no one wanted to see that. Ferra always says I have the rhythm of a chihuahua wearing ice-skates. I think it's an unfair comment (for the chihuahua). It was true that I couldn't sing, but my dancing was far worse. When the Void was handing out rhythm, I was last in line. I was so far back in the line that you'd need a curved telescope to see me, waiting patiently with a look of foolish hope on my face.

"I need to go." I started to stand up, but Morgan caught my wrist and pulled me down again.

"No way," she said. "No way you're going anywhere."

"I need to get home."

To my haunted house, my dying pot plant, my empty bed.

"One more drink," she said to the waiter, and he bustled to the bar.

THE ONE DRINK turned into more, as they do, and when Morgan and I left the bar we were three sheets to the wind. The breeze had picked up, turning the night cold, and Morgan and I quickly hugged on the sidewalk and jumped into our cabs, promising to chat the next day to compare hangovers.

I climbed into a sleek black sedan and said *hi* to the driver, hoping the booze fumes wouldn't make him as drunk as I felt. When he didn't answer, I tried to get a look at his face, but the screen between us distorted the view. He pulled out of the parking space and joined the main road. Then I realized I hadn't checked the license plate of the car. I had just assumed it was my Uber and jumped in.

"Stop the car," I said, feeling suddenly stone cold sober. He kept driving.

"Stop the bloody car!" I shouted, and tried to open the door, but it was locked. I fumbled for my wand, which is never a good idea after drinking. I know from unfortunate personal experience that slurred spells can lead to a whole heap of trouble.

He pushed a button on his dash and the screen slid down, silently.

"Jacquelyn," he said. It was the Voice. The stalker.

"Filius Canis," I whispered.

Darick shrugged. "I've been called worse."

"You understand Latin."

"Doesn't any self-respecting stalker understand Latin?" he said.

"What are you doing here?"

He looked at me via his rearview mirror and ran a hand through his hair. "Isn't it obvious? I'm taking you home."

"I don't need you to take me home. I called a cab."

"I know."

There he goes, being infuriating again.

"I didn't like the idea of you getting into a car with a stranger," Darick said. "Especially in your condition."

"You *are* a stranger. Just because you worked out where I live doesn't make you any less of a stranger." My inner belligerent drunk was clearly making an appearance. "And exactly what *condition* are you referring to?"

"You're vulnerable at the moment," he said, turning a corner and slowing down for a pedestrian to cross the road. I felt like telling him to get lost, but then a lump appeared in my throat and I couldn't talk past it. I kept quiet for the rest of the trip; there was no way I was going to cry in front of him.

I woke up when the car stopped and the engine cut. Darick opened my door and picked me up. I was going to protest, but the feeling of being weightless in his rock-solid arms, safe and protected, was too good to argue with. I put my arms around his neck and rested my head on his chest. We flew up to the top floor in the Swift, where he nudged open my front door and laid me on my bed. Even though I was awake, he removed my coat and pulled off my boots, and pulled the blanket up to my chin. Gizmo scampered to his favorite spot on the couch, and Ghost threw the book on the floor with more force than usual. I had obviously missed my curfew.

I lay there, watching Darick as he pottered around, pouring me a glass of water for my bedside table, making sure the ferret was settled. I could deny it all I wanted when I was sober, but the truth was that being around him made me feel safer than I'd felt in forever. The truth was that when he was taking my coat off, I wished he'd taken everything else off, too.

"You're making this a habit," I said.

"Ha." He sat down in his chair, in my bedroom.

"You're not going to watch me sleep again, are you?" I asked.

"No," he said, glancing at his watch. "I need to be somewhere."

But he didn't move; he was waiting for me to fall asleep. I wished he'd climb into bed with me, wished he would wrap his arms around me and we could fall asleep like that. I realized I needed that, needed him. But when I opened my eyes again, he was gone.

CHAPTER 30

THE MORNINGLARK HARP

I woke up with a grim sense of purpose. I had to shake my rather brutal hangover, and go and tell the Belore kids about their father. They had left a dozen messages on my phone while I had been sleeping off the tequila.

I heard the twins screaming before I knocked on the door. It was unlocked, so I rushed in. I followed the horrified wailing through the messy house and found the three of them on the floor in the study. Three white masks of devastation.

"What's happened?" I asked, out of breath. "What's going on?"

Eafaris and Pepin sat there, cradling their collapsed mother's head in their arms. I dropped down to my knees and searched for Francis Belore's pulse, but I couldn't find it. The Morninglark Harp played its wistful tune.

"What happened?" I asked again. My head was thudding, my eyes dry and scratchy, but my discomfort faded when I saw Francis's limp body. I called emergency services, but I knew it was too late.

"She just collapsed," said Eafaris.

"She wouldn't stop dancing," cried Pepin.

"We tried to phone you," said Eafaris. There was no hint of blame in his voice, just desperation, but I felt wracked by guilt all the same.

"We tried to stop her, but she said the spell would only work if she kept dancing till Daddy came home."

If my head felt like splitting open, my heart felt swollen to bursting point. I couldn't stand the pain in the room, augmented by my own loss. I moved Francis's body to the couch and put a pillow under her head, then sat down with the children and cried with them.

"Dad's dead, too," said Eafaris, and Pepin looked at me sharply.

"Is that what you came to tell us?"

I took Ametrix's amulet out of my pocket and gave it to her. "I'm sorry."

She flinched, as if the Dragon's Eye amulet had burnt her, then doubled over in grief, clutching the Dragon's Eye in her tender palm. Pepin wailed so loudly then, and Eafaris hugged her and didn't let go. I threw my arms around them and sobbed, too. We wept till our eyes were pink and puffy and our throats dry, and we heard the siren of the ambulance approaching.

I phoned Ferra and asked her to come and get the kids, and to take care of them till the Council's social services branch could be notified. She agreed without hesitating, as I knew she would.

"I'll Portal there right now," she said. "I'll take care of the wee ones."

"Thank you," I sniffed.

"Oh, Jinx. This must be so hard on you."

It's harder on the Belore twins, I thought.

"Come and see me later," she said. "Your crossbow is ready for you, and it sounds like you're going to need it."

I walked back into the study and lifted the harp. "I'm taking this," I said, and the kids nodded. Then came the difficult part: leaving two kids alone who had just lost both of their parents. I was shaking, inside and out. Gizmo squeaked, which gave me an idea.

"I need your help," I said. "I need you to look after Gizmo while I investigate. It's too dangerous for him to come along."

They nodded and took him from me. The ferret snuggled into Pepin's chest and she kissed the top of his head. She stopped crying.

Eafaris put his arm over his sister's shoulder. "We'll take good care of him."

Hopefully Gizmo would be able to distract them from their heartbreak, if only a little. I ruffled his fur and said goodbye.

"Quickly pack a few of your things," I said. A couple of home comforts would be a small consolation, but a consolation nonetheless. "Pajamas. Toothbrush. Your favorite toy."

They both looked at me with blank expressions. *A toy?* I imagined them thinking. *What good is a toy, when Mom and Dad are gone forever?*

But I knew the value of things from home, even if they were just *things.*

"A trusted friend is coming to look after you," I told the twins. "She's a dwarf with red hair named Ferra. You can trust her. Don't go with anyone else."

"Don't leave us," said Pepin. "Please."

The guilt and grief pulled at me, hard, and my insides ached.

I took out the envelope of money they had given me when I first met them and tried to push it into Eafaris's hands, but he shook his head and pushed it back toward me.

· · ·

"Keep it," he said. "Keep looking for the person who did this."

"I will," I said, looking him in the eyes. "I'll find them if it's the last thing I do."

Ferra arrived and started to matronly boss everyone about, and I ruffled the kids' hair, and left.

CHAPTER 31
POPCORN CONFETTI

I had the magic harp and I knew exactly who I was going to use it on. I gunned it to Goblin City and made my way directly to the Rainbow Popcorn Barn. I roared as I kicked over the stand, and the multi-colored snacks spilled out onto the ground like confetti at a goblin bris.

It would have made a veritable feast for ferrets; if Gizmo had been with me he would have wasted no time in jumping down to help clean up the mess. I missed his warm little body in my pocket and I looked forward to when life would return to normal.

Although... who was I kidding? I'd never had a normal life. Why start now?

The goblin pedestrians milling around stopped and stared at me. I didn't care. I was going to get answers even if I had to force them out of the greasy gob's mouth.

"Salty!" I yelled, and she gasped. I was clutching the Morninglark Harp under my arm and her eyes grew wide at the sight of it. "We are going to have a frank conversation," I said. "We can do it here, in the middle of bloody Goblin City," I motioned at the bumper cars and the spinning cups and saucers, "or we can do it somewhere more private."

SaltySnap stuttered and mumbled, which stoked my anger. I strode toward her and lifted her by her stupid collar.

"You decide," I whispered. "But I'm not leaving here without answers."

Nilve SaltySnap reluctantly left her wrecked popcorn stand, and I followed her past the rollercoaster and the log ride. We walked past the mini-train station and into the House of Horrors. It was supposed to be a scary tram-ride—not dissimilar to the real one in the Orc SubRealm—but with cheesy models of wart-nosed witches and dusty zombies, and cheap colored lights and sound effects that were probably recorded in the 70s. We bypassed the groaning model of Frankenstein's monster and found a small room at the back, behind a black curtain. It had a tumbledown table, and two chairs. The tram wheeled by, out of sight, every minute, and I heard the same chorus each time: wicked witch laughing; zombie marching; Frankenstein groaning.

"What do you want with me, Wizard?" Nilve asked.

"You know what I want," I said, pacing the tiny room like a madwoman. "I want the bloody truth!"

The goblin pulled her soggy macaroni lips in a grimace, as if the very idea of truth was distasteful to her.

The tram shuddered; the goblins screamed. The witch, the zombie, the monster.

"You're going to tell me everything you know about Ametrix Belore's murder, or you'll find yourself in a very similar position to him."

Salty froze. "Ametrix is dead?"

"Don't act as if you didn't know, you treacherous little gimp!" I kicked the wall. It hurt.

"I didn't know," she said, shaking her head. "I didn't know."

"And how am I to believe anything that comes out of that slimy mouth of yours?"

"I knew he was missing. It was on the news. I don't know who took him."

I got really close to her, close enough to smell her pond-scum breath. "Tell me, Salty, are we playing our game?"

"Wh-what game?"

"The cute thing we do when you lie out of your needle-teeth and then I know the opposite is the answer?"

"No," she said. "No game. I don't know who killed the Wizard Belore. I swear."

"Do I need to use this harp on you?"

Her eyes flashed at me. "No," she shook her head. "No."

I was bluffing, of course. I wouldn't know the first thing about using the harp to force the truth from someone. I knew it was possible, I just didn't know how to do it. According to legend there were over a thousand different tunes, each with a thousand different magical outcomes. With my musical ability I thought it was best not to try my luck. The last thing I needed was a supernatural tidal wave crashing through Jo'burg city just because I couldn't hold a note.

"Don't play the harp," pleaded Salty.

"Then for *faex* sake, tell me what it is that you are so desperate to hide. I can see it! It's written all over your sludgy face."

She hesitated again.

"I'm not messing around, Slimer. This is your last chance." I held up the harp and pretended I was about to strum it. The strange thing was that even though I had no inclination to play the thing, my fingers had other ideas. They moved toward the strings of their own accord.

"Don't!" she said, clapping her hands over her ears. "Please, don't. I'll tell you what I know. But—"

I yanked my hand away. "But?"

"But it's not about Belore. I didn't know about the missing wizard. I don't know who killed him."

I lost my temper and pushed over the table. My fingers itched to play the harp. The tram shuttled past, we both waited for the screams.

I spoke through clenched jaws. "Tell me something you *do* know."

Her voice was soft. "The Crown."

I feigned indifference. "What crown?"

"The HighFire Crown. The one in your pocket."

How did she know it was there?

"What about it?"

The witch laughed, the zombie marched. Nilve gestured at the chair near to me.

"I think you'd better sit down."

I wanted to be on the move and getting things done. I didn't want to sit in a claustrophobic room with a smelly popcorn goblin. But I needed to know what she had to say, so I clenched my teeth and sat down.

"I know this will be difficult for you to believe," Salty said.

That made me think of a generous pinch of salt, and again how snails react when you sprinkled it on their skin.

"Pavaris paid Qwynkle to steal the Crown."

"What?" My head practically spun on my shoulders. "You're lying."

"I'm not!"

"That doesn't make any sense."

"It does," said Salty.

"Rubbish. He'd never! That Crown is everything to him."

"Pavaris was in debt. Even with the Crown, his consortium was crumbling. Three of his newspapers went out of business last year, remember?"

I remembered.

"His stock price has been falling—"

"But that still doesn't explain why he'd pay a goblin gang to steal the Crown." As the words left my mouth, I realized SaltySnap was telling the truth. Estelar had claimed insurance on that break-in, and who knows how much the High-Fire Crown had been insured for. It would be enough for him to do some serious damage control; perhaps plug some holes in his leaking empire. It was also the only possible answer to a question that had been bugging me from the beginning. How had the thief managed to get past the elf security enchantment? Simple. Estelar had just not set it on the night he had instructed Qwynkle to sneak in. He had set the whole thing up.

I recalled how bad I had felt for him, watching him sink deeper and deeper into despair, his house into ruin. In the end it had all been his doing.

"He planned to have the Crown stolen, claim the insurance, then have me find it again and return it to him."

"I assume so, Wizard."

"Why didn't you tell me, before? I was almost killed for it, you know." It stung: the knowledge that I had been used as a pawn in the elf's game, and I hadn't had a cooking clue.

"Don't you see?" she asked. "Don't you see why I lied, and why the gang at the Dome were so intent on stopping you from taking it? We couldn't let you find the Crown, because you'd give it back to the elf."

"You didn't want me to give it back to Estelar."

"Once the news was out that the Crown was in circulation, everyone wanted to get their hands on it."

I remembered the teal-caped vampire and the dobermans in the drained swimming pool, and I shuddered.

"Including a clan of particularly bloodthirsty vampires," I said. "And that would be a disaster."

Nilve nodded. "Now you see. We had to protect the Realm."

THE VAMPIRES WERE PLANNING something bold, I could feel it in the pit of my roiling stomach. They were doing everything they could to gather as much power as possible. I wouldn't be surprised if they were stealing and storing a host of magical items for their own benefit, like Nazis in a war.

The tram rattled, the goblins screamed, the witch cackled. I picked up the Morninglark Harp, ready to leave.

"The gang leader," I said. "Qwynkle," I said in a low voice. "Is he still alive?"

Salty nodded, and I wish she hadn't.

"He'll come after me," I said, anxiety thrumming in my chest.

"Yes," she said. "But not yet."

"Not yet?"

"He was badly hurt in the accident at the Dome. He's in the hospital. He lost a leg."

I almost felt sorry for him. Then I remembered how he had tried to kill me and the sympathy disappeared. I started making my way out of the House of Horrors, harp under my arm.

"Wizard," SaltySnap said, and I turned around. "I know what Qwynkle is like. He will come after you. Before the hospital even thinks of discharging him he'll be in a dark corner somewhere, waiting to pounce."

"You're trying to scare me," I said. (It was working).

She shook her head. "No."

"Well," I said, thinking of the vampires that were after me. "He can get in line."

I felt my fear and my magic building. The vampires were coming for me, a vengeful goblin was coming for me, and I was going to be ready.

CHAPTER 32

HAPPY WIFE, HAPPY LIFE

W hen I arrived at *The Copper Cog and Ale*, the downcast Belore twins were playing in the garden with Gizmo and Ferra's kids.

"We've talked it over," announced Ferra, throwing a tea towel over her shoulder. "I'm adopting them. Eafy and Pip."

"What?" I said. "You've only know them for, what? Twenty minutes? Plus, you've got twelve kids of your own!"

She shrugged. "Och. Twelve, fourteen... you get to a point where you just stop counting."

I stood there, blinking.

"Besides," she said. "It's handy to have some tall kids around to reach the higher shelves in the pantry."

Despite everything, I laughed. There were difficult times ahead, dark times. A double funeral, and counseling for the kids. Denial, anger, acceptance. Not to mention a clan of powerful vampires poised to kill me for the HighFire Crown.

"Come on, Wizard," she said, and punched me on the arm. "Let's go get your crossbow."

I followed Ferra inside the pub and greeted her husband, Fighour. Fig Fernak was usually so busy in his brewery at the back of the property that no-one ever saw him. Customers used to joke with Ferra, asking if her husband was a 'fig'-ment of her imagination. Of course, the multitude of children they had was proof of his existence, as was the excellent beer that flowed every night in the steampunk pub for magical creatures. Fig was hammering away at some contraption and greeted me back with a grunt. Despite being height-challenged, he's as strong as an ox, and his skin is tattooed with Celtic ink and the names of his children.

"How does Fig feel about the adoption?" I asked.

"He'll not mind at all."

"You haven't discussed it?"

"No need," she said. "Happy wife, happy life. Besides, he's got a new bee in his bonnet," said Ferra, motioning at the toiling dwarf. "He thought of a new invention in the middle of the night and has spent all morning on it."

"What is it?"

She shrugged. "Your guess is as good as mine."

The Fernaks were a tribe of inventors and engineers. I loved the family for very many reasons, one being that they kept me in supply of the most advanced tech magical weapons which had saved my bacon time and time again. I wasn't often invited into Ferra's workshop—a magical weapon manufacturing room is a dangerous place to be—but she tugged my hand and I went gratefully along. We moved behind the bar and through the hobbit-sized kitchen, where a handful of her children were baking spice cookies.

"To cheer up the twins," said Eileen, a mousy child with a serious expression.

Ferra tossed a cookie to me, and I caught it, bumping my head on the low ceiling. It was fragrant and sugary and still warm from the oven.

"Too much nutmeg!" she said after taking a bite, and the kids nodded. "Not enough salted butter." The dwarf children nodded again. "But apart from that, they're absolutely delicious. Well done, skunks!"

AT THE OPPOSITE end of the kitchen there was an arched door which led to Ferra's office. I was reminded of Don Vito's man-cave, and the maudlin cook who was stirring the pot of singing clam sauce. Something was still worrying me about that case. In my mind, I had washed my hands of it, but still, there was a niggle I couldn't quite put my finger on.

· · ·

INSIDE THE OFFICE there was a heavy brass security door. A steampunk version of what you might find at a bank vault. It had a combination lock and a turning wheel, like a ship's helm. Ferra wiped her hands on the towel hanging on her shoulder, and while the dwarf punched in the twelve-digit code, I looked at the neat framed embroidery swatch hanging on the opposite wall. It was an Arthur C. Clarke quote. Stitched in copper wire, it said: "Any sufficiently advanced technology is indistinguishable from magic."

"*Patentibus*," she said. The seal released with a hiss, and we went inside.

CHAPTER 33
A PAIR OF MAGICAL SOCKS

Ferra called it her workshop, but in reality it was a cutting edge high-tech lab that would get any engineer drooling. As spacious as a unicorn barn, with clean lines and white light, and touch-sensitive storage space under every available surface. It was years before I was allowed access, and in all that time I imagined the dwarf's workshop to be flagstone-walled, dimly lit, low-ceilinged, with a fire in the corner for smelting the ore she was so fond of using. The steampunk theme was great for the pub, but for her lab, Ferra preferred a more scientific approach.

"I've made a few modifications to your crossbow," she said with a glint in her eye.

I thought of the day the weapon decided to redecorate my apartment with its arrows. "What kind of modifications?"

Ferra touched the counter in front of us and it slid open to reveal my shiny new weapon. She scooped it up and looked through the viewfinder. "It's more intuitive now, for one."

My face must have conveyed my concern.

She put her hand on her leather-clad hip. "What's wrong?"

"My wand is intuitive," I said. "It gets me into trouble, sometimes."

"That wand is fifth generation," she said, glancing at my utility belt. "It's bound to have its... eccentricities."

Ferra looked down the flight groove of the crossbow and seemed content with what she saw, and handed it over. Despite my reservations, it felt wonderful in my hands. Super light, but at the same time solid enough to do some real damage. The cables seemed to be zinging with energy.

"So, the default setting is heat-seeking," said Ferra, "but I designed it so that it'll respond easily to your elemental magic."

She clicked a button on the counter and an archer's target appeared on the blank wall opposite us. The bull's-eye glowed red with warmth that radiated out in circles. "Go on," she said, winking. "Give it a go."

I adjusted my grip and held the scope up to my face, pointing at the bull's-eye. I had always been top of the class in archery at The Copperfield Institute—even won the national championship and had the cheesy arrow-through-apple trophy to prove it—but the episode with Desdemona at the Jupiter Drawing Room had given me a serious case of self-doubt.

I put my finger on the trigger and took aim. Just as I was about to shoot, Ferra elbowed me and knocked the crossbow sideways as the arrow left the weapon. I scrunched up my face and waited for it to embed itself in Ferra's expensive lab equipment, but instead it swerved, righted its course, and hit the middle of the target.

"Wow," I said. "That could come in handy."

Ferra pressed the button again and the wall across from us moved, and a new target replaced the old one. "Now try some magic."

I grimaced. I didn't want to damage anything. "In here?"

Ferra's hands were back on her hips. "Where else?"

She had a point. It's not like you can go slinging spells randomly in the city. I lifted it again and aligned the arrow head with the target. I closed my eyes, breathed in deeply and thought of the Belore Twins. As I felt the grief rise I channeled it down my arms and through my hands, which were thrumming on the cool black metal. Then I opened my eyes again and said "*Fiat Fulgur,*" as I pulled the trigger. It felt like the room exploded.

IT WAS as if a lightning bolt had hit us from above and traveled through me and the weapon toward the target. It smashed into the middle of the circle and burst into flames. My arm felt scorched inside, my fingers were numb.

Breathless, lost for words, I looked over at Ferra while the wall burned.

She gave me a naughty look. "Well. That worked a little better than I had expected."

Smiling, she grabbed a cherry-red fire extinguisher from the wall, pulled the pin out with her teeth, and blasted the fire with a cloud of sodium bicarbonate. Then she thunked the canister down on the counter beside us, the wall shifted, and a new target appeared. "Try a different spell."

I flexed my fingers a couple times to try to get the feeling back. "I'm not sure my hand will survive another one."

"You need to get used to its power," she said. "And I can't let you take it without testing it first."

I took another breath, brought the crossbow up, and rested the stock against my shoulder. I lined it up, blinking at the scope, cycling through the different spells in my head. My finger pushed against the trigger.

"*Glaciem Exquiris!*"

This time a jet of ice flew out of the crossbow, sheared the air, and speared the bull's-eye with a satisfying thwack. I moved closer to the target and saw that the missile was a stake made out of ice.

"You're a genius, Ferra Fernak," I said.

She waved her hand, dismissing the compliment. "That's not all, by the way. Fire and ice, I mean. You can think of new spells on the fly and they'll probably work, from trick arrows to poison bolts. It's a good little weapon you've got there."

I looked at her with wide eyes. "I owe you so big time. Thank you."

"Nonsense." Ferra smiled, cheeks shining. "I enjoy it."

As if I had been thanking her for knitting me a pair of magical socks instead of making my weapon the most kick-ass crossbow in the entire history of vampire slaying. I didn't want to gush too much, though. It wasn't the first time Ferra had saved my life, and I was pretty sure it wouldn't be the last. Besides, dwarves hate gushers.

She glanced at my wand again. "Do you want me to look at that for you?"

"I don't know," I said. "What will you do?"

"I'd have to strip it, first, before I do anything else. Then I'd try—"

"Oh," I said, thinking of my mother. I wanted every hint of her that I had left. "No. Thanks."

"All right," Ferra said gently, then thumped me on the back, knocking the air out of my lungs. "All right, lass. Let me know if you ever change your mind."

I knew I wouldn't.

"In the meantime, I have one more thing for you. It's silly, really, but might come in handy in your... line of work."

My ears pricked up. I was always keen to hear about Ferra's new inventions, especially if they were going to help me ash vampires.

"It's more about prevention than cure," she said, holding up a piece of dark fabric.

At first I thought: *Oh, she did make me socks, after all.*

But then the thing changed shape, like black silk origami. Like a pack of novelty cards that are stuck together. Then it changed again, reshuffling itself into another origami shape, as if it was playing in Ferra's palm.

She laughed. "It's still new. Like a puppy. Eager to please, but can't decide what it wants to be."

"What is it?" I asked.

"Nano-tech something-or-other," she said.

"Something or other?"

"There's no name for it yet, as far as I know. Just a silly thing I was playing with in my spare time. I call it Nano, for short."

I wanted to say: *you have a thriving business, twelve children (and counting), and you have spare time?* But what struck me more was how she had invented something so completely new that it didn't have a name yet, and here she was playing it down as if she had indeed just knitted a pair of socks. That said, I still didn't know what it was. I looked more closely, and saw three buttons on it that matched my trench coat.

"In theory, it can be anything. It's made from suggestible nanites, with baked-in conjuring magic, so you can will it to be something and it will—usually—obey." She put the thing on the counter, the dark material striking against the white. "Nano. Plate," she said, and it rearranged itself into a plate, with the three buttons acting as decoration on the edge. "Nano. Cup," she said, and it sculpted itself into a cup. "Nano. Bunny," she said, and it became a polyart sculpture of a rabbit. Ferra shrugged. "Sometimes it likes to be creative. It's better at some things than others."

The rabbit melted into a puddle of water, and then built itself up again into a tall, velvet-petaled rose. "And it's a little unpredictable."

It was like nothing I'd ever seen before. "It's beautiful," I said.

"I have some different kinds, some different versions that I'm tweaking, but this one is for your trench coat," she said. "I made that coat bulletproof," Ferra nodded at the coat I was wearing that had saved my life a hundred times over, "but it still leaves certain parts of your body vulnerable. With this," she picked up the rose, "you'll be able to protect your neck and face."

I looked at the rose.

"Nano. Jax mask," said Ferra, and the rose turned into a mask the perfect size and shape for my face. "In place," she said, and the mask whipped onto my face, opening apertures for my eyes, nostrils and mouth. It was massively disconcerting to have the thing up against my face, but I guessed that in another Goblin Gang drive-by shooting I would probably overlook that feeling in the general hope of staying alive.

"Nano. Melt," the dwarf said, and the mask melted away into its black puddle on the counter. "So, you can use it as anything, really, but I made this one to be a collar on your trench coat. To protect your throat, and also so you can keep it really close—within whispering distance—if you need it."

"Nano. Collar, in place," I said, and it flew up in the air and swirled around my throat, attaching perfectly to my existing collar, except that this one covered my whole neck, right up to the base of my chin, reminding me of some of the Victorian costumes I had tried on before going undercover at the Jupiter Drawing Room. I thought it would feel restrictive, that I would battle to breathe with something *unpredictable* up against my throat like that, but really it was comforting. Bulletproof, bomb-proof, vamp-fang proof. Along with my new, improved, crossbow, it made me feel invincible.

"That's incredible," I said.

Ferra took my hand. "You're doing a good thing, Jinx," she said. "Important work. You mustn't feel alone. We're all behind you."

Sometimes I thought that Ferra glimpsed the darkness inside me, but other times, like this, I wondered if she thought I was more worthy than I really was. It didn't matter, not really. I needed all the support I could get if I wanted to find out what happened to Ametrix, and stay alive doing it.

"And when you need help," she said, "you need to ask for it."

I looked into her eyes, the ones I know so well: burnt caramel flecked with gold. The memories that Obsidian Hill cut into me still glowed in my chest. I was ready to face the vampires responsible.

"You've always been a loner, Jinxie Knight, and that's okay. But there's too much up against you in this. You shouldn't rely solely on your magic, or your pain. You can't do this on your own."

But Ferra was wrong. I've always been alone, would always be alone. And I'd kill every last vampire I could get my hands on, on my own.

It was my destiny to die alone. The darkness told me that, and I knew it was true.

CHAPTER 34

THE TRICK

I left the Copper Cog, waving to the Belore twins as I went.

"I'll be back later," I called to them, forcing a smile. "We'll go out for a milkshake. Take care of Gizmo!"

They looked at me with faces blank with despair, and I swallowed the lump in my throat. Ferra waved and put the harp —which I had given her for safekeeping—on the counter of the bar. Fig was still hard at work on his midnight-dream-inspired invention. My stomach sank, seeing the look on Eafaris and Pepin's faces. I wanted to say something to them, something to make them feel better, but when I opened my mouth I found there were no words of comfort. I couldn't help thinking, over and over again, of how I had been in a similar position to them. The Belore twins wouldn't be with the Fernaks for long. Despite Ferra's best intentions, a social worker representative, sent by the Council, would arrive soon enough to assess the situation, and take the kids away to the Copperfield Institute. I knew that just as the Copperfield scout had nabbed me that day on my way to Mr. Hot Dog, he or she would take Eafaris and Pepin, too.

When I arrived, dirty, hungry, smelling of the street, I lashed out at anyone who approached me. I truly lived up to my "Feral" classification. I was a wild cat, hissing and scratching at anyone who came near me. I was angry, and terrified, and didn't understand why I had been kidnapped off the street, but I soon came to understand that the people there wanted what was best for me, whether I knew what that was, or not. There were other orphans there, but it was mostly a dumping ground for the Touched children of closeted Touched parents who didn't know how to handle their children's burgeoning magic.

The establishment seemed brutal at first, as the wardens held a hose to my goose-pimpled body, tut-tutting about my grubbiness and bruises. Then the de-lousing shampoo that smelled like tar and stung my eyes, followed by a rough, starched uniform over my scrubbed pink skin. I was scared and confused. Who were these people, and what did they want with me? The Ferals had told me about Bad People, and how they were always on the periphery of the area we traversed. Sometimes, stranger danger broke through our boundary. Once, just before Christmas, a Bad Person took Wandile. I remember the time of year because the city was stinking hot but the shop windows had their fake snow sprayed on their depressingly limp window displays. I remember looking at some cheap plastic mistletoe and hoping that Wandi would come back with some kind of happy explanation for her sudden disappearance. *My parents came and found me!* or, *I found a hundred bucks on the floor and went to buy everyone lunch.* But that didn't happen. We were so happy to see her again when she came back, a few hours after she disappeared, but she wouldn't say where she had been, and her eyes had an empty look they had never had before.

Another Feral, Sam, wasn't so lucky. He went off with a man with a lisp who whispered something in his ear, and didn't return at all. Again, we said how fortunate Sam was, how he must have somehow found a wonderful life, but deep down we knew it wasn't true. There was evidence all over the streets we lived on that Bad People existed, and I never did get the picture of Sam's empty sleeping bag out of my head.

When the scout grabbed me off the street like that I thought it was my time to die, too, and I didn't fight it as hard as I thought I would. The truth was that I was tired of scraping out a meager existence in the city center, never knowing where my next meal was coming from, being haunted by nightmares of the scarred vampire in my parents' bedroom. A part of me said: *if it's my time to die, so be it.* Another part of me kicked and screamed and refused to take it lying down.

I knew what was in store for the Belore twins: the hard-faced Council representative, the struggle, the initiation and then, finally, the acceptance. The Institute was the best place for them, just as it had been for me, although it was difficult to believe at the time. I hated being locked in, and I chafed under the rigid rules of the school, but it was comforting having a bed to sleep in every night, and teachers to lay a comforting hand on my shoulder. From the Ferals I learnt parkour, and quick and dirty magic, perfect for picking pockets and sneaking stolen food, essential for our survival. From the Copperfield Institute I learnt the more academic side of sorcery: elementary magic, and traditional Latin incantations, and the combination has made for an interesting arsenal of spells.

Directress Copperfield was always an intimidating figure. Flawless mahogany skin and ivory-colored braids and wand. She was eighty in the shade when I attended the school but I hear she is still there, heading it up with her world-renowned titanium wand (which just happens to match her spine). You can say anything you like about the Institute, but for as long as Directress Copperfield is there, you know it is beyond reproach.

We had our regular lessons there: Theory of Magic, Prac., Hedge Chem, Potions, Occult History, not to mention our extra murals of archery (my favorite), banner athletics, and magical slipstreaming, but when the directress appeared in our classroom we knew the lesson would be an important one. Suffice to say we'd sit up straight if she walked in to give a lesson.

"You need to always consider the keel," she said one day, and she had looked me in the eye. I hadn't known what a "keel" was so I just stared right back, ears on stalks.

Everyone knew I was an ex-guttersnipe, so I got away with cheeky behavior a little more than most.

"Consider the keel," she said again, and used her wand as a piece of chalk and drew a simple sailboat in the air before us. She tapped at the bottom of the boat, and it turned upside down.

"The upside-down, the flip-side, the *is* that *isn't*."

I think we all just gawked back at her with our mouths open. We still didn't know what she was talking about. The directress waved away the air sketch and shook her head. "There will come a time in your life," she said, looking again directly at me, "when you will need to see the situation for what it really is. And that is not always the upright picture, the picture that was painted for you, but the *real* structure, the thing that floats it."

"So you're saying," said Orphan Bishop, a brown-haired boy in the front row with braces on his teeth, "to look beyond the surface."

"Yes," said Copperfield, pleased. "Very good, Bishop."

"In fact," said the directress, walking across the room, the bottom hem of her full skirt dragging along the dusty floor, "there's a rhyme I recite to remind myself not to allow my attention to be reflected off the façade of a thing. A very simple mantra, of sorts, which I will now teach to you."

The classroom was silent, waiting.

"Cold Fire," she said, and smiled at the class. "Dark Bone. Black Mist."

The class repeated after her: *Cold Fire; Dark Bone; Black Mist.*

She was pleased. "Look for the turn, the trick, the twist."

Again, the class repeated after her. *Cold Fire; Dark Bone; Black Mist. Look for the turn, the trick, the twist.*

THE MEMORY BROUGHT me to a standstill. I stood outside the *Copper Cog* as cars whizzed by in the road before me, my mind whirring with the new perspective. This is what I had been missing. No matter how many times we were made to repeat that mantra, I had forgotten it. Deep down, it was in my mind, in my memory, but not center-stage enough to inform my investigations. But now I realized it was what I had been missing. I had missed it in the Pavaris case, and I had a strong sense of foreboding that I had missed it in the Or'Capone case, too. Something had bothered me about The Godfather case from the beginning. It was like a spark went off in my head, and I knew I had to get to the Khargol house in Illovo as fast as my bike could get me there.

WHEN I ARRIVED, the restaurant was closed, and all the lights in the house above were off. I noticed they had upgraded their security since the fateful drive-by. There wasn't a single window not covered with burglar bars. I rang the doorbell, but no one answered. I remembered the Pavaris mansion with a shudder.

"Hello?" I called, hoping they weren't asleep. An orc is grumpy on a good day. Waking an orc—disturbing his beauty rest—is practically unforgivable. People may have been beheaded for less.

"Hello?" I called again, stabbing the button with my index finger. Still nothing, not even the faraway sound of the bell ringing inside. I stood out there in the cold, dark, night, breathing out condensation like smoke, wondering if I was crazy. The Khargols were probably sound asleep, and there I was, ready to break down their door because I had a bad feeling about a lesson I got when I was sub-twelve years old.

I turned the handle, fully expecting it to be locked, but it turned smoothly and the door opened. I stumbled inside, trying to find the light switches on the walls.

"Hello?" I called. Where were the ubiquitous security guards? The last thing I needed was to be pumped full of lead for breaking and entering on a whim.

But there were no guards with guns, and no switches on the walls. My penlight was still out of juice, so I unclipped my wand from my belt and held it out before me.

"*Illuminem*," I said, and the tip of my wand glowed with a warm white light. The entrance lounge looked undisturbed. I kept walking, feeling apprehensive and ridiculous at the same time. Someone would turn on the lights, I thought, and I'd be stuck there, frozen under the glare of the lightbulb, like an awkward game of Musical Statues, and have to explain that I was breaking into the Orc Mafia Boss's three-story apartment just because I had a bad feeling I couldn't shake.

I crept through the entrance hall and into a lounge, reaching the kitchen. When I saw ingredients still on the counter—wilted basil, turning gray; a congealing jar of passata, an onion half-chopped—I knew something was wrong. Singed meatballs lay in burned-black sauce in a tray in the oven. I used the glowing wand to light my way up the narrow steps to the Khargol bedroom, dreading what I might find. The smell of raw onion and smoke followed me. I walked slowly, trying to keep calm, even though I felt my heart pounding in my chest. The panic made me feel uncomfortably hot, and breathless. I paused halfway up, and reminded myself to breathe. I had my wand. I had my crossbow on my back. I would be fine. Still, my anxiety spiked, my fear rustled in my ears.

"Sugar?" I called when I got to the top of the stairs. "Vito?"

I made my way to where I thought the bedroom was, on the second floor. As I stepped over the threshold, there was a shriek which almost made me hit the ceiling. My internal organs almost jumped out of my chest. When I looked down, a dark shape bolted out from under me. A black cat. Or rather: a black cat with a sore tail.

I was in the Khargols' bedroom. I tried to flick on the lights but they were dead. There was a shape in the bed. A motion-less body. I moved closer.

"Don Vito?" I said, wondering again what on earth I was doing there.

I expected him to stir, or snore, or sit up and shoot me with the pistol he's known for storing underneath his pillow, but he did none of that. Instead, he lay on his back, his face pointed to the ceiling, his arm outstretched to where Shagar would usually be sleeping. Closer I crept, closer, until I could see his face. It looked pale and waxen, and reminded me of the models at the magical items display at the Dome: the mermaid out of water; the ancient hermit-like wizard. I reached out my hand and touched his arm, and when my skin touched his, I knew he was dead.

CHAPTER 35
DARK BONE

I extinguished my wand's light and took my phone out of my pocket. I scrolled to Darick's number, and he picked up after the second ring.

"Well, hello," he said in that golden-syrup voice of his. "How is my favorite Wizard?"

I didn't have time to think about the fluttering in my stomach, and how much I had missed him.

"The Godfather's dead," I whispered into the phone. I felt like I was in a trance.

"What?"

"Don Vito Khargol," I said, slightly louder. "He's dead."

"Are you sure?" he asked.

"His heart isn't beating."

He covered the mouthpiece while he swore. "Where are you?"

"His house. Illovo."

"I'm close," he said. "Don't move. I'll be there in five minutes."

I STEPPED CLOSER to the bed and inspected Vito's face: his blue-cheese veins and swollen eyelids. A wave of nausea hit me, so I undid the top few buttons of my coat and pulled it open so that I could breathe freely, and directed my Nano to my top pocket. I lit my wand again and looked at Don Vito's lips. They looked slightly purple. Not too unusual on a dead orc, I'll grant you, but there was something about them that bothered me. I looked closer; they were definitely purple. I steeled myself, then pushed my fingers into his mouth, which felt as disgusting on my bare skin as it sounds. It made an unattractive squelching sound as I levered open his lips and inspected his gums, which were the same shade. Then I parted his eyelids, and my suspicion was confirmed. The whites of his eyes were shot through with purple capillaries. Indigo Violent.

It's one of the most potent poisons available on the black magic market, and the only reason it's relatively easy to score nowadays is because Vito had been underhanded. The one-nippled sinhead orc at the SubRealm had told me that the Don had been trading in illegal goods, which included, amongst other Council-banned substances: VV, Magus, and Indigo Violent. The Godfather had been poisoned by his own ambition. But, worse than that, he had been betrayed by the woman he had trusted most. I knew as I looked at Vito lying there that I wouldn't be breaking the news to his wife about his murder because she knew about it already. Sugar Shagar had been the one to poison her husband. Just one drop on the lips would be more than enough to send Vito off to sleep with the fishes.

Dark Bone.

The treachery of it stabbed me in the chest. All that acting, that pretending to be the worried wife, when she had been planning his murder all along. I heard a shuffling noise behind me and turned, ready to greet Darick, but in his place stood a slimy goblin with a peg-leg.

"Qwynkle," I said, involuntarily taking a step back, and gripping my wand tighter. "What the hex are you doing here?"

My instinct told me to take him out right there and then. Goblins in a dark house are menacing enough, and grudge-bearing goblins are particularly dangerous. But he was unarmed, as far as I could tell, and I needed information.

He frowned at me. "Isn't it obvious, Wizard? I thought you would have worked it all out by now."

"Shagar Khargol paid you and your goblin gang to stage that drive-by."

"Yes."

"That's why you were paid before the shooting. Because it was staged. It didn't matter if you hit your target or not. It was all for show, driving by like that on a busy road, smashing the glass front to pieces. It was a scene out of a 50s mob film."

"Yes," said Qwynkle. "Although I did try. I gave it my best shot."

He clutched his potbelly and grinned, showing off his brown needle teeth. Goblins have an unhealthy appreciation of puns.

"Shagar wanted it to look like it was a goblin hit," I said. "So that when she killed him in his sleep everyone would think the goblins were responsible."

He nodded.

"Why? When word gets out that Vito is dead there will be civil war."

Qwynkle spat out a laugh. "Do you think she cares about that? Orcs only care about themselves."

"Right," I said. "And, let me guess: Goblins are pillars of community spirit. Especially when they drive by Italian restaurants with AK47s."

"Sugar doesn't care because she's so blinded by what she wants... and there is only one thing that orc cares about."

At first I couldn't figure out what he meant, but then flash memories sparked in my mind. The way she looked at

Gnarg, the way she spoke to him. Then I remembered the joke about Gnarg sleeping in the Khargols' bed with them.

"She's run away with Vito's personal body guard," I said.

Qwynkle crinkled his eyes. "They say you're a clever wizard," he said. "But, honestly, I think you're a little on the slow side."

I thought of Shagar's hand on her swollen belly and wondered if Gnarg was the father of her baby. Not that any of it mattered. The damage had been done.

I pointed my wand at Qwynkle, and he put his hands up. "Get away from me," I said. "I've had enough trouble tonight."

"On no," he said. "I'm not going anywhere. You're the whole reason I'm here." He whipped off his peg-leg and thrust it in my direction, and then the room was lit up by an explosion.

CHAPTER 36
SURRENDER

The first bullet hit me in the chest, and I reeled backwards, falling to the floor. It happened so quickly I hardly had time to react. I fell down, dropping my wand, and its light went out like a torch with a smashed bulb. The combination of the darkness and the pain overwhelmed me suddenly and as the barely visible silhouette of Qwynkle hopped toward me I thought I was going to die. My chest was on fire. I cursed myself for unbuttoning the top of my coat, and I cursed the goblin for being such a treacherous bastard. He had his modified peg-leg gun pointed straight at my face and I knew he wouldn't hesitate to kill me right there and then. His other hand shot out and offered me a greasy palm. For a second I thought he was offering to help me stand up—which would, admittedly, be a strange thing to do after shooting someone, but I wasn't thinking straight—then I realized what he wanted.

"The HighFire Crown," he snarled. "Give it to me, and I'll let you live."

"Even if I believed you," I growled back, battling to speak through the pain. "It still wouldn't happen."

I tried to reach surreptitiously for the crossbow on my back, but the fresh gunshot wound didn't allow my arm that action. My wand was somewhere on the floor, lost in the dark.

"Give it to me!" he shouted, and lunged for my neck. He wanted to strangle me, but a second before his fingers reached me I thought of my Nano, which was within whispering distance in my top pocket.

"Nano. Collar, in place," I said, and the thing flew around my neck just in time. His approaching needle teeth gave me an even better idea. "Spiked collar!" I said, visualizing the sharp spines of a sea urchin. Qwynkle's fingers found my Nano just as it shot out its thorns and he screamed in pain as they skewered his miry hands. As he hollered, droplets of goblin saliva showered my face, and I thought I probably would have preferred it if the bullet had killed me outright, because being on the receiving end of that might just have been a fate worse than death. Taking advantage of his distraction, I kicked him away from me and jumped up, and the pain of the gunshot sheared through me. Without his artificial leg, Qwynkle lost his balance and fell down, but he didn't let go of his weapon. He fired again—another orange gunpowder explosion—and the bullet ricocheted off something in the room and rushed through the air right next to my cheek. I tried to reach for my crossbow, but my right arm was still not taking calls.

"Wand!" I said, and my mother's silver spellstick flew into my hand.

QWYNKLE AIMED at me and shot again. This time I dodged it. Yet another blast, and a bullet flew at me in the dark. The only hint I had regarding its direction was the bright cadmium explosion that erupted from the end of the weapon. I pulled the top of my trench coat closed. "Nano! Mask, in place!" I shouted, and the Nano wrapped itself around my face. Yet another blast, and a bullet flew at me in the dark. The only hint I had regarding its direction was the bright cadmium explosion that erupted from the end of the weapon. The next bullet hit me under my left eye. The mask had stopped the projectile from entering my skull, but the force of it was like a heavyweight punch. I heard and felt my cheekbone crack, and my head snapped backwards, knocking me to the ground again. I couldn't see well before with the lights off, but now I had stars crowding my vision and I couldn't see anything at all.

I lay on the bedroom carpet of the Khargol bedroom, bleeding, blinded, a white hot glow in my chest, my eye socket fizzing with pain. I felt like I didn't have anything left to fight with; my energy drained away along with my blood. I didn't want to die like that, but I started thinking that perhaps I wouldn't have a choice. Qwynkle moved in what sounded like a limping crawl toward me. I tried to lift my wand to defend myself but neither of my arms were working anymore. Perhaps my body had died and my brain hadn't yet got the memo. It was just a matter of time before my mind shut down, if Qwynkle didn't speed up the process with another bullet. Either way, I realized I was on my way to join Don Vito in the Underworld, dispatched by a greedy goblin to boot, and the thought of that made me angry. Angry enough to try one last spell, even though I knew it wouldn't save my life.

"*Fiat Fulgur,*" I said. It came out in a feeble whisper. My numb hands sparked. I tried to gather what little strength I had left. I used the agony that was radiating through my dying body. With a gargantuan effort, I lifted my wand an inch off the floor. "*Fiat Fulgar!*" I said again. It was barely a whisper, but the pain coursing through my body magnified the spell in a way I'd never experienced before and without much energy from me the lightning crashed out of my wand and rushed directly into Qwynkle's peg-leg pistol, detonating it in his bleeding hands. The blast knocked him up off the floor and backwards. He cracked his head against the wall, then slid down onto the floor, unconscious.

I SLUMPED BACK into my pool of blood.

"Nano. Tourniquet," I said, and it detached itself from my face and wrapped itself tightly against the hole in my chest. It worked well, but I thought it was too late to make any real difference: I could feel my blood pressure was dangerously low, and dropping. The thought of how funny-not-funny it was that I had survived so many dangerous vampire attacks but in the end succumbed to the treachery of a slimeball with dirty daggers for teeth and an unhealthy appreciation of puns.

Then I remembered standing on the pavement with Shagar, after being chased down by Gnarg.

Can you imagine, she had said, *being killed by a goblin with such a stupid name?*

I may have laughed out loud, just a little. It hurt. And then my smile disappeared in the fog of pain and I could feel the surrounding darkness sucking me in, slowly at first, then faster and faster, until all I could do was surrender.

CHAPTER 37
HALLOWEEN HEAVEN

The lights in the Underworld were dazzling; much brighter than I had expected. My body was still wracked with pain, which was disappointing. It seemed that the Afterlife was not all it was cracked up to be. I had expected an intense blue sky, mesmerizing music like that played by the Morninglark Harp, and the occasional goblin ankle-biter dressed like an angel, or a skeleton, or both.

As a child I had imagined the Next World to be like a kind of Halloween-themed Heaven, with plenty to eat and drink, and no suffering. I was wrong. The joke was on me: trick, rather than treat.

I blinked, and groaned, and my vision came slowly into focus. There was a white ceiling, and below that, a wall with blood spatter. A dead Orc Mafia Boss lay in his triple king-sized bed. A goblin's face came into view, startling me. My instinct was to jump up and fight, but my body refused to move.

Hex, I thought, *am I stuck in some kind of limbo? Some cursed Groundhog Day where I'll have to fight and lose to a psychotic goblin over and over again in perpetuity?*

But then I realized the face was not Qwynkle's, but Nilve SaltySnap's.

"What are you doing here?" I croaked.

"Shush," she said, putting something soft underneath my throbbing head. I knew by the way she was frowning that I was in bad shape. Despite the tourniquet wrapped tightly against my gunshot wound, the pool of blood had spread out all around me: a Rorschach pattern in red.

"Qwynkle cut the lights," she said. "I fixed them."

They're really bright, I wanted to say. Instead I said: "I thought I was going to die."

Salty shrugged, and her meaning was clear: *You were probably right.*

"I called emergency services," she said, but I could tell she didn't think I'd stay alive till then. I thought of those orc paramedics at the Dome, and the young man who was so kind and gentle with me. They must have rescued Qwynkle that day, too. I tried to sit up on my elbows, but the pain rushed through my ribcage the moment I moved. I wasn't going anywhere. I wasn't going anywhere fast.

"Don't move," said SaltySnap.

"Is he dead?" I asked, looking over at Qwynkle.

Nilve made her way over to him and checked for a pulse.

"Still breathing?" I asked.

"Still breathing," she said.

I swear that bloody goblin was born with nine lives. Salty muttered something under her breath. I still didn't understand what she was doing there.

"Did you come to help Qwynkle?" I asked.

SaltySnap looked down at her belt and unsheathed an emerald-glass dagger. She stepped slowly and deliberately toward Qwynkle, kneeled down to where his body was splayed on the carpet, and with a practiced motion she slit his throat, deeply and decisively.

"I don't understand what's happening," I said. Goblins were known for being as thick as thieves—probably because most of the creatures are, literally, thieves—but if Nilve was about to press a knife to either of our throats I had fully expected it to be mine.

"We have a history," said Nilve, wiping Qwynkle's dark blood off the knife with a clean white hand towel embroidered with gold thread. *V&S.*

"I don't understand," I said again.

The dagger glinted as she slid it back into its leather scabbard. "You don't need to understand."

A TALL SHADOW arrived at the door.

"What—" said Darick, shocked at the blood-stained carpet. "What happened?"

If I was indeed going to die, I thought, at least I got to hear his voice again, which seemed to stream into the room like a breeze of audible gold.

I blinked at him, ready to smile, but saw that he was bleeding, too. His clothes were ripped and he had a nasty gash on his right cheek.

"What took you so long?" I asked.

He moved his chin over his shoulder to gesture outside. "It was hell getting in here."

"Vito's bodyguards?"

"I wish," said Darick. "That would have been easier. They've all been knocked out by some kind of sleeping spell."

"What's out there?" asked Nilve, frowning again.

"Jax's favorite," he said, inspecting a deep cut on his arm. "And we're surrounded. It's like a bloody vampire convention out there. And they're not leaving till they get what they want."

I thought of the HighFire Crown glowing in my infinity pocket; realized I would've been dead without it. The red carpet beneath me reminded me that I'd still most likely die, anyway. After all, there's only so much a magical crown can do.

"Goblin," he said to Salty. "Make sure all the windows and doors are locked."

She blinked at him, bristling at taking orders from a human and scared of venturing to the rest of the house alone. But she didn't sulk for long. Her instinct for survival trumped her petulance, and she scurried out of the room.

Darick came over to me and I saw the muscle in his jaw ripple, his forehead crease. "What have they done to you?"

His anger, and his sympathy, made my eyes prickle with tears. But now was not the time to give into anguish. Darick pulled the bed covers around Don Vito's dead body and hauled the bundle onto the floor. Then he came to pick me up, and I was again in his arms. He lifted me up and laid me gently on the Khargol bed, ripping my shirt open to get a better look at the gunshot wound. The Nano tourniquet came away in his hands and he inhaled sharply.

"How bad is it?" I asked, but he didn't answer me. He lifted me into a sitting position to check the exit wound, then laid me gently down again.

"You've lost a lot of blood," he said. "I don't know what kind of bullet that is, but... it did a lot of damage. And it's still inside you."

Judging by the look on his face I could see he was surprised I was still alive. He moved his hands to my face and adjusted the angle of my chin to inspect my cheekbone, the distension of which had caused my eye to swell shut.

"Broken," he said, more to himself than anyone else.

SaltySnap arrived back in the room, breathing so hard she was practically hyperventilating.

"They're everywhere," she said. "At every window."

Thank the Void the Khargols had burglary bars installed on every window, and every door. Darick looked at me with something terrible in his eyes, an emotion I couldn't interpret.

"Jax," he said. "I'm going to have to take the bullet out."

"No," I said, shaking my head. "Wait for the ambulance."

His voice was soft. "The ambulance isn't coming."

I pictured then how the vampires would have destroyed the vehicle and the paramedics in it. They hadn't stood a chance.

Darick began scrubbing his hands in the en-suite bathroom. I felt like saying, *Don't take it out. Just leave me to die here in The Godfather's bed. Just wrap yourself around me while I drift off to Halloween Heaven.* But I knew I wasn't ready to die, I was just scared. Scared of more pain, scared of living though this, just to be pulled apart by the multiplying vampires outside.

"Look for alcohol," he said to Nilve. "And antibiotics. Penicillin, amoxycillin, anything." She rushed toward the drinks cabinet and came back with half a bottle of expensive orc vodka with a gold label. She left it spinning on the bedside table, then left in search of medicine.

Darick was back with white bath towels, and hands smelling of lemongrass, as if he were preparing for a session in Pavaris's spa bathroom instead of a backstreet surgery. He splashed the alcohol on his hands, rubbed them together, then he loomed over me, and my heart started sprinting. He laid his hands on either side of the injury, and I felt the pain dissipate. It didn't disappear altogether, but the radiating circles of pain got smaller, easier to manage.

"Oh," I said, blinking at him. His face didn't register my comment. All his focus was on the hole in my chest. I knew what he was going to say before he said it.

"This is going to hurt."

I took a deep breath as he plunged his hand into my chest, and I screamed. I didn't mean to, didn't want to distract him, but the sound shrieked out of my body before I could stop it. It was too much, it was all too much, as the pure agony painted my vision white and then red, and I felt like I would never see again, move again, breathe again. And just as my body was about to explode with the excruciation, Darick's voice, far in the distance, said: "Got it."

His hand slid out, painted slippery scarlet, and he held up the missile to the light. It looked nothing like a spent bullet.

It was a silver planet, a bursting star. It was ugly and beautiful and Darick had just extricated it from my broken body. I stared at his face, which mirrored mine in its exhaustion and relief, and started to feel woozy. Had this really happened?

He put it in his pocket, disappeared from my view, and I heard water gushing in the bathroom again. Then he was back and he laid his clean hands on me again, this time covering the wound. I felt an intense tugging inside my body underneath the heat of his palms, as if I was under a non-sedating anesthetic and a surgeon was working on my organs: rearranging, ablating, stitching. Darick's face was pure concentration. There was more tugging and snapping and then it faded, and I felt the damaged skin on my chest zip up until it was sealed completely.

NILVE STOOD at my bedside with boxes of medication. Her mouth was hanging open.

"You're a Mage," I said to Darick.

"A healer," said Salty.

I felt amazed and light-headed and a little bit in love.

Darick shrugged. "Sometimes I'm a healer." I finished his sentence in my head: *and sometimes I'm a killer.* Because I had witnessed Darick in action, fighting vampires, and he was the most efficient assassin I'd ever laid eyes on.

Seemingly satisfied with the healed wound on my chest, he moved his hands to my face. He cradled my cheeks as if he was about to kiss me on the lips, and I felt my cheekbone fizz as the fracture melded together. The swelling went down, and I was able to see out of my left eye again. I looked into Darick's eyes, clear enough to swim in, and he took my hand. Then he moved his other hand to cover my eyes and said "Sleep."

No, I wanted to say. *There is no time to sleep. There are vampires outside and I need to—*

But my brain short-circuited and I felt like I was dying all over again. But this time Darick was with me, my hand warm in his. Dying like this was on the bright side of bitter. I saw in my imagination the intense blue sky and the ankle-biters dressed as ghouls. I heard the harp playing.

Oh, being dead was like Halloween Heaven after all.

"Trick or treat," I said, and lost consciousness.

CHAPTER 38
THE CURSED MILKSHAKE

When I woke up, I was clear-headed and almost pain-free. Darick was sitting on a chair, watching me, in his usual pose.

"Sorry I had to knock you out there," he said. "Your body needed a few minutes to consolidate the healing."

"You saved me," I said.

"I know, I know," Darick said, ruffling his hair. "You don't need saving."

We traded skew smiles, despite the situation we were in. As if to underscore the danger, there was a smashing of glass from downstairs. The sound reminded me of the broken vase in the Belore house, and Francis Belore's sad, limp body on the hardwood floor. I hopped off the bed and buttoned up my trench coat. Checked that my Nano was in my top pocket.

"They'll be able to break in soon," said Nilve. "They'll get crowbars. Blow torches. Angle-grinders. It's just a matter of time."

"I need to think," I said, touching my newly-healed cheekbone. I had spent the last hour in so much pain I had lost control of the situation and any idea of a strategy. I had to re-orient myself to what was happening. Before I had time to even begin to process what I had been through, my phone started ringing in my pocket. I grabbed it, and saw it was *The Copper Cog & Ale* calling.

"Ferra!" I said, relieved to just think about the steadfast dwarf. I had the urge to tell her what had just happened, but I knew there was no time for that.

"Jinx," said Ferra. "How are you?"

In my head I quickly ran through the events, trying to make them more real: *I found the Orc Godfather, dead in his bed, poisoned in his sleep by his wife and personal bodyguard. A double-betrayal by the people he trusted most. There was a vengeful goblin waiting for me. He had cut the power to the house. We fought, and he shot me. A different goblin showed up and slit his throat. I almost died, but then my stalker appeared and saved my life. Which sounds great, apart from the dozens of vampires crowding outside the house, trying to break in so that they can kill us all and steal the HighFire Crown.*

"Good," I lied.

"Well I'm just ringing to ask when you'll bring the twins back. We've got a nice warm dinner waiting for them—and for you, if you like!—minted lamb chops, and sweet potato apple cinnamash. And spice cookies for—"

It felt like my stomach dropped onto the floor, right there on the stained Khargol bedroom carpet.

"What?"

"No rush, Jinxie, I just wanted to—"

"Ferra," I said carefully, my hand on my chest. "I left the twins with you. You were looking after them. I don't—"

"Jinx?"

"Ferra?"

"I don't understand what you mean." Ferra's voice sounded suddenly thin.

My heart was stuck in my throat.

"Let's start again," Ferra said. "You came to the *Copper Cog* to collect the twins for that milkshake you promised them. You said you'd bring them back in an hour. It's been two hours, so I'm phoning to check if you are all right. *Are* you all right?"

"I didn't pick them up," I said, shock still hazing my understanding of what was going on. "I didn't pick them up for the milkshake."

The cursed milkshake.

"The kids—*my kids*—saw you with their own eyes," said

Ferra. "They said that the twins cheered up. They said you waved and said you'd be back in an hour."

"Oh my—" Dread bubbled inside me, boiling like a violent sea.

"It wasn't you." Ferra whispered, understanding finally dawning for both of us, terrifying us. "Someone else took them. Someone who looked like you."

"Someone using a Glamour," I said, finally realizing what had happened. A vampire, posing as me, had kidnapped the Belore kids. I knew exactly what the ransom would be.

"Oh, Jinx," said Ferra, about to apologize.

"Can you ask Gizmo to find them?" I asked, desperate, but I already knew the answer was no.

"Gizmo is with the twins," Ferra said.

Of course he was. Adrenaline mainlined through my body. "I've gotta go."

"Jinx," said Ferra. "She took the Morninglark Harp, too."

CHAPTER 39

THE SILVANO CLAN

I dropped the phone on the floor.

"What is it?" Darick and Salty asked at the same time.

"The Belore twins," I said. "Ametrix's children. They've been kidnapped."

Darick's face looked gray. The laceration on his cheek was healed and barely visible.

"They took Gizmo," I said. "And the Morninglark Harp, too."

SaltySnap's eyes stretched wide. "The harp?" she asked. "You can destroy a whole city with that harp."

"I wouldn't put it past them," I said.

There was another smashing sound, and tinkling of glass shards on tiles. There was a loud thumping on the wall, as if they were trying to break it down from outside. I needed to decide what to do, quickly, or the vampires would do that for me. I wished for the hundred-thousandth time that I was good at Portal Magic. Then my gaze fell on the goblin beside me, who just happened to be the most proficient gateway-creator I knew.

"Salty," I said. "You need to portal us to where the twins are."

"I don't know where the twins are!" she said. She was shaking. "Besides, if I portal us anywhere it will leave a tail, and we'll be in even more trouble. At least here, we have some protection."

She had a point. If the vampires used our portal tail they'd all be right behind us wherever we traveled to, and we'd be surrounded. There was more banging and crashing on the wall.

"The Belore kids," I said.

Darick frowned at me.

"They're in one of the teal pocket realms."

"What the what?" asked Nilve. "Are you speaking in code? Or did you just hit your head too hard?"

I blinked at her, trying to puzzle together my theory.

"Last night," I said. "Gizmo directed me to a strange place. A graveyard. Obsidian Hill Cemetery. But it wasn't real."

"What?" asked Salty again. I could tell she wasn't a very patient listener. I got the feeling she wanted to just slap me on the side of my head and tell me to get to the point. And I didn't blame her, with the threat outside getting ever closer, but my thoughts weren't clear in my mind, yet.

"When I stepped through that gate at Obsidian Hill," I said. "Time stopped on the clock on my phone. And when I left, it started again. Also, when I was there, I kept running and running, and I never got anywhere. That means I inadvertently stepped into a pocket realm, right?"

"I would say *right,* apart from the well-known fact that you don't just *stumble* into a pocket realm. You need strong Portal Magic to enter. And that's only if you actually *find* the portal, which is next to impossible, if you're not invited by the creator."

"And I didn't have an invitation. Or any Portal Magic."

"Right," said Salty.

"But what if," I said, sliding my hand into my infinity pocket and bringing out the Crown. "What if the Crown acted as my portal key? Then I wouldn't need to have any Portal Magic. I wouldn't need anything but this."

Darick nodded. "Yes. But that would mean that the Crown is the underlying magical item of that pocket."

"I was never supposed to find that place," I said. "No one was. But with the combination of Gizmo's magic and the Crown I was able to enter it. That's how I found Ametrix

Belore's dead body, drained of blood. And that's how I knew it belonged to vampires."

"You called it a teal pocket realm," said Darick. "What does that mean?"

"Ever since I got this thing," I said, looking at the Crown, "I've noticed that all the vampires trying to get it have this light blue color on the underside of their capes."

"That's the same as the vampires outside, now," said Darick.

"Light blue?" says Salty. "That's the Silvano Clan."

"The Silvano clan," I said. "Then it's them. They're the ones who will do anything to get their hands on this."

"That is not good news," says Salty, still shaking.

I looked at her for an explanation.

"The Silvano Clan is headed up by Acheron Baldassare," she said. "Think of the most evil, violent, bloodthirsty vampire you've ever met. Acheron would make that vamp look like Florence Nightingale on supernatural steroids. But more worrying than that," said Salty, "is that he is supremely ambitious."

"Great," I said. "Just great."

"Hang on," said Darick. "So you think the kids are being held at that graveyard?"

The idea of the kids being there made me shudder. I remembered the cold dark forest and the giant spiderweb, and the ring of freshly dug graves.

"No. That's where they're hiding the bodies."

"Which bodies?"

"The wizards they're killing. The Silvano Clan are killing wizards for their blood. Magus is the most potent magical blood there is, and they've decided to help themselves to it."

"It's Acheron," said SaltySnap. "He's preparing to take over the Realm."

"Stealing magical items," said Darick. "Harvesting Magus."

"He wants the Silvano Clan to rule the Realm, and he'll do anything to get what he wants."

"Holy hex," I said. Suddenly the reality of getting the Belore twins back safely—or of even surviving the night—seemed a lot less likely. There were sounds from downstairs, different than before. I realized with a twist in my guts that the vampires had broken into the house. I ran to the bedroom door and slammed it shut. Darick shored it up by pushing a chest of drawers against it.

"If the kids aren't at Obsidian Hill," said Darick, "then where are they?"

I looked at the Crown, still in my hand. "I think I know."

CHAPTER 40

THE FRACTURED POCKET REALM

I spoke quickly, hoping that my theory held up.

"Estelar Pavaris had no idea how powerful the High-Fire Crown was. No one did. When he lifted the elf security enchantment and allowed it to be stolen, he gave the Silvano Clan the perfect opportunity to draw on its magic to create their pocket realm."

"But they've never had the Crown," said SaltySnap. "Qwynkle had it before you."

"The Crown is so powerful that you don't need to be in actual possession of it to draw on its power. The pot plant on my kitchen windowsill started thriving even when the Crown was nowhere near it. The fact that it was no longer being protected by Pavaris's enchanted room was enough for the vampires to siphon what they needed. It was made vulnerable, and the clan took advantage."

Darick rubbed his face. "But they need to actually possess the Crown to stabilize the pocket. Relying on a distant connection to a magical item is too risky. Pocket realms can pop in and out of existence if you don't maintain them with enough energy; and if you're in a pocket when it disappears, you disappear along with it."

We stood in the Khargol bedroom, looking at each other. I was so on edge I may as well have been standing on the serious side of a razor blade.

"When the HighFire Crown broke," I said, "I think it fractured the Silvano pocket realm. Obsidian Hill was... missing certain elements."

"Like what?" asked SaltySnap.

"There was a giant spiderweb, but no spider. And when I ran, looking for Gizmo, it was like I was in a hamster wheel. I kept churning the ground but not getting anywhere."

"So you think the Silvano pocket realm broke into pieces. The graveyard was originally part of the main pocket."

"Makes sense," Darick said. "How many pieces did the Crown break into?"

"Three pieces," I said. "One main section, and two smaller bits."

"Okay," said Darick. "So there is probably a main pocket realm, and two smaller ones."

I bit my nails. "But how do we know where the Belore Twins are?"

"Impossible to know," he said.

"Not really," said SaltySnap. We both turned to her, and she looked at us with her big, bloodshot eyes. "We'll use the Crown as the portal key, and something of the Belore children's as a guidepost."

"I don't have anything," I said. "The harp was stolen by the same woman who kidnapped the twins."

The attackers were outside the bedroom door, now. Thumping on it, splintering the wood. We had to go.

"It doesn't have to be a magical item," said Salty. "Anything will do."

I searched my mind while the others watched me. I was about to give up and shake my head when I remembered the envelope of cash. I brought it out of my coat pocket and showed it to Salty. The paper was worn, now, and leathery. It had my name on it in blue ink and childish handwriting.

"Perfect!" said the goblin. "Hurry up. Hold hands." She closed her eyes and started reciting her gateway incantation. A fist broke through the top panel of the door, and the smell of vampires swirled into the room like red toxic smoke. Salty flinched and stopped the spell, her eyes flew open.

"Keep going!" I said to her, and she scrunched her eyes closed again and continued.

"Wait," said Darick, and Salty opened one annoyed eye at him.

"Do we know what we are doing?" he asked. "I mean, we don't know where we'll land up, and these vamps might follow us through the portal tail."

"Do we know what we're doing? No." I said. "But the children are being held by the same people who killed their father, and I won't let them die."

Our eyes met and I felt how strong our connection was. I remembered how he had healed me. I owed him my life, but I was asking him to risk his. The expression on his face was so intense, it made my magic flare inside me. I stretched out my hand to him, and he took it.

CHAPTER 41

DEADWING

SaltySnap's Portal Magic was as potent as always, and we were whipped up into the air, hung there in slow-motion for a moment, then flung along time and space as if we were lint in a vacuum cleaner. Most experienced portal-travelers advise to keep your eyes shut during a gateway trip to avoid motion sickness and vertigo, but I never could resist the beautiful scenery. The darkest depths of space lit up by the Northern Lights; banished specters stuck onto the outside of the tube-like sucker fish in a tank, forever hopeful of release. Warm rain and cold lightning; air smelling like ozone; silver stars that reminded me of the bullet Darick found resting in my chest. And just as you get used to the rushing in your ears you slow down and there is absolute silence. Silence like you've never experienced before, so all-encompassing that you think you have stopped existing. That's when the pressure bears down on you, pushing against every inch of your skin, hollowing your cheeks, pressing against your eyeballs until you think your skeleton will crumble under the force of it, and just when you think you can't handle any more it gives you one last squeeze and expels you. Less experienced gateway practitioners will dump you on the floor of your chosen destination and expect gratitude for the trip. Nilve SaltySnap's magic is more sophisticated than that. As we lurched toward the black rocks below us she caught us in her phantom net and lowered us carefully to the ground. Which was lucky, because the rocks were gigantic and sharp-edged, and I was pretty sure a rough landing on them would be lethal.

We were inside the bowels of some kind of mountain with a blue disk of sky for the ceiling. It was a vast space, like an arena, and there was no one else in sight. I wished that Gizmo was with us. I missed him, and his talent would have really come in handy.

"It's a volcano," said Darick, and I felt stupid for not realizing that before. We started walking, hoping no one had followed us via our portal tail. Depending on the strength of magic used, tails can stay open for hours, which means anyone who recognizes the opening can hitch a ride. Lucky break for them, unlucky break for us.

When we reached the center of the volcano floor something shifted: like we stepped into a parallel reality. Same space, same volcano, but we were no longer alone. A dozen teal-caped vampires appeared out of thin air, and they were striding in our direction. I pulled my crossbow off my back so quickly I even surprised myself. I pointed it at the vampire closest to us. He looked like the leader, with a glinting diamond brooch on his cape and a look of smugness I couldn't wait to wipe off his face. Darick drew his gun, and Salty, her emerald-glass shard dagger. The leader held up a steady palm in my direction.

"Please," he rasped. "There is no need for violence."

I would have laughed if I wasn't so sure we were all about to die.

"No need for violence?" I said. "Do you think we're here to disco?"

"I know very well why you are here, Wizard," he said. He looked into my eyes and his name came to me. *Deadwing.* "And we will be happy to oblige."

We kept walking backwards, and the vampires kept advancing. Soon, we were up against the rugged volcano wall. I shook the hair out of my eyes. I wanted to make certain that I had one hundred percent clear vision when I shot my high-tech arrow through his stone cold heart. My fingers clutched the crossbow. It thrummed in my hands. "Happy to oblige?" I said. "That's a new one. What are you talking about?"

"No one has to die today," Deadwing said.

"I think we have a difference in opinion, there," I said, lifting my weapon so that I could see his face through the scope of my bow. His palm was still up, and I imagined shooting an arrow right through it. It didn't seem to unsettle him.

Deadwing, I thought, *an apt name for an evil vampire's wingman.*

"I'm assuming you came here for the dead wizard's children?"

"That dead wizard," I said. "That wizard you *killed* has a name." I felt the anger rising in my tender chest.

Deadwing lifted his chin at a vampire off to the side, and the man made some sweeping gestures and opened some invisible curtains, revealing the Belore Twins, who jumped and stumbled when they saw me. They were crying, their hands tied behind their backs, and their mouths were sealed with duct tape. My heart contracted. The anger grew, ballooning my lungs and turning my stomach.

"Let them go!" I shouted. "How dare you?"

Have you no shame? I wondered.

Shame is for the weak, he replied, without talking.

"Let them go," I said again, and Deadwing shrugged.

"You are very welcome to them. I have no need for them." He touched the pad of his thumb to his tongue. "They are too young for my taste."

The children sobbed and walked gingerly in our direction. Pepin, overcome with emotion, stumbled to the ground, and Eafaris helped her up.

"You know what I want in return," said Deadwing. "Please don't make the transaction more difficult than it has to be."

"Transaction?" I said. "They're *children*."

The vampire sighed. He was getting tired of me. I didn't give a flying *faex*.

I held out my hand to the twins, who were now halfway between us and the vampires.

"Stop!" shouted Deadwing, but the kids didn't listen. "Stop!" he shouted again, but it only made them start running toward us. "Impedio!" he shouted, and a stream of magic left his palm and hit the children from the back, freezing them. Their bodies completely still, their faces snapshots of terror.

I became angry enough to attack, but tried to keep my emotion in check. When I had lost control in the parking basement at the Dome I had lost control of my magic. I couldn't afford to do that again.

"You can have the children," said Deadwing, angling his face to the side. "If you give me the Crown."

I held my crossbow in my left hand and rooted for the Crown with my right. I felt Darick's hand on my shoulder.

"You can't," he said. "You can't give him the Crown."

"If I don't give it to him," I said. "The children will die."

"If you give it to him the whole Realm will be destroyed.

Acheron will be able to control us all. Do you think he'll let the wizard children live?"

Deadwing moved closer to us. I looked again at his flashing diamond pin and saw that the symbol was the same one that had been branded onto Liz Durison's chest. That confounded me, but I didn't have time to work it out. Suffice to say that the Silvanos were evil incarnate and I had the one thing they needed to take over the city, the country, the entire Realm.

Darick didn't let go of my arm. "Would you be able to live with that?"

"Of course not!" I said. It came out as a sob even though I swear I wasn't crying.

"You can't do it, Jax!" he said. "Think of your parents."

His words hit me like a wave of ice water. I tore my eyes off Deadwing and looked at Darick. Unwelcome images flashed in on my mind: Dad with that gash in his neck, Mom's waxen face. The scarred vampire watching me from the corner of the room. You'd think they'd fade in time, the memories, but they were as bright and clear as the day it happened. "What the hell do you know about my parents?"

"I know enough to tell you that if you hand that Crown to the enemy you will never forgive yourself."

Deadwing took a step closer.

"So, what?" I said to him. "We sacrifice the children?"

Darick's face was anguished, his eyes dark. He leaned into me, put his lips next to my ear.

"No," he whispered. "We fight."

CHAPTER 42
DANCING SKELETON

I didn't need any more prompting than that. I let go of the Crown in my pocket and gripped the crossbow with both hands. Darick turned his pistol on the vampires in one fluid motion. As if we were one, we began firing.

A vampire was running toward us from the side, so I swiped my bow toward him and yelled *"Fiat Fulgur!"* A bolt of lightning surged through my body and out through the bow, and the white-hot current flew right into the vampire's torso, and he exploded.

"Fiat Fulgar! Fiat Fulgar! Fiat Fulgar!" I shouted, and the bolts instantaneously ashed three more vampires heading our way. Darick shot four or five and they fell down onto the black rocky ground beneath them.

Deadwing didn't move. He just stood there, watching with his arms crossed, as if he were invincible.

Despite being height-challenged, Salty was able to jump up and stab a vampire in the chest. She must have hit the sweet spot because he, too, exploded into sparks, and the ash rained down on us like confetti at a vampire funeral.

There were only a few of them left, now, and they were slightly less confident in their approach. Darick, Salty and I took a breath, ready to finish the fight. But then a vamp who had been hiding in the dark recesses behind the goblin jumped on top of her, knocking her to the ground. SaltySnap hit her head on the volcanic rock and passed out, her body splayed, her face pointing at the circle of sky. The sneaky vampire took her dagger, crouched over her, and was about to plunge it into her heart when Darick shot him, twice, and his whole body listed to the side and turned to cinders. A tall, thin vamp, one who had been hanging back from the battle so far, reluctantly made his way toward me. He had some kind of—what I guessed was enchanted—metal shield on his chest, one that would prevent a fire spell from killing him outright. That suited me, because my wrists and hands were numb and black: burnt out from being lightning conductors.

I breathed in, readying myself. These were the vampires that killed Ametrix. They had killed at least a dozen other wizards, just to harvest their blood, and had tried to kill me. The rage bubbling up fueled my resolve and my magic.

"Glaciem Exquiris!" I shouted, and a cold wave shot out of my arm, traveled along the barrel, and blasted out of the

crossbow in the form of a sharp icicle. It jettisoned through the air and sought the vampire's heat. The frozen stake penetrated his throat with such force that it shot right though his neck and out the other side, shattering on the ground behind him. He grabbed at the spurting wound, but the projectile had done too much damage, and his jetting blood painted his fingers dark red. He gargled, his eyes wide with shock, as he crumpled to the ground, then burst into flames. Only ash and his rocking chest shield remained.

DEADWING STILL SEEMED UNFAZED, which made me worry. He certainly knew something that we didn't, or he'd be fleeing, or fighting, or begging for his life.

"What is it, Deadwing?" I asked. "What is it you're not telling us?"

He didn't answer, of course, just kept his smug face at that annoying angle until I wanted to detonate it with a fireball. There was one other vampire in the crater, but he kept his distance. Clearly he wasn't as arrogant or dumb as his fellow brethren.

Three of us versus two of them, and we were armed. I saw one of Pepin's fingers wiggle. Deadwing's spell was wearing off, and the twins would be able to move soon.

Deadwing gestured at the surviving vamp, and the man opened another invisible curtain. It revealed the Morninglark Harp, which he picked up and brought over to his leader.

Pepin's hand was free now, and so was Eafaris's foot. My heart thudded in my chest. It was so loud that I felt for a moment that I couldn't hear anything else. It felt like the rocky walls of the cavernous volcano were closing in on us, and there was a silver shimmer in the air.

"You see that?" asked Salty, who had regained consciousness but didn't get up off the floor. Her injured head spilled greasy blood that shone on the stony ground.

"Salty!" I said. "Are you okay?"

Darick moved slowly toward her to help her up, but she could hardly stand.

"That shimmer?" she said. "This pocket realm is fading. We need to get out of here." She grimaced in pain and held her head. "If this pocket stops existing, we will, too."

"Once you hand over the Crown," said Deadwing, "this pocket will be as good as new. You won't have to worry about disappearing along with it."

I looked at him, gritted my teeth. I didn't have to say the word out loud.

Never.

Deadwing pursed his lips. His hand traveled slowly to the harp in the other vampire's hands, and he took it and plucked one of the strings. The sound was impossibly beautiful. How one chord could carry so much meaning, so much harmony, seemed at once impossible and wholly perfect. He plucked another, and another, and the figures carved into the wooden arch of the harp began to sway, and the volcano was filled with the most evocative melody I had ever heard. It felt like the music entered my body and penetrated every molecule, coating my DNA. The music's power was evident all around us, painting the dark space in golden pink light: a mountain sunset. I felt it tugging at me, caressing me, urging me forward.

I TRIED to resist the music of the Morninglark Harp, but it was impossible. It drew my body forward, forward, toward it. I dropped my crossbow, and Darick dropped his gun. I tried to struggle against it, but it was like trying to fight love, or beauty, or birth. The music flowed over me, into me. It embraced my goose-pimpled skin. Before I knew it, I was dancing toward it. I looked over at Darick for help, but he was being pulled along, too. We exchanged glances, our eyes mirroring each other's fear. I fought the urge to just give in. The idea of surrendering to the music was so incredibly tempting. It took every ounce of willpower and strength I had to fight it. I tried to cover my ears but it made no difference to the sound of the harp, as if you didn't even need ears to listen to it. As if the music washed over your body and was absorbed by your skin and your dancing skeleton.

The silver shimmered in the air.

Don't think of the music, I told myself. *The beauty is a trap. Black Mist. Think of the murder, the mayhem. Think of the twins cradling their dead mother on the floor.*

STILL, I danced toward Deadwing.

CHAPTER 43

VENTUM EXQUIRIS

I danced right up to Deadwing, close enough to touch him, and he reached into my coat with the confidence of a lover. He came up empty handed.

Suddenly his smugness disappeared. "Where is it?" he snarled. He searched every one of my coat pockets without luck. Fortunately, he didn't know how infinity pockets worked. When he got to my top pocket, he pulled out my Nano.

"Nano. Noose! Deadwing, in place!" I shouted, and the Nano turned itself into a thick black rope and tied itself around Deadwing's neck.

"What?" he said, his fingers flying up to touch it.

"Tighter," I said, and it began to strangle him.

The other vampire, the clever one, was at our side in a flash. I hate it when vampires bolt like that; it never fails to unnerve me. He tried to wrestle the Nano-noose off Dead-wing's purple-veined neck, but he only succeeded in making it worse. Maybe he wasn't so bright, after all. Deadwing was spluttering and choking while Darick and I danced before him. The harp clattered to the ground, which made our dancing more energetic, less rhythmic. Were we going to dance ourselves to death?

The air shimmered before us. I looked at my blackened palm, which was flickering, too. Nope. We wouldn't have time for such a protracted death sway. This pocket was deteriorating fast. As if on cue, a gigantic piece of rock cracked and detached from the volcano wall opposite us and crashed to the ground, sending up an atom-bomb cloud of shards and brown dust. The floor became warm, and began to give way. I thought I was imagining it, thought it was part of the harp's magic, making my soles hot and the floor soft. But when I looked down I saw that the previously solid lava we were standing on was melting. My feet glimmered against the heat.

The volcano was crumbling, the lava was coming back to life. Deadwing swung and struggled, his eyes popping, trying to loosen the rope around his neck. I looked for the children, but couldn't see them. The spell must have worn off. But where were they? Towers of steam began to shoot out of the ground like bowled-over fire hydrants. That's when the other coven of vampires appeared.

They were the ones from outside the Khargol house. They'd found our portal tail, after all. Still dancing, our weapons lost, we couldn't defend ourselves. The temperature was getting unbearable. The smart-not-smart vampire was back in my line of vision. He hissed at me.

"Give it to me!" he shouted.

I was right. Not smart.

"No means no, you *filius canis*," I said. "Didn't your mother teach you that?"

He hissed at me again, a full-throated, vicious sound, and showed me his dirty fangs. My body was so repulsed by it that I stumbled, and, weakened by the music, I fell. The other vampires saw me go down and they descended on me. There must have been ten vamps on top of me, hissing and snapping their jaws. One of the vampires, a female, looked at my neck with clear desire, opened her mouth wide so that I could see her sharp teeth, and got ready to plunge them into my throat.

"Nano! Collar!" I shouted, and the Nano flew off Deadwing's neck and flittered around my neck like a silk handkerchief. It attached to the collar of my coat, extending up to my chin. The female vampire hesitated, giving me just enough time to jump into a squat and unclip my wand.

"*Ventum Exquiris!*" I shouted, feet still tapping beneath me, and the gale spell flung the vampires off and away from me. Some of them hit the rock walls, some landed badly on the hot black rocks surrounding us. I saw that Darick and Salty were also covered with vamps.

"*Ventum Exquiris!*" I shouted. "*Ventum Exquiris!*" and their attackers were blasted off, too. One of the vampires landed in a splash pool of molten lava and he screamed as he combusted, throwing cinders and ash into the hot, shimmering air.

I had managed to ash at least ten of them, but more kept coming. I searched desperately for my crossbow. Darick was dragging Salty's motionless body away, but there was no safe place to put her. I never thought I'd care if Nilve Salty-Snap lived or died, but I found that now I did. Reluctant friendships aside, the goblin needed to be alive in order to portal us back home, but chances weren't looking good.

The vampires approached again, hissing, ready to finish me off, their desire for the Crown overtaken now by bloodlust. They wanted every part of me, every drop of blood, every limb. I could feel it in their gaze. My hands were burnt and brittle-feeling, as if they had been frostbitten despite the heat that surrounded us. I didn't know if I was able to perform any more spells.

A vampire dashed suddenly to Darick. He was helping Salty, and didn't raise his arms in time to defend himself. The vampire sunk his fangs into Darick's neck, and Darick shouted in agony.

"No!" I shouted, running to him. "No!"

Another vampire joined the feast, and Darick's knees buckled. Then there were five vamps over him, like vultures, and I could tell by the spread of his legs on the ground that he was no longer conscious. I pointed my wand toward them, ready to send another gale their way, when it was snatched out of my hand.

Deadwing.

His eyes were bloodshot, his throat a purple gash. He no longer had a voice. The harp still played its tune; I could hardly hear it, but I felt it in my body, which was still not under my full control. I looked over at Darick who was being feasted on by the savage creatures. I stopped breathing. My hand traveled to my chest where he had healed me, and my heart ached.

Give me the Crown, Deadwing said to me, without moving his lips. *And I will call them off.*

"Darick would rather die than have me give it to you," I said.

But what do you *want?* Deadwing asked, holding my mother's silver wand in his hands.

I stared at his swollen face, his depraved eyes, and my stomach tumbled.

I wanted Darick to live. I reached into my infinity pocket and pulled out the Crown.

CHAPTER 44
THE DEATH SPELL

I thought I was dreaming when the orcs started appearing. Dressed in the smart black Khargol bodyguard uniform and bristling with weapons. I looked up to see that the portal tail was still open. Even if Salty was unable to get us back home, we'd be able to use the tail to return, if we were quick enough. The orcs clutched their guns and began firing. I thought they had arrived to kill me, but they were gunning down the vampires.

Deadwing put out his hand to take the Crown from mine. The air between us flickered and glittered.

The orcs didn't waste any time in detonating the vampires. Bullets zinged all over the cave, ashing vamps and dislodging more of the rock face, causing it to crash down. The lava below us was almost too hot to stand on, but the leather-soled orcs didn't seem to mind. One of them swiped at the vampires who were on Darick, and they moved away, hissing, then he pumped them full of bullets and slung

Darick over his shoulder. Another orc picked Salty up and did the same thing. They moved in the direction of the portal.

Out of the corner of my eye I saw a stone-faced Pepin sneak up and grab the Morninglark Harp. Without hesitating, she lobbed it into a pool of lava, and it began to burn with green and violet sparks. The music faded, and I suddenly felt stronger; my body stopped jerking, and my mind cleared. Deadwing frowned and looked over his shoulder. Eafaris stood there, holding out his father's amulet. Pepin rushed to join him, and they held hands. They both had an intense look of concentration on their faces, and their mouths were moving in unison, but I couldn't hear what they were saying. Then I caught the end of the incantation, and I realized what it was.

Deadwing stood there, blinking in shock.

"... *nunc defungor*."

The Death Spell. It was the most dangerous spell in the book. One that I shied away from using, even in the face of vicious vampires, because if it's not delivered absolutely perfectly it can backfire and kill you instantly. It's not advisable to sling the Death Spell—even if you are an accomplished wizard in a predictable environment—never mind by emotional untrained child wizards, in a crumbling volcano, in an unstable pocket realm. As soon as I realized what the twins were saying, and saw the tell-tale red spark dart out of Ametrix's amulet—glowing like an angry dragon's eye—I gasped, grabbed my wand from Deadwing's hands, tore open my trench coat, and launched myself at them. I knocked the twins to the ground and wrapped my coat around them.

"Nano. Helmet," I whispered, just in time for the deafening explosion.

CHAPTER 45
VOLAS

The blast knocked me onto my side, but the coat protected us from the shrapnel. When I was able to stand and shake off the dust I was covered in, I saw the volcano was littered with dead bodies, vamps and orcs alike. The Belore twins' bodies lay to the left of me, and what was left of Deadwing's, to the right. The surviving orcs were limping and staggering to the portal door, which was now shrinking by the second. A vast lake of lava separated me from the glittering ring of light.

I put the Crown back into my infinity pocket and ran over to Pepin's motionless body. I scooped her up, throwing her over my shoulder as the orcs had done with Darick. It was more difficult to pick up Eafaris, but I managed to sling him onto my hip. I didn't have time to check for a pulse, but I wasn't optimistic, not after such a wild Death Spell. Out of breath, I ran up to the ledge of lava that had not yet melted and looked across at the bubbling flow. Just standing there seared my cheeks and singed my hair. I looked up at the closing portal, out of reach, out of time.

There was no one left in the scorching volcano but us. No one to help. Eafaris slid down my hip and I had to haul him up again. I took a deep breath and the hot air burnt my lungs. I would need every drop of magic left in my body to escape this hell. I felt the deadweight of the bodies of the children and I felt their suffering. I thought of Salty and Darick, and wasn't sure if they were alive or dead. I thought of my parents and the lifetime of love I had lost, and the pain was more searing than the heat of the molten rock glowing before me. The pain poured out of my inflamed, throbbing heart and pushed through my veins like boiling blood, reaching every inch of my being, until my limbs and fingers were singing with magic.

I crouched down, held my father's pentacle ring, and used my best parkour launch to jump into the air. At the same time I yelled "*Volas!*" and the spell lifted me and catapulted us across the lake of liquid fire, and we landed safely on the other side, but what was left of the still-solid lava cracked open and threatened to swallow us. The children's bodies were getting too heavy to carry but I shouted as I hoisted them up again and kept going, closely avoiding a jet of steam and reaching the portal door. Already, it looked too small for us to get through, but I wrenched Pepin off my shoulder and forced her through, then did the same with her brother's body. The closing ring wasn't wide enough for my body, but I tried to force my way through it, anyway.

Head first, arms by my side, as if I was a baby in a burning birth canal.

I got stuck. Something in my coat was stopping me from making progress, and the portal loop was crushing the life out of me. My legs were burning, my shoes melting. I tried harder to move forward but it was no use. I was stuck with just my head and shoulders through, and the ring would cut me in half if I didn't get out of its way. I knew what the obstacle was; I knew what the Void wanted. With my upper arms pinned to my sides, I struggled to get it out of my pocket, but then eventually the Crown was in my hand, and I had to let it go.

Suddenly I wasn't stuck anymore. The ring squeezed my ribs and pelvis as it tried to close around me, but I closed my eyes and remembered how I had fought my way through the rubble at the Dome, and the silk cocoon of the monster spider-web, and I kept rocking and pushing and pulling, inch by inch, until eventually my hips scraped through, and I quickly pulled my legs in after me. An intense mixture of relief and regret felt like a splash of cold water on my burning face. The vacuum began to pull at us. I reached out to Eafaris to see if he was alive, but as my hand reached his, Gizmo jumped out from under his jacket and nodded at me, cleaning his whiskers.

"Gizmo!" I said. He hopped into my burnt hands and I felt like crying, I was so happy to see him. I thought: *I'll feed you as many overpriced salted peanuts as you want. I'll never let you go again,* but the ferret had other ideas. He ran along my arm, toward the portal ring that was now the size of a bangle.

"Gizmo! No!" I shouted.

But, as I was slow to learn, magical albino ferrets don't like taking orders. He took a flying jump and dove through the gateway, after the tumbling HighFire Crown.

EPILOGUE

A SILVER PLANET

When I got back to my apartment that night, there was a note nailed to the door from Uragh, my stinky orc landlord, thanking me for six months of rent paid in advance, scribbled on the back of a king-sized triple-decker cheeseburger wrapper. If he had been surprised, I was doubly so. I had no idea who had deposited the money, and, after what I had just been though, I didn't have the mental bandwidth to even guess. I was just relieved to have a shower and a bed to sleep in.

The apartment was clean, and the bed had been turned down. I touched the crisp white linen and the fluffed pillow. My pajamas were folded up neatly, waiting for me. I collapsed on the end of the bed and stared up at the stained ceiling, pretending I was gazing at scudding clouds instead of decade-old water damage that Uragh would never dream of repairing. I could smell the laundry detergent and the sunshine on the linen.

"Thank you, Ghost," I said, and I heard the red book falling to the floor. I thought it was a gentler shove than usual, but that may have been my imagination. I looked at my teak bedpost, scored with hundreds of notches—of vampire kills, not lovers—but I didn't have the energy to add any more. Besides, I had no idea how many vamps I had ashed that day. More than ever before, that was sure, but I couldn't bring myself to be happy about it. Not with the Belore twins in the hospital ICU and Darick and Gizmo missing. Then there was Estelar. I shouldn't care about him, especially after how he had deceived me, but I had a soft spot for the elf. According to the Forage newsfeed on my phone, his house had collapsed, and he had to move back in with his parents, who were 140 years old in the shade. Poor Pavaris.

I sat up with a sad sigh and peeled off my scorched clothes, and wrapped my dressing gown around my shattered body.

Try not to think too much, I told myself. *Just shower and sleep. Everything will seem better in the morning.*

And I didn't have to sleep with one eye open this time, because the Khargol security guard who had escorted me home was busy fixing the lock on the front door. He was adding a couple of extra ones, too, made from indestructible orc steel, and said he'd stand guard for the night. I wasn't sure that was necessary, but I wasn't going to argue. When I asked the leader of the orc guards—they call him "Boss"—why they had come in through the portal to help us, he said that when I had saved Don Vito's life the first time, he had instructed them to protect me, or die trying.

But now the Don's dead, I had said.

His instructions remain, Boss muttered, and then insisted one of his men accompany me home.

I thanked the Void for Boss. Apart from the fact that he had saved my life, he was also doing a good job at holding the orc society together. As soon as I had told him what had happened with Shagar—who was still on the run, and I imagined her basking in the sun on one of the Khargol Isles, Piña Un-Colada in one hand, pregnant belly in the other, while Gnarg massaged her swollen cocktail-sausage toes— Boss had sent out a press release covering up how the Don had died. Heart attack, I believe he said, but I can't be sure. It would keep the Khargol loyalists from baying for blood, and give us a window before the Hammerskins starting plotting a *coup.* He seemed smart, for an orc.

We had all stood speechless, crowded, in the Khargol bedroom, after being flung there by the portal, and I had done a head-count. Eleven orcs, one goblin, two wizard children, all in bad shape. There was no mage.

Where is Darick? I had asked the orcs, but they just shrugged and shook their heads. *Is he lost?* I asked. *In the portal? Or did he make it here and then disappear?* But no one knew the answer. I didn't know if he was alive or dead, or lost forever. I swallowed hard and reminded myself to get some rest. I was going to need it if I was going to go looking for him.

~

THERE WAS a hard knock on the door. A loud, clumsy noise, which I interpreted as orc knuckles. I tightened the belt of my gown and opened the door. The Khargol security guard stood there, his grumpy gherkin face looking especially displeased.

"Boy here," said the guard. "I get rid of him?"

"What?"

"Miss Knight," said a meek voice from the right. I looked down. It was Bron.

I sighed. "No," I said to the orc. "It's okay."

Bron peered up at me with hopeful eyes. "Have you thought about it, yet, Miss Knight?"

"I've told you a hundred times, Bron," I said. "I don't have to think about it. The answer is no."

His face fell.

"Now, scram. I've got things to do, and standing in the doorway arguing with a waif is not one of them."

"I won't ask anything of you," he begged. "I'll only ever help. All I want is to learn."

"Bron. It's nothing personal. I've just had the longest day in the history of forever, and I just don't have the time or energy to train an apprentice."

"Please!" he said. "You don't even have to train me. I'll just keep quiet and—"

"I doubt that," I said.

"... and I'll just watch and learn. I promise!"

I shook my head. "Sorry, Bron, I just can't." I started closing the door, and Bron put his dirty sneaker in the way. The orc stiffened, ready to pick the boy up by the scruff of his neck and hurl him off the balcony.

"Wait!" Bron pleaded. "I have something I want to show you."

I sighed again and opened the door, motioning for the orc to stand down. I crossed my arms and looked at the boy, grimy clothes covering his skinny frame. I didn't even have an apple I could give him.

"Well?" I said. "I'm getting old, here."

He looked hopeful again, and there was a glimmer of mischief in his jade-colored eyes. He closed them, and bunched his hands into fists. His brown skin turned darker before our eyes, then a texture began appearing all over him.

"Bron?" I said, but I could tell he couldn't hear me. His skin continued to darken and the texture became more pronounced, until a few of the ridges popped out of his skin and I flinched. His face bubbled with the strange weave, too, and I found it difficult to watch.

But then there was a snap in the air, and the sound of birds' wings taking flight, and Bron vanished right in front of us, and then there was a raven perched on the balcony balustrade, looking at me with beady black eyes, turning his beak and squawking.

"Bron?" I said again, holding out my hand. The raven flapped its handsome wings and came to sit on my burnt fingers. His feathers were dark and sparkly: the color of the night.

There was another snapping sound, and Bron the boy was standing before us again. I just stared at him, breathless. "You're a shape-shifter."

The stunned orc looked like someone had just told him his mother was a werewolf and then snapped his underwear.

"Go home," I said to Bron.

"But—"

"Go home, Bron. And come back tomorrow. You'll start your apprenticeship in the morning."

His eyes shone. "Really? Really, Mrs. Knight? You mean it?"

"Call me Jacquelyn," I said. "Jax."

I rubbed my damaged fingers together, flexed my brittle wrists.

My name is Jacquelyn Denna Knight, and I turn my pain into magic.

. . .

"Now, scamper, before I change my mind."

Bron cast a quick smile my way and then disappeared in a snap of shiny black wings. A small feather floated to the floor.

"Wizard," said the orc, and I wondered if he was going to lecture me about the safety risk of taking on guttersnipe apprentices from off the street. Instead he opened his hand to reveal a small jewelry box.

"Who is this from?" I asked, but he shrugged. It had been left outside the door.

"Also, message from Boss."

"Yes?"

"Wizard children stable. Also: Goblin. Alive."

Thank the Void, I thought. My muscles sagged in relief. The Belore twins would, despite all odds, live, and so would my favorite goblin.

The phrase quirked my lips into a smile. If you had told me I'd have a "favorite goblin" a week ago I would have spat coffee out of my nose. I smiled and thanked the orc and took the box inside, opening the ribbon as I walked. I sat down at the rickety kitchen table and pulled off the lid. Inside, on a pillow of cream silk, lay a silver bracelet with a single charm. It was the bullet that Darick had taken out of my open chest. A silver planet. Ugly, beautiful.

I hugged it to my chest and wept. Darick was alive, and he'd be back. This charm was his promise to me.

IN THE SHOWER I scrubbed the dirt and carbon dust off my skin, careful not to open any of the just-healing cuts. The water comforted and stung me in equal measure. I heard my phone ringing, so I turned off the water and leapt out, hoping it was Darick, or Ferra, and not wanting to miss the call. *Scorpion Unit* said the caller ID.

"Jax," said Morgan's voice, as tense as I'd ever heard it. "We've got a problem."

I stood there, dripping water onto the gray, balding carpet, picturing Liz Durison's pale dead body lying in the refrigerator at the city morgue, branded with the vampire anarchy symbol.

"Morgan," I said into the phone. "More bodies?"

"More bodies." The strain was like an electric current through the phone. "From all over the city."

"A serial killer," I said.

"More than one killer," said Morgan. "A serial killer cult."

"*Faex*," I said. I don't think Morgan minded anymore if I swore in Latin. I could have sworn in Gaelic Orc Gibberish for all she cared. I needed to get on the case, and quickly.

"All killed in the same way?" I asked. "Branded in the same way?"

"Yes," said Morgan. "But there's something else."

Now it was my turn to tense up. Something told me that I didn't want to hear what was coming next. I waited, but Morgan didn't speak.

"Morgan?" I prompted. "What is it?"

"The bodies," she said. "The dead women. They all look like you."

THE END

Interested in what happens next?

Book 2 is available! It's called The Dream Drinker, and it's waiting for you.

See you on the other side of the Veil!

ALSO BY JT LAWRENCE

FICTION

WHEN TOMORROW CALLS

• SERIES •

(Futuristic kidnapping thriller)

The Stepford Florist: A Novelette

The Sigma Surrogate

1. Why You Were Taken

2. How We Found You

3. What Have We Done

When Tomorrow Calls Box Set: Books 1 - 3

(complete)

URBAN FANTASY

BLOOD MAGIC

(complete 6-book series)

1. The HighFire Crown

2. The Dream Drinker

3. The Witch Hunter

4. The Ember Isles

5. The Chaos Jar

6. The New Dawn Throne

CURSEBREAKER

(complete 6-book series)

1. The Dusk Reapers

2. The Haunted Portal

3. The EverShade Ring

4. The Obsidian Castle

5. The Pick Pocket's Curse

6. The Eternal Betrayal

STANDALONE NOVELS

The Memory of Water

(steamy psychological thriller)

Grey Magic

(witchy magical realism)

EverDark

(urban fantasy)

~

SHORT STORY COLLECTIONS

Sticky Fingers

Sticky Fingers 2

Sticky Fingers 3

Sticky Fingers 4

Sticky Fingers 5

Sticky Fingers 6

Sticky Fingers: The Complete Collection:

Books 1 - 6: 72 Short Stories

~

NON-FICTION

The Underachieving Ovary

(memoir)

The Indie Author Game Plan

~